1

The Field Researchers series
by A.E. Hellstorm

In the Hands of the Unknown
Lost

IN THE HANDS OF THE UNKNOWN

a novel about

the Field Researchers of the Golden Fleece Society

inspired by the world of H.P. Lovecraft

by A.E. Hellstorm

Copyright

Acknowledgment

There are some people whom I would like to thank. Because of their actions, this book is now in your hands, ready to read.

Nikolai Smith, Victor Vargas, and Ian Tweedale gave me my hope back that with a few small changes, my book was publishable in its own right.

Sarah Lynne Bowman took valuable time to proofread the book, for which I am grateful.

Jenna Innes, Emma Fryksmark, and Melody Bell gave me lots of great advice without which this book would not be the same.

Dr. Cecilia Gordan gave me valuable insight on medical procedures.

Chris Wilson read through my first shaky chapters and told me to go on.

Logan Ferguson graciously gave me permission to use his RPG character, Dr. Florian Atzmüller, whom we might see more of in book four.

Years ago, Martin Lysén introduced me to the world of H.P. Lovecraft as the role-playing game Delta Green, and I've been in love with it ever since.

My father, Roald Vincent Irenes Sköld, gave me the first insight that people you know can write books, not only read them. I still treasure the only book for young adults he published before he died.

My husband, Mikael Hellström, has always been there for me and believed in my writing even when I myself doubted.

Thank you, /Eleonora

Part One

beginning

Chapter 1

The heat of the day was slowly fading away, and the air at the middle of the bridge started to cool down. Miriam wished that she had a jacket to cover her bare arms with. Goosebumps appeared on her sunburnt skin and made it stretch uncomfortably. She should be well on her way home, taking a shower, putting on sun lotion, and heating up the leftover Chinese food from yesterday. Instead, she was standing here, three hours after work, trying to think of nothing while watching the water lazily drifting by some twenty yards below her, brownish in color. Behind her, the traffic flowed slowly but steady, copying the river below. 'Rush hour' was such a wrong word for the phenomenon going on around her, she thought.

The city skyline on her left reflected the dying sun in glass and metal, but the city skyline on her right was already hidden in shadow. It was not logical, of course, but the fact that she was heading towards the sunlit part of the city made her breathe easier. She turned her head towards the golden skyscrapers, followed every single one of them with her gaze, counting them as she always did when she walked this way from work.

"... twenty-nine, thirty, thirty-one, thirty-two." Thirty-two visible with their windows viewing her mindlessly. Miriam's sense of relative security disappeared, and she shuddered. The unexpected sound of the cell phone made her jolt. She grabbed it hastily to silence it. "Yes?"

"Claire?" Caesar's deep voice caressed her, made her heart dance happily in her chest.

"Mhm."

"I need you down at the morgue. The autopsy is finished."

Something in his voice made the air feel even cooler, and she embraced herself to stop the hair on her arms from standing up.

"Have you called Cyrus or should I?" Her voice was calm and steady, much to her own surprise.

"Don't worry about him. I'll call. Just get over here, will you?"

"I'm on my way."

"And Claire...?" Caesar's voice became emotionless. "Don't eat."

As a sinking sensation spread in her stomach, she asked anxiously: "What do you mean, 'don't eat'?" but he had already hung up on her. Tetchy, she scowled at the cell, before turning her back on the sunlit part of the city and began to walk the short way back to work.

The morgue was silent except for the never-ending buzzing of the air conditioner. Miriam fastened the last button on her FBI jacket while she took the empty stairs down to the lower level where the autopsy room was located. Through the doors' windows, she saw Cyrus leaning against the wall, arms crossed over his chest and his face as unreadable as always. His copper-red hair had a metallic luster from the cold fluorescent tubes. Miriam grimaced when she realized that he was there alone and for a moment she hesitated to go in, but he had already seen her. She gave up an inaudible sigh, pushed the doors open and then stopped abruptly, choking. Her stomach churned, and she swallowed hard to gain control over it.

"Oh, my..." she said faintly. "What's that smell?"

A thick layer of something that was almost visible hung around the room: a stench that resembled sour milk left in the fridge for weeks combined with rotten fish. Cyrus gave her half a joyless smile.

"Nice, eh. Don't worry, you'll get used to it."

Miriam scoffed and didn't meet his gaze. Although Cyrus was twenty-seven and thus three years younger than her, he always made her feel insecure and nervous. She wished for the hundredth time in a row that she could read him, but he kept his feelings tightly controlled.

8

"So…" She inspected the autopsy room, desperately trying to ignore the stench. The examined body of the young, extremely obese girl they'd got transferred to them earlier that day, lay on a bier covered with a sheet. On a metal table next to it, were clean tools neatly organized in a line beside a big red plastic bucket that seemed out of place. It looked more like it belonged in a cleaning closet than in a morgue. "Where's Caesar?"

"Buying donuts and coffee." Miriam raised an eyebrow. Cyrus shrugged. "Don't look at me. I'm not the one working in this stench." He gave her another glance. "Did you hear that I went back to question her parents?"

"Mhm. Did you get anything new?"

Cyrus smirked. "They've moved out."

"What?" Miriam stared at him. "Moved out?"

"Yep, the whole place is as empty as a mousetrap."

"Moved out?" she said again, unbelievingly. "But what about her?" She nodded towards the motionless body under the sheet.

"Come on, Claire. The girl's dead. Apparently they didn't care about paying for the funeral."

Miriam got a lump in her throat that had nothing to do with the odor. She had been working with crimes like this one for six years, and she still didn't understand how people's minds worked. That's why she just investigated the crime scenes and never questioned the people involved. A deep sigh heaved in her chest as she turned her back on the bier, grabbed the only chair in the room and sat down. Cyrus' stare at the body was clinical and intense as if he could see through the sheet and into her dead mind, locating the secrets the girl had hidden. Maybe he could. Miriam looked at Cyrus; Cyrus looked at the dead girl. Silence fell in the room while they waited for Caesar to return.

Not even ten minutes later, Caesar's robust, comforting body was seen outside the window, to Miriam's relief. He waved with a half-eaten donut in his hand towards them, then swallowed it and gulped down the rest of the coffee before coming into the autopsy room.

"Good!" he said to no one in particular. Then his eyes crinkled as he gave her one of his warm, pleasant smiles. He went to wash his hands at the sink and put on a clean laboratory coat. The white coat brought forward the silver tinges in his dark hair that always reminded her of an elderly hero in a Jane Austen novel. He handed over two coats and pairs of latex gloves to her and Cyrus. "Let's get to work."

They all stepped up to the bier. Caesar's sympathetic face lost its comforting empathy, and in its place, a facade that showed only mild professional curiosity appeared. He cleared his throat and removed the sheet from the dead girls' face.

"Emilia Sabrina Stevenson. Female. Ten years old. Caucasian. Parents: Robert and Stella Stevenson. Father called nine-one-one on the evening of July ninth to report his daughter's death. We got our hands on it four days later, July thirteenth. She had not been examined at that time."

Caesar pulled up the girl's right eyelid. Miriam gasped and stared at the eye as she felt cold shivers running down her spine.

"Holy…" Cyrus' voice sounded shaken. He reached out a hand and grazed the girl's cheek, but removed it instantly and stared at Caesar, his detached mask gone. "It's been four days. Why doesn't she look dead?"

Caesar acknowledged him with a calm nod and held up his hand. As he continued, Miriam couldn't take her eyes from the girl's face. She felt a sick kind of fascination looking into that eye, so vividly alive, so vividly watching, in the dead face. It was as if the girl's mind had not left her at death's entrance, as if it was still there, trapped inside of her.

"Henry Wittinger, FBI Forensic Pathologist, conducted the autopsy July thirteenth. I noticed…" He cleared his voice. "Forensic Pathologist Wittinger…" he corrected himself before continuing. "Forensic Pathologist Wittinger noticed some very unusual things during the autopsy. The eyes were still moist and had not shrunk into their sockets." Caesar let the girl's eyelid close and took up an arm. He reached for a scalpel and a small metal bucket and made a diminutive incision at the wrist. Blood dripped into the bucket. Miriam stared uneasily at it. "The blood had not yet coagulated."

With a gentle touch, he placed the arm on the bier again and dabbed a piece of gauze at the wound, drying up the trickling blood. Then he made a movement as if pulling down the sheet from her abdomen, but halted and scrutinized Cyrus and Miriam.

"Mr. Stevenson said that Emilia complained about a stomach ache when she came home from summer school. He had dismissed it since she used to experience psychosomatic responses to schoolyard bullying. Two hours later, Emilia fell on the floor, screaming in agony, and before Mr. Stevenson got to dial nine-one-one, she was dead." Caesar sighed, pulled down the sheet and uncovered the enormous bluish white belly. It was clinically opened up to expose the stomach and the intestinal area. "I haven't touched this area because I wanted you to see this in situ. I have seen numerous strange things during my many years at Field Research Team C2, but this..."

The stench was stronger here, and Miriam took an involuntarily step back, but Cyrus frowned and bent over the stomach, apparently oblivious to the odor.

"What am I looking at, C?"

"She has been eaten alive from the inside."

Cyrus froze. Then he turned his head slowly towards the older man and stared at him, bewildered. "You're sure of this?"

"Yes."

Caesar reached for the red plastic bucket that was still standing on the metal table and removed the lid. Something made a splashing sound from it. Miriam made a nervous giggle.

11

"Do I want to see this?" Her voice expressed only a slight tension.

"No."

Caesar gave her a sympathetic glance, but didn't impose. Cyrus took the few steps to the bucket, looked into it a short moment, and moved back, visibly pale. Miriam sensed that well-known impact of fear grabbing her by the stomach as she forced herself to come closer.

"They were wriggling around in there when I opened her up, ferocious in their hunger, trying to eat anything they could get at." Caesar had that emotionless voice again. "Strangely enough, they haven't eaten each other. I thought they would."

At last, she got to the bucket and had a reluctant view of the interior. Several dark-green eel-like creatures swam around in water that had the consistency of mucus. The stench threw itself upon her. She choked, gasping desperately for air, and Caesar put the lid on again. He watched them gravely.

"Go home now, take the evening and early morning off from work. We'll assemble again at ten a.m. I want you to determine if you have ever seen something similar to this – at all – somewhere in your previous Research Projects or during your Star Student years. Cyrus, I'm thinking especially of you here, since you were transferred from FRT N5 and have investigated RPs Claire and I have not been involved in."

Cyrus nodded with a reflective demeanor. "Yes, sir. I will do my best." He glanced back at the red bucket. "How the hell did they get in her?"

"That's an excellent question, Cyrus, which I don't have an answer to. My closest hypothesis would be that she took a swim somewhere, and they drilled into her body, just after hatching. I've heard of something similar happening in Egypt... or was it India? But that was some other kind of creature." He sighed and for once he looked his actual age, tired and wrinkled. "You don't have your car today, Claire?"

Miriam shook her head and tried to find her voice. "It's still at the workshop." The words sounded hoarse.

"I'll drive you home. Let me just clean up in here and we'll be on our way."

Cyrus nodded at them and left. Miriam waited just long enough for him to disappear before she went into the women's changing room and took a quick shower to get rid of the stench that seemed to linger on her skin. She was happy that she always kept extra clothes in her locker for situations like this one.

Henry waited in his car, with wet hair and smelling faintly of that eau de cologne she liked so much. They stopped at a restaurant, the Mongolian on Fifty-Second Street that was Henry's favorite, on their way to her place. They didn't talk about work at all. Instead, they continued to make plans for their upcoming vacation in late August, both well aware that they might have to change them and disappoint Miriam's family again this year.

Night had fallen when they got home to Miriam's penthouse-inspired apartment. Henry took another shower, a long one, and went to bed, absently kissing her on the corner of her mouth. Miriam was tired, but too restless to be able to relax. Instead, she took a mug of steaming chamomile tea with a generous spoon of ecological honey and went out to the terrace. The scent that rose up from the daffodil-yellow stoneware was soothing. Miriam stood at the baluster high above the quiet street with the mug resting in her hands, taking deep breaths of the gentle, inviting air. It was that kind of warm, velvety night that only July could provide. *Almost Mediterranean*, she thought dreamingly and felt a deep longing for Crete in her heart. If she'd been younger, she would have been roaming around town with friends. Now, she was content spending the early night on her terrace while the love of her life slept soundly in her bed.

A light-brown strand of hair had escaped from her hairpins and rested on her sunburnt shoulder. As she let her thoughts wander, old memories of childhood pleasantries showed up: sleeping in the hammock on the veranda under the stars; swimming in the balmy lake with its deep green water; taking walks in the nearby wood with Petronilla, her beloved golden retriever… A soft smile lit up Miriam's face, smoothed it out, and made it look as young and naïve as it used to be, six years ago.

Behind her, numerous soft table lamps lighted up the apartment. A mild scent of the twenty or so different potted plants filled the air, melding together with the fragrant smell of the planted spices on the terrace. The walls were elegantly decorated with Minoan art, her favorite era in history. Classical music on low volume wrapped around her like a warm blanket. At this moment, Miriam was perfectly happy, and she didn't want to go to bed just yet even though it was two o' clock in the morning.

Inside the open bedroom door, she saw the contour of Henry's body under the duvet, and she was relieved that he was here this night. He provided such a safe and tender embrace in which to hide and tonight she needed that. Usually, her old, ragged teddy could sooth her, but this was not one of those nights. Instinctively she knew this would be the last calm day in a long time. She had been a member of the secretive Golden Fleece Society far too long not to recognize the signs.

Her thoughts wandered unwillingly back to the dead girl lying alone in the cold, dark morgue with her lifelike eyes closed, and she shuddered. This was definitely one of those weird cases that sometimes got transferred to them from the local PD, and she didn't like the feeling of it one bit. Miriam swept the soft red nightgown closer around her in an attempt to quiet her suddenly pounding heart. The thin, silky fabric embraced her soothingly and the deep reassuring breaths she drew in as she surrendered to the strains of Vivaldi helped her calm down again. Her gaze wandered back to Henry, as it always did when she felt anxious, but it didn't really help her now. He had been so fascinated, so engulfed with the girl, under that mask of professionalism. *No, not the girl*; she

14

thought and frowned, *the eels and the death they brought to her.* A violent shudder made the tea splash in the mug. Sometimes, Henry was so engaged in the projects that he never stopped being Field Researcher Caesar of Field Researcher Team C2, who graduated Star Students with Honors more than thirty years ago now and had been a member of the Golden Fleece Society ever since. It was at those times she felt lonelier than ever, and she was aware that those times were just around the corner again. The CD had played its last track. The disc buzzed some short seconds before replaying the first track again. When was it that she stopped turning off the lights and started playing calm music on repeat through the whole night? It must have been at the end of her fourth year as a Star Student when she was on her research assistantship with the FBI-agents from FRT B9. She shrugged uneasily at the flashing memory of her first real-life nightmare. The former Star Students of B9 had not shied away from showing her the real deal, and it had left deep bite marks on her left thigh that no zoologist would be able to recognize. The big, jagged scar had become a constant reminder of how much deeper and frightening reality was than most people ever saw or perceived.

In the end, it didn't really matter, she decided. The important thing was that the light and the music helped her relax and sleep without too many nightmares, and if any kind of unwelcome nightly visitors decided to show up, she would not be taken by surprise in a dark room.

The anxious frown smoothed out, and the soft smile returned when she once again looked at Henry, this gentle, affectionate and loving man. How he could still be that way after over thirty years as a part of team C2, was beyond her, but the fact that he was filled her with hope and a great deal of respect. Even as far back as when she was a student she had heard rumors about him; being the only Field Researcher who had never been transferred to another Field Researcher Team. She had been star struck, to say the least, when she got the honor of being part of his team after she graduated as a full-fledged member of the Golden Fleece Society six years ago. He had been the one who had given her the name Claire, because of the beaming light he saw in her soul, he told her. Ever since had he acted as her friend and later her lover, while the others, Cecilia, and Conrad, had ignored her at best and treated her with suspicion at worst. It had taken a year to come close to Cecilia, and she never really got to know Conrad. They were both gone now. Cindy had replaced Conrad. She lasted two years. Miriam had visited her once at the Lincoln Asylum. Seeing Cindy in the white straightjacket wildly trying to get out of it and not recognizing her own reflection was like seeing an image of herself five, ten, or even as many as twenty years from now. She never went back there again. Cyrus got transferred from the shattered FRT N5 after Cecilia… drowned… two summers ago. Miriam didn't know how long he had been at N5 or what had happened to his team, but his strained and controlled personality made her believe that he wasn't a new graduate. Throughout all the horror and grief she had been through, Henry stood steadfast and safe, and she loved him for that and for all the kindness he showed her.

Miriam forced herself to let go of the dark thoughts. Another deep sigh made her body unwind again, and she could finally go inside, lock the three different security locks, and curl up behind Henry's broad back. Sleep came gradually to her, but when it came, it was as soft and warm as an old friend.

That night she dreamt of it all: the beginning. She was twenty-one and pretty as a flower, as her mother said when Miriam graduated from the prestigious Western Shore University. Her father blinked at her and told her that big brain of hers was far more significant than her rosy cheeks, her wavy brown hair, and those big eyes, dark as night.

"It's easy to disarm a person in any given situation without them noticing as long as you use your brain, sweetheart."

Her mother scoffed lovingly and kissed her on both cheeks. "I'm so proud of you, HaY'Karah."

Her sister just beamed at her, sharing the delight and pride and excitement with the family's baby girl.

In her dream, she drifted away to that important moment when the headmaster took the stage to announce who amongst the one hundred and ten hopeful graduates would become the Star Student. This was what Miriam had worked for, lived for, cried for, and even breathed for since her first week. This was why she chose Western Shore to begin with and not Harvard, Yale, or Princeton. She felt nauseated by the fluttering butterflies in her stomach when the headmaster smiled towards the audience and started to talk.

"As headmaster of one of America's finest universities, it is always my utmost pleasure to announce which graduate has achieved admittance to our one-of-a-kind highest education program: The Star Students, a program different from anything any other university has to offer. Today, this honor goes to graduate Noreah Christine Hatfield. Congratulations, Miss Hatfield. Please approach to the podium to receive your ring and your new robe."

Even as she applauded together with all the others in the audience, Miriam's eyes burned with the treacherous tears that she desperately tried to hold back as her stomach grew heavy and sour. She hadn't made it. All that work, all that passion, all those dreams had been for nothing. The girl entering the scene looked dazed with being the chosen one and she walked as if in a dream. The headmaster opened the box with the tiny ring adorned with stars, put it on the girl's left little finger, and placed the thick, ocean-blue mantle over her shoulders. On the front left side, the words Golden Fleece Society were embroidered in gold. The audience' applause was deafening. The girl turned around, smiled as if her face might split in two, bowed, and took a couple of steps towards the stairs when the headmaster started to talk again.

"This year is very exciting indeed. This year, we could not choose. Instead, we have not only one future Star Student, but two. Congratulations, Miriam Glukel Goldblum. Please approach to the podium to receive your ring and robe."

At first, Miriam stood absolutely dumbstruck, but then her sister gave a wild cry and hugged her intensely.

"It's you, Mimi! It's you! Come on, up with you!"

With tears finally free to flow, she walked towards the stage.

17

Chapter 2

The sun was abundantly drenching the small briefing room in light this lunch hour. Cyrus stood at the window with some paperwork in his hands, but instead of reading, he was watching the slow-flowing river below while Caesar neatly laid the cloth-covered table. The aroma from the Indonesian take-out food that filled the room made Miriam's mouth water and her stomach growl.

"So, team," Caesar said when everyone was seated with a plate filled with food in front of them. "What have we got?"

Cyrus waved with his fork while chewing. He swallowed and took a mouthful of ginger ale.

"I don't have anything that could spread any light on the creatures, but I did an experiment this morning," he said at last and wiped his mouth with a napkin before neatly laying his cutlery at the side of the plate as if he wasn't hungry anymore. "I went to the butcher and got myself some intestines: sheep, cow, pig and hen. First, I fed the eels, or whatever they are, the cow intestines. Nothing happened."

"They didn't eat it?" Miriam asked surprised.

"No. Cow was not what they wanted." The way Cyrus said that made Miriam freeze for a second and the hair on her arms stand up. Caesar watched Cyrus with concentration. "So, I tried sheep and hen. Same result. My suspicion then turned into certainty."

"What about the pig?" Miriam asked reluctantly and wasn't sure if she wanted to hear the answer.

"Oh, that worked all right, I guess," Cyrus said with a strange kind of smile. "But what they really wanted was… this." He held up his finger where a Band-Aid was put on. "I dropped some of my own blood into that bucket, and they went totally berserk."

An uneasy silence filled the room for a moment.

"So..." Caesar said thoughtfully. "They can feed on pigs because of their similarity to humans, but humans are their hosts. That's why they didn't feed on each other."

"Right." Cyrus' voice was filled with dark humor. "And since we don't know how they spread, we need to find the girl's parents. Who knows, they might be hosts to these monsters as well. Heck, we might all need an X-ray, as far as I can tell."

Miriam scoffed and scowled at him. "That's ridiculous! We weren't even near those creatures. If they don't spread by merely looking at us, I wouldn't be concerned."

Caesar interrupted smoothly, apparently wanting to avoid another of their countless arguments. "And what about you, Claire? What have you got?"

She gave Cyrus a last annoyed glance before turning to Caesar, practically with her back towards Cyrus. In the corner of her eye, she saw him smirk, and she scowled again.

"I contacted Anna at the Faculty this morning with a description of the eels and how they were found. She gave me the contact information for a former Star Student - a Professor Bruchheimer at the Museum of Natural History. I'll meet him after lunch to get his professional opinion. Anna also gave me very brief information about two other apparently similar cases: one in India and one in Finland."

Cyrus frowned intrigued. "Huh. Interesting geographical spread. India, Finland, and the U.S. And 'apparently similar'?"

Miriam turned towards him again. "Yes. GFS didn't get to see the cases themselves, so it's only testimonies from the locals that we have to work with. Sorry."

Cyrus shrugged with a half-grin. "Well, why would it be easy?"

Miriam couldn't help smiling back at him, as usual reluctantly charmed by that boyish demeanor he sometimes put on.

"You want to come too?" she asked with a conciliatory gesture. "Or do you have something else to work on?"

"Nah, I can come. Could be interesting hearing this guy's opinion."

"Good." Caesar rose from the table and gathered their plates. "I'll work more on the girl. Don't take all the eels with you. Leave me a couple to dig into."

The drive to the museum was as usual conducted in awkward silence, and Miriam had second – and third and even fourth – thoughts of asking Cyrus to come with her. *I'm always falling into that trap*, she thought grumpily and stared out of the window, avoiding his emotionless face. At least they didn't argue about anything this time. Well... arguing wasn't really what they were doing, she thought in honesty. It was rather an endless battle of who of them could frustrate the other one the most. Combined with the awkward silences Cyrus had mastered to perfection, he managed to get on her nerves like no one else.

At the museum, they were let in without any problems at all, and a security guard showed them the way to Professor Bruchheimer's office. Miriam knocked on the door while Cyrus stood a step behind her with the box containing the eels.

"Professor Bruchheimer?"

The wrinkled face that was peeping out at them from the chink in the door was painted with suspicion.

"Who are you?"

Miriam tried a comforting smile. "I'm Field Researcher Claire from the Star Student FRT C2. We spoke earlier today. About the..."

"Shh!" The professor popped his head out a bit further and scrutinized the sterile hallway. Then he fixed his gaze on Miriam's forehead.

"Did you say anything about bringing someone else?" he whispered in an accusing tone, glancing hastily towards

Cyrus, not meeting his eyes. "It's only you two? No one else?"

"Just us, Professor. May we come in?"

He shot another peek at the empty corridor before pulling in his head and opening the door just wide enough for the two slender agents to squeeze in. The elderly man closed the door hurriedly behind them and locked it. Cyrus and Miriam exchanged looks. The small windowless room was reeking of old cigar smoke. Taxidermic animals and creatures in glass jars were all over the bookshelves that filled every wall, packed in between books and binders.

"So..." Professor Bruchheimer wiped off his hands nervously on his worn-out chestnut corduroy jacket. Miriam held out her hand.

"I'm Field Researcher Claire, as I said, and this is Field Researcher Cyrus." The professor stared blankly at her hand, not giving any sign of taking it. Miriam let her hand sink again, feeling awkward enough to blush. She tried to hide it as she nodded towards Cyrus who held the box containing the eels. "As I explained earlier we need to identify the creatures in that box."

"Yes, yes. Please put them on the table."

He hasted towards the cluttered table in the middle of the room and started to shove papers towards the right end of the table. Some of them fell down on the floor. Miriam reached down and picked them up. Before she had a chance to react, the professor snatched them furiously out of her hands.

"Don't you dare touch those!" Even in his anger, he never looked her in her eyes, but focused on a spot on her forehead.

"I'm sorry," Miriam said humbly. "I just wanted to help..."

"Help? Help me fiddlesticks! You don't know what you're dealing with here, and you don't want to know either, so keep your dirty hands where I can see them, young lady."

Cyrus, who had put the white box on the clean fleck on the table, gave her a warning glance and interrupted smoothly. "So, Professor, I've unpacked the eels now, if you would please like to examine them."

The old man turned around, still with an angry expression on his face. "What?" His eyes fell on the open box. "Yes. Yes, of course."

As he moved towards the table again with the papers protectively clutched to his chest, Miriam rolled her eyes at his back, still with angrily blushing cheeks, and gave a soundless sigh. Professor Bruchheimer reached for his glasses, a pair of rubber gloves, a couple of doctor's instruments, and bent over the box.

"I take it that they're in the bucket, still alive?" he asked, turning slightly to Cyrus while putting on the gloves and trying the lid.

"They were alive when I packed them this afternoon, that's for sure."

The bucket opened, and Miriam smelled the slight odor from within. Then a long, silent pause occurred, in which the two agents observed the professor's motionless frame before he quietly moaned and rubbed his face.

"No, not again. Not again." His voice was almost a whisper. Miriam urgently took the few steps to his side. His face had suddenly become pale, and he was staring into the bucket with fear. Faint splashing sounds were heard from it. "Wait!" he said suddenly. "There are only four! Why only four? There should be six." White in his face he turned towards Cyrus. "There should be six! Have any of them escaped?"

Cyrus held up a calming hand. "Nothing to worry about, Professor. The other two are in good hands."

A brittle chuckle found its way out of the old man's throat. "You don't know what this is, do you? There are no 'good' hands when it comes to these creatures." With a frightened expression, he looked down into the bucket again. "I don't need to examine them. I know what they are, even though they don't have a scientific name nor are they identified in any book of biological species that I have read. They get planted in a human as larvae, and according to my guess – that's the best you can get from me – the time it takes for them to hatch is different depending on the human and her diet. How long? I don't know. A month? A year? Who knows? When they hatch, they eat everything they can get their mouths on, and when the victim dies – in horrible pain – they live as long as the body is not totally decomposed. After that, they die. If they are not plucked out, of course. The good thing is that even if they're deadly once inside a human, they need help to spread. That's why I'd say they're not naturally developed – they're cultivated. Where? I don't know. By whom? Who knows?" Professor Bruchheimer sighed with a painful expression on his face. "I've seen them before, in Finland. A whole family was being devoured by them. No one was saved, not even the little baby. A terrible thing to do to people." The pained expression vanished, and he glanced at them. "No one in the village spoke, but there were… indications… of a bigger… group… that the family appeared to belong to. A group that wasn't satisfied with them. And that's all you get from me. Now, I hope that you'll excuse me. No…" he said towards Miriam, "I'm not in the mood to play *Jeopardy* today, so please spare me your questions. I don't know anything more of interest to you anyway." After shoving them out of the barely opened door, the professor paused and looked at the box in Cyrus' hands. "Salt. That's what eats them. Just melting. Good thing, salt." He glanced quickly at the empty corridor and without another word he shoved the door closed and locked it behind them.

Out in the parking lot, Cyrus and Miriam secured themselves into Cyrus' old bottle green Volkswagen. Even though the sun turned the small car into a sauna, they chose to keep the windows closed.

"You really should get yourself an AC," Miriam puffed as he drove out on Lincoln Avenue.

"Yeah? Well, tell the Society to raise my wages and I'll think about it."

The usual awkward silence fell for a while. Miriam wiped away sweat from her forehead, while thinking about the old professor, locked up in his office.

"You know," Cyrus said thoughtfully at length, his eyes fixed on the road, "I feel sorry for him. A biologist, working alone and not in a team. Always in the dark. Always having slightly too much information, but never getting the full picture. Always aware that you one day might speak to the wrong person and get whacked."

Miriam glanced at him, but didn't see any expression on his face that corresponded to the sympathetic tone in his voice. She looked out of the window again.

"Sometimes not knowing the whole picture would be a blessing," she mumbled to the window.

"Did you notice what the old fox didn't mention, Claire?" he asked as if he hadn't caught what she said. Curious, she turned towards him. Cyrus smiled. "He didn't lie. Not a single white one slipped out of his mouth. He knows that most of us pick up lies as easily as spreading jam on a sandwich. That sly bastard." His tone was bland, but he was still smiling to himself. "I think I'll let you off at HQ and go back for another little chat."

"Cyrus!" protested Miriam.

He gave her a side-glance. "He didn't like you, Claire, and he certainly didn't trust you. You must have noticed that?"

She scoffed, annoyed by his tone, and for a second, she quietly debated with herself before giving in to curiosity. "Well, go on, tell me. What did I miss?" This time, she could read him, and that didn't make her day any better. He was clearly amused.

"All right. He said there should be six eels, not four. Why is he so sure that six is the correct quantity, especially if they were planted by someone? Why not five or seven? What's so special about the number six? That's the first."

"And the second?" asked Miriam, listening attentively, her irritation forgotten.

"If they can't breed, why was he so terrified that they might be on the loose?"

"Huh…" Miriam frowned intrigued at this new angle.

"And the third… but this has nothing to do with the professor's knowledge; we really need to get to the Stevenson parents. Whether they planted the eels in their daughter or not, they have information we need."

"I'll work on that today, then," Miriam said and viewed him anticipatory from the side, unable to keep her goodies any longer. "Did you see what he kept in his bookcase, by the way, Cy?"

"No, what?"

She smiled just a little triumphantly. "He had a couple of glass jars with our friends the eels in them."

"Really? Way to go! See anything else?" The sincerity in his voice turned her victory to ashes, and she shrugged grumpily.

"Nothing that I think has anything to do with our RP. A lot of strange animals, some that I'm not sure I've seen before, but then I'm not a biologist. Lots of books in Latin and German and Greek. I think there were some in Russian and maybe Arabic as well and a couple in other languages. The papers he was so afraid I might read were encrypted."

Cyrus chuckled. "Yep, an old fox, that's for sure."

"Other things were interesting too. The whole room reeked of cigar smoke, but he didn't have any tobacco stains on his hands and everything in the room was organized in a specific pattern. I noticed it, but didn't have the time to make any sense out of it. It's not important, though."

Cyrus suddenly got a strange look on his face. "You're sure about the lack of stains?"

"Yes. Why?"

She could see him clenching his teeth. "He never said that he was the professor, Claire." Miriam inhaled aghast as if someone had kicked her in the guts. "It's probably nothing,

25

but… Almost there now. As soon as I let you off, I'll go back. You know, just to check things out."

She scowled at him. "You shouldn't go alone. You know that."

"I won't get anything out of him with you there." Miriam frowned, but didn't say anything. He was probably right, even though it annoyed her to admit it. With another glance at her, he said: "Don't worry. Nothing will happen."

"You'd better be right," she muttered and had the pleasure of seeing him blush.

Another silence fell in the car; a tense, worried silence. Miriam tried to think about what she had said to the old man on the phone, but she couldn't remember if she had mentioned the girl or what the eels had done to her before they came to see him. Not that the last part mattered, she thought. He seemed to know more about what the eels did to people than he was comfortable with.

"Stay in touch, Cy," she said when she reluctantly left the car. He gave her one of his humorless smiles, and she heard him say: "Will do." before he closed the door and drove off. She watched him disappear around the corner with a nagging feeling that she should have gone with him nonetheless. Then she shrugged and tried to get rid of the foreboding sensation before entering the FBI building, where she took the stairs to her office. There was work to be done while she waited.

The rest of the early afternoon, she sat restlessly at the computer, trying to concentrate on her work, while checking the time every other minute. A little more than an hour had passed since she parted from Cyrus and he had not yet called her. It didn't take more than half an hour to return to the Museum of Natural History, so he should have had at least forty minutes to do whatever he needed to do by now. For at least the twentieth time, she berated herself for letting him go alone, for not pushing hard enough for the option to at least sit in his car while he was in there. She should have gone with him; that was the plain fact. She knew – no, they

26

both knew – how dangerous it could be entering a scene that might be of interest to the Society when all three of them were there together – and now she had let him go off by himself. Both previous times he'd entered a site alone, it had ended catastrophically bad. If something happened to him now, she would never forgive herself, no matter how much she disliked him. Miriam checked the time again. Five more minutes – that was all she was going to give him before calling him, not a second more.

She clicked on another link at the FBI's citizens archive page to try to steer her thoughts away from Cyrus. So far, she hadn't found much. Robert Stevenson. Age: thirty-two. Profession: carpenter. No criminal record. Spouse: Stella Stevenson. Born: Stella Alba – now that was a silly name if she'd ever heard one. Age: thirty-four. Profession: waitress. No criminal record. Married: December twelve, nineteen ninety-two. Nothing outstanding. Just one of millions of similar couples all over the U.S. There was only one thing that was weird, one thing that evoked a tingling sensation of something wrong. The child was not listed. That made no sense at all.

Sometimes the FBI kept fake pages for certain people. Why the Stevenson's would be among them, Miriam had a hard time understanding. They had not been unique in any way: a lower class family, not very educated, struggling to make ends meet. Still, there was something else there, something that made her sense that there was more to this family than met the eye. Whatever it could be, Miriam wanted to be sure that she didn't overlook anything on the regular pages before going into the special FBI sites and maybe even contacting the Golden Fleece Society's information source within the Faculty.

While she waited for the web page to load, she nervously tapped a pen on the desk and checked the time again, like poking a bad tooth with her tongue. She would give him two more minutes before she called, she decided. Her gaze went back to the stagnant computer screen. She

27

couldn't believe the time it took for it to load today. The staccato tapping became more restless, and her thoughts returned to Cyrus again. As usual, when she was nervous, she berated herself. Letting him go alone was a stupid, stupid thing to do! Last time he went somewhere alone they'd all paid for it, not just him. Another glance at the time showed her that it was just one more minute now before she could call him. Her gaze shot back to the screen. Still nothing. What was it with that damned page? Miriam tried to move the cursor to reload, but nothing happened.

"*A brock!*" she growled in Yiddish and kicked the computer tower in frustration. Just as she reached for the cell phone, it rang and made her heart stand still. When she started to breathe again, she saw the number in the display window, and it filled her with a relief so great that her limbs went limp.

"Cyrus!"

"Okay, I admit, I'm stupid!" Cyrus voice on the other side was clearly upset, and he panted as if he was running.

"What...?"

"I didn't pick up the signals! There must have been signals!"

"Cyrus, please, what happened? Are you running?"

She could hear him sigh and then a loud brushing sound near the phone's head when he ran his hand through his hair, a clear sign that he felt out of control.

"What do you mean 'running'? I'm not running. What are you talking about?" He took a deep breath as to compose himself. "I asked the museum's security staff to show me a picture of the good professor..."

"It wasn't him," Miriam said with a calm she didn't feel.

"No. So I had them unlock his office... The guy was apparently in a hurry after we left. It looks like a tornado has gone through it. I've blocked it off until you can get a look at it, but Claire, you need to take Caesar with you and meet me at the real professor's house. He doesn't answer the phone."

Miriam went cold. "Where are you now?"

"Still in his office, but I'm leaving right away. Should be there in about twenty."

"We'll meet you there, Cy."

"Address is eighty-four twelve, one-hundred-and-seventieth street."

She scribbled it down on her memo pad. "Right. We're leaving a.s.a.p. And Cy, it wasn't your fault."

Cyrus just scoffed before hanging up on her.

Chapter 3

It only took a minute after Caesar turned left on eighty-fourth Avenue and drove down the one-hundred-and-seventieth street before Miriam spotted the small sandstone house where Professor Bruchheimer lived. It looked even smaller than it actually was, flanked as it was by two red-bricked houses, four stories high.

"New England style," Caesar commented as he parked the car and lowered the volume on Ella Fitzgerald.

"Mhm," Miriam agreed, but was more interested in the house with its neatly cared for yard and its bright marigolds shining in the flowerbeds. It would have looked inviting had the blinds at the front not been down. "It looks like the professor hasn't emptied his mailbox for a couple of days," she remarked.

"I guess that he's not lucky enough to be on a business trip."

Miriam gave Caesar somewhat of an amused look.

"That's something Cyrus could've said, you know," she said with half a smile.

"That's true," he admitted. "And speaking of Cyrus, where is he?" He checked the empty street. "No sign of either him or his car."

"I hope he didn't go in on his own." Miriam couldn't really hide the concern in her voice. Caesar squeezed her hand.

"Don't worry, Mimi," he said, and the use of her pet name made her feel warm and loved. "He hasn't done anything that stupid since... well... the two last projects."

She giggled nervously, once more vividly remembering the disasters he had caused back then.

"Aw, thanks, Henry. That made me feel much better."

Caesar chuckled, reached for his cell phone, and dialed Cyrus' number. One signal sounded, then two, three.

He was just about to hang up when she heard Cyrus' muffled voice answering at the other end of the line.

"I'll be with you in ten minutes."

Caesar gave Miriam another smile and shrugged. "Well then, no need for us to sit here. Let's go and check the surroundings."

They stepped out of the car and crossed the street to the white painted wooden fence that surrounded Professor Bruchheimer's house. The mailbox was indeed overloaded. Miriam glanced at it.

"I'd say that it's probably best to start with the door. Who knows, he might just be sick and in bed." She opened the gate and started up the small graveled path that led to the veranda and the front door. "Beautiful stones in this gravel," Miriam reflected. "This man really cares for his home. And look at the grass and the flowers. They're very well cared for. Someone watered them recently. They'd be wilting in this heat otherwise. Probably not a neighbor since a neighbor would have brought in his mail."

Caesar nodded. "Most likely *Green Oasis Company.*"

The sound of an approaching car caught their attention. Cyrus' old Volkswagen parked carelessly behind Caesar's black Opel Vectra. Cyrus unfurled himself from the vehicle and strolled determinedly towards them.

"Quickest ten minutes I've ever seen," Miriam remarked, and Caesar smiled, amused.

"Bloody peak hours," Cyrus commented casually as he joined them on the path and nodded towards the house. "Have you been inside yet?"

"We were just going to take a look," Caesar replied.

Miriam studied Cyrus' face. It looked flushed and weirdly bloated. The improbable thought of him drinking while on duty occurred to her. The speculation made her ashamed of herself. He had never consumed alcohol as far as she knew. Maybe he was sick?

"You all right?" she asked concerned.

"Oh, yes," he answered with a smug smile. She frowned, not certain if he was making fun of her.

"Are you sure? You look sick."

Cyrus moved abruptly and towered over her. Miriam crouched involuntarily and backed away.

"Mind your own business, Miriam, and I'll mind mine," he lashed out at her, eyes glaring with anger. Miriam stiffened, shocked by the attack. Caesar stared confounded at Cyrus.

"That was very much uncalled for," he said coldly, but Cyrus just shrugged.

"Whatever."

When they looked at him, both speechless for a moment by this unusual behavior, he folded his arms and glared provocatively back. Miriam didn't know what to think. He acted like a spoiled teenager, a side he had never shown before. *He must be drunk*, she thought again, even though she didn't believe it and he didn't smell of alcohol. As the silence stretched out, he shrugged once more.

"You have to come to the museum when we're done, Miriam," he said.

The odd use of her real name instead of her FRT name irked her immensely, and she glared at him on the edge of anger.

"Can you stop calling me that?"

The surprised expression on his face had to be faked, and it nearly made her go over the edge. Caesar's hand on her arm was soothing, and instead of lashing out at Cyrus, she turned her back to him.

"Whatever," he sneered at her. "Just come and get the damn things, bitch!"

She swirled around with her fists clenched, hot with anger.

"That's enough," Caesar interrupted with a deep scowl on his forehead. "Let's work as a team now, but you and I will have a talk tomorrow. This is not acceptable."

Cyrus just shrugged and muttered: "Whatever." under his breath again. Miriam stared at him unbelievingly while her anger slowly vanished. He was like a completely different person than the professional FBI agent she knew. Yes, they had their moments, but nothing like this. He had never called her 'bitch' or anything like it before. He didn't do that, no matter how frustrated he was. Had something happened at the museum? Had he got personal news that put him off balance? Clearly something was wrong. She surprised herself by wishing they were close enough for her to ask him and lend him support if he needed. As it was now, she could just helplessly let the situation cool down and let Caesar take care of it. She embraced herself mentally and adopted her own professional outlook. She was not going to be dragged down by him. Caesar observed them emotionlessly.

"Shall we?" he asked coolly, and both of them nodded.

They continued up the path and went up onto the veranda. Caesar knocked firmly on the door, and it opened up slowly from the force of his knock. Miriam shared a glance with him and released the gun from her holster while she quietly stepped behind the door. For some reason, Cyrus did not react on the cue, and she waved him on so that he eventually trod to the other side of the doorway. Caesar glared at him, but then he drew a deep breath and opened the door wide.

"Professor Bruchheimer?" he called out. "FBI. Please come to the door."

The seconds went by and the only thing answering them from the inside of the house was a deep silence. Miriam's heart pounded, and her forehead was getting moist. She watched Caesar intently. He finally returned their gaze and said calmly: "We're going in. Are you prepared?"

They both nodded. Caesar raised his gun and stepped into the narrow hall. Miriam followed closely with Cyrus covering the back. Caesar tread cautiously through the hall and stopped just before the doorway. A quick peek around the corner at both sides produced nothing. He beckoned the others to come after him as he stepped into the next room.

The living room was lit up by the sinking sun and bathed in a golden light that was reflected on the wooden floor. A vase on the coffee table contained withered tulips; amber-colored petals covered the wooden surface. An ancient looking clock ticked quietly in the corner. Caesar headed towards the open archway that seemed to lead to the kitchen. A startled, rattling sound was heard as he closed in. He stopped right there, making another quick peek into the kitchen. A flutter of wings and an anxious chirp greeted him.

"Just a canary," he whispered, and Miriam suddenly remembered to breathe again. When they cautiously entered the kitchen, Miriam saw the first sign of something unusual. The yellow canary was flying around in an extraordinarily big cage and on top of it, an open box with birdseed lay as if it had been dropped there. A huge pile had run out of it and onto the cage floor. She pointed it out, and Caesar nodded.

The kitchen was neatly cleaned with no dishes in the sink or in the plate rack. It felt as if it was swimming in a green-colored shadow cast by the richly leafed birch right outside the window. A tablecloth of bright yellow gingham adorned the table and a clear glass vase with no water, and wilting white tulips stood in the middle of it. It was a kitchen Miriam would have liked to be invited to dinner in.

She took a short step and opened the fridge. A quick glance revealed lots of almost fresh vegetables and fruits that were neatly packaged in open cardboard boxes. A bottle of milk and a pitcher of juice with a grayish tinge to it stood on the lowest shelf. There was no meat or fish on any of the clean shelves. The professor was either a vegetarian or bought all his meat and fish directly from the market. The obvious difference between his neatly organized living space and his chaotic workspace struck her as odd, but interesting. She met Caesar's look and shrugged to indicate that there were no interesting revelations in the fridge.

Cyrus stood leaning heavily against the wall beside the birdcage with a bored expression as he watched the outside view from the window. Miriam scowled at him and bit her lip nervously. *What's wrong with him?* she thought again. The canary hopped from branch to branch with anxious chirps. It didn't have any water in its container, Miriam noticed with another concerned frown.

On the other side of the table, two doors led out of the kitchen. Caesar waved towards the closest of them. Miriam nodded and started to follow him, gun ready. She hadn't taken many steps before she realized with surprise that Cyrus still stood at the window, seemingly lost to the world in his own thoughts. She tapped Caesar's shoulder and pointed towards him. Caesar looked flabbergasted, but scowled and took the few steps back to the window and tapped Cyrus harshly on the shoulder. The younger man jolted, and his eyes flashed angrily. Caesar mouthed the word "Focus!" and Cyrus' heated expression changed into a condescending one as he met his leader's glare. Never had Miriam seen so many different expressions on his face and in such a short time period, and to see him being condescending towards Caesar? That had never happened. If she was certain about one thing when it came to Cyrus, it was about his deep respect towards the older man. Once again, she bit her lip and looked back and forth between the two men. The tension born between the three of them that very second hit her like a bullet and their presence in this house suddenly felt more dangerous than it did just a minute ago. She had never entered a possibly dangerous crime scene with a team she sensed that she couldn't completely trust would cover her back. Not once since Cyrus joined their team a year and a half ago had she liked him, but she had always been aware of his loyalty to the team and his determination to keep it safe. That had made her feel protected and secure. That feeling was totally gone now. Sweat broke out on her forehead, and when Cyrus suddenly turned an unusual unsympathetic gaze towards her, she saw disdain in his eyes. It took all her willpower, but she slowly turned her back on him and followed Caesar's lead, gun held tightly in hands not as steady as they usually were.

Caesar was already at the door, waving impatiently at them. Miriam hurried as silently as possible to the right-hand side of the door, while Cyrus casually made his way to the left. Caesar's dark expression when he looked at the younger man didn't bode well. Nervousness tickled her spine as the tension between the three of them rose with every second.

After a short glance towards both of them, Caesar opened the door. A small office revealed itself with three bookcases on the right side and a desk with the dark luster of wild cherry in the middle of the room. At the window, a honey-colored armchair, worn and comfortable, was placed beside a rustic end table and a floor lamp. The room smelled deeply of cigar smoke. Miriam could see an ashtray of mild orange agate on the desk, empty, but clearly used.

Caesar waved towards the last door. Miriam and Cyrus took their usual positions on each side of it. There was a moment of calm and suddenly Miriam knew what they would find behind this regular-looking white door. The ominous stillness of violent death leaked out from it, so intense that she could almost see it. The foreboding gripped her so strongly that she nearly choked and had to gasp for breath. The stern look on Caesar's face told her that he sensed it too. Cyrus contemplated the door thoughtfully and absent-mindedly put his gun in its holster. Miriam lifted her own gun into position, even though she was quite sure she wouldn't need it. Whatever had happened in there had already passed. Three pairs of eyes met each other in silent agreement, and Caesar opened the door.

The dark and sweet smell of blood was the first thing that greeted them when the bedroom was finally revealed before them. No one moved as they tried to take in the sight that met them. Someone was lying on the narrow bed. A man or a woman, Miriam couldn't tell. The skin of the face had been carefully carved off, as had the genitals. The chest area had been carved bloody with numerous symbols she didn't recognize, while the abdomen had been opened and the intestines were taken out. They had been placed around the body in an egg-shape with the heart above the head, the lungs at the elbows and the stomach at the feet. Connected to them all were the entrails. A still burning grave candle, a withered bouquet of forget-me-nots, and a small glass vial filled with coagulated blood stood on each side of the heart. Blood had also been used to write the words on the cafe-latte-colored walls, one word on each wall: *Mother Accept Our Offering* with the word *Mother* at the head.

Not a sound disturbed the stillness. Miriam had the troubled feeling of entering an unholy religious site and her hand unconsciously reached for the Star of David she hadn't worn since her late teens. Caesar put away his gun with a deep sigh.

"We're much too late to use these," he said. "Let's get to work." He turned to her. "You work the room as usual while we talk to the neighbors. Leave the body to me. I'll take care of it after you're done here."

"Okay," she agreed hoarsely and cleared her throat. Caesar ushered Cyrus out of the room. Miriam wondered why Cyrus didn't argue about questioning the neighbors together with Caesar since that was his area of expertise, but he didn't even frown, even though it must have hurt his feelings to suddenly not be trusted. With a shrug at the whole situation, she looked around the room once more, taking in the details and distancing herself emotionally from the site before leaving to get her camera and tools. On her way out, she passed the canary again. It sat by the empty water tank and chirped when she closed in on it.

"Oh, you're thirsty. Poor little one. Let me just process the sink before I give you fresh water."

She hurried out to the car, grabbed her equipment and went straight back to the kitchen again. To her astonishment, there was not a single trace of blood in the sink and just one pair of fingerprints. After gathering a sample,

37

she went on to fill up the small water tank. The canary threw himself at it and drank eagerly.

"Poor you," Miriam said. "How long have you been without water? Thank goodness for the air conditioning. You'd probably be dead without it. What will happen to you when we go? We can't just leave you here." She looked at the drinking bird and made her decision. "You wouldn't complain very much if I took you home to my place, right? I used to have a budgie when I was little. I guess you're not that different." The bird ignored her wholeheartedly and continued his relationship with the water. Miriam smiled to herself and left the kitchen.

Two hours later she packed the samples and the camera's full memory card into the trunk of Caesar's car while the blanket-covered birdcage was carried into the back seat. As soon as it was placed in the car, Cyrus went straight to his own car, waiting for her for the trip to the museum. Miriam closed the trunk, leaned towards it with a tired sigh, and drew her hand over her eyes.

"Are you all right?" Caesar shut the door and came to her side, touching her arm a couple of seconds before letting go, but it meant a lot to her. He never touched her if they weren't on their own. On the other hand, his big frame obscured her, and no one could see that he touched her, she realized and sighed quietly, wishing for something more, as usual.

"Yeah, I guess. I'm just tired. It's just that... um... these weird RPs... they're getting to me."

To her surprise, Caesar took her hand and squeezed it gently

"That's your problem, Mimi, your weakness. You're always getting too personal. Your kindness and empathy are assets in every other job, but to manage as one of us, you have to shut it off. Cyrus is a great example of that."

She sighed again, seeking comfort in the warmth of his hand.

38

"I know. I know. But I still don't grasp how to do that. It's like the poor professor inside – if indeed it is the professor. I can't help but think of his last hours, of the pain, the terror, the hope that it would end with him still alive, that someone would come to stop it, the last moments when he realizes that this is really, really the end..." A tear fell down her cheek. Caesar dried it gently. "And then the poor canary hearing the screams and feeling the agony... Sometimes I cannot bear this, what people do to each other."

Another tear fell and then one more. Caesar's voice was very soft. "We all feel that way from time to time, Mimi. That's why we accepted becoming researchers: to be able to protect people. That's why we continue because we have more insight now, we have more power and are better able to help people. We can't save everyone, but our work is not in vain. Do you remember the last case we had before Cyrus joined us?"

"How could I forget?" Miriam sniveled. "We lost Cecilia then."

"Yes, but we managed to save fifty children who would have died without us. That's worth fighting for, Mimi, and it's worth dying for. You know that Cecilia believed that."

She nodded. Another deep sigh heaved within her chest, and she dried her eyes with the back of her hand. Caesar lent her one of his big checkered handkerchiefs for her to blow her nose.

"Thanks," she said, muffled, with her face buried in the cloth. "I'd better get going. It would be nice to be home before midnight."

Caesar gave her a last squeeze before letting her hand go. "Where do you want the bird?"

"Put it in the living room near the windows so he can see the view, but leave the blanket on for now. I'll remove it in the morning."

"All right."

"Are you staying the night?" she asked and felt her cheeks heat. Quickly she looked down, didn't want him to see her blush.

"Possibly, if you want to."

She nodded. "Thanks. Oh, and could you please give the samples to the lab before going home? I'd like to have at least some of the results tomorrow, if possible."

He raised a couple of dissatisfied eyebrows at her, and she felt her cheeks heat again, but this time in embarrassment.

"They don't work that fast, you know that, Mimi, but I can hand them in if you want to. I intended to follow Andy and his angels back to the morgue anyway. They should be finished any time now. Hey, Andy!" he shouted to the middle-aged detective standing at one of the police cars further away. "How long do you think it will take?"

Andrew Gorlois strolled over to them. He and his team had worked for twenty minutes, gathering the evidence and removing the body.

"Oh, not long now, Henry. Ten minutes at the most. The girls have covered practically everything by now." He gave them a curious glance. "You guys always get your hands on such weird stuff. Ritualistic murder? You think we have a serial killer on the loose or is it a single case?"

Caesar shrugged to show his ignorance.

"You're probably as knowledgeable as we are right now."

"For sure. Brief us as soon as you get anything, will you? We need to stop the bastard if he turns out to be a playful fellow."

"That you can count on," Caesar said sternly and met the detective's intelligent, searching gaze. "And you," he turned to Miriam, "need to go. I think someone's getting restless."

She followed his look and saw Cyrus standing outside his car looking their way.

"Um, right."

40

"Yeah," Andy said, turning towards the house. "I'll get the girls to hurry up."

When he left them, Caesar lowered his voice, still watching Cyrus. "By the way, Claire, keep your eyes open tonight."

A worried pang in her stomach made her cringe. "What do you mean?"

Caesar hesitated, but then he frowned and shook his head. "Just that. Keep your eyes open tonight. And call me when you get home."

She nodded slowly while the insecurity bubbled up inside her again as she grabbed her toolbox and camera and headed for Cyrus and the trip to the museum.

Chapter 4

It was the throbbing pain in Miriam's head that woke her up. She blinked, trying to get her sleepy, scattered mind awake and functioning. As she lay staring out into the gray half-light, she realized that something was wrong. There were no sunlight and no lamps shining on her face. She lifted her head and a flash of pain made her groan. With a grimace, she let her head sink back onto the pillow again while she gently rubbed her eyes and temples. Migraine? She hadn't suffered from migraines since she was a teenager. Was that why she hadn't switched on the lights? She couldn't remember. At last, she managed to sit up and look around in the dusky room while cradling her aching head. Everything appeared to be normal, except that the blinds were folded. She never did that anymore.

"Henry?" Her voice sounded hoarse and was not louder than a whisper. She gargled and tried again, stronger this time. "Henry?"

Only silence answered her. The apartment felt empty. He must have left without waking her up. He did that sometimes when he thought that she needed more sleep than usual. This was the first time he folded the blinds, though. She'd have to tell him not to do that again. Miriam put her feet on the naked hardwood floor with the intention of heading for the window when the cell phone rang. She grimaced again and put a hand to her throbbing temple. Where was the phone? The sound didn't come from its regular place at the bedside table. She must have left it in her jacket. Irritation started to rise when she saw that her clothes were not thrown on the chair as usual. Where were they? What had gotten into Henry, messing around with her routine like this? He knew how much she relied on her routines. The cell phone rang and rang. She tried to localize the sound, confused by the unfamiliar dusky light in the room and the pounding headache.

"*A brock!*" she growled when the sound abruptly stopped. At last, she saw her clothes, hanging half hidden on the hanger behind the bedroom door. She glared at them. When had Henry become this meticulous about her habits? The cell phone rang again. This time, she managed to reach it in time, digging into the jacket pocket.

"Hello?"

"Hi, Claire. Ready for a trip to the museum?" Cyrus' voice sounded rested and cheerful.

"The museum?" Miriam rubbed her temple again.

"Yeah, to collect the evidence. Remember?"

"Um..." Hadn't they done that yesterday? She tried to recollect her thoughts. No, that's right. Cyrus had driven her home instead. She couldn't remember why they changed their minds, but the image in her head of him letting her off at her house was crystal clear. "Right."

"All right. Need a ride?"

"Sure. And thanks," she added as an afterthought.

"I'll be there in twenty."

He hung up, and she went straight to the window. Sunlight flooded in and bathed her face with warmth when she pulled up the blinds. She gave up a deep, relieved sigh and allowed herself a few seconds to just bask in the light, letting her whole body relax before heading for the pleasures of a hot, soothing shower.

Twenty minutes and one Tylenol 3 later, she was clean, dressed, and enjoying a bagel and coffee from the café on the opposite street while she waited for Cyrus to show up. The migraine throbbed somewhere underneath that thick, soft blanket the painkiller had created, but she could live with it and even function. She had taken the time to give the canary fresh water and birdseed, as well as a few moments of chatting, before leaving the apartment. Later today, she thought, she was going to stop by a pet store to get a book about canaries and some supplies. It felt good having a pet around again. She wouldn't be able to keep it, of course. No one knew if she would just disappear during a case again

43

someday and be gone for a week or two, or maybe as long as a month this time, without any way of notifying anyone; that would leave the bird to die a slow and painful death. Maybe her sister could take him? Bethany, being a veterinarian, loved animals and would be more than happy for an excuse to finally get a bird into her house. Miriam imagined that Ted, her brother-in-law, would mutter a lot under his breath, but he had more than once said that Beth coming home with a pet someday was inevitable. "Resistance is futile," he had confessed with a deep sigh last Christmas.

Miriam thought about the bright yellow color of the bird and how happy the sight of him had made her when she removed the blanket from the cage this morning. He had looked at her with those clear pit coal eyes and chirped lively as if he greeted her. She would call him Luce, she decided, and Beth was only to borrow him.

Cyrus' car drove up beside her, and she got in.

"Morning," she said as she buckled her seat belt, determined to keep the atmosphere polite and agreeable today.

"Yeah," Cyrus answered.

"Slept well?"

"Well enough," He started to back out.

"Good," Miriam said and couldn't find something else to say. For a while, they drove in that familiar silence that at least Miriam thought was uncomfortable, but Cyrus never seemed to be bothered by, something that irritated her immensely. At least he appeared to be himself today. Whatever news he'd gotten the day before, he had composed himself and, apparently, the meeting with Caesar this morning had helped too. She was relieved that they were on speaking terms again. Well, she admitted to herself, 'speaking terms' was something she never was on with Cyrus, but uncomfortable silence was way better than fighting. Miriam sighed inaudibly and wished for the thousandth time that he had a radio in the car, or that he at least would talk about the weather or something, or that her own car would finally be repaired so that she wouldn't be trapped like this.

"Interesting scenario yesterday," he commented suddenly and immediately she inconsequently wished that he had kept his silence.

"Mhm."

"Ritualistic. Wonder if it has anything to do with our project. Bet my head it's not related at all. Would be too simple."

"Hm." Miriam sounded skeptical. "Maybe. But it's a real strange coincidence in that case."

"Yeah?" He glanced at her. "Well, coincidences happen all the time."

"Not in our job."

"They can happen, Claire."

Miriam put up her hands in a defensive gesture. "I'm not saying it's not a coincidence. I'm just saying that it's not very likely."

Cyrus suddenly turned into a narrow alley and parked abruptly. Miriam watched him, surprised. He looked back with an angry flare in his eyes. *So much for agreeable atmosphere...* she thought and watched him guardedly.

"Why are you arguing with me?" he asked with a demanding voice, and she gave him an alarmed look. He never lost his temper. What was going on with him?

"Um, Cyrus, I'm not arguing. We're discussing the project, right?" she said cautiously, but he made a dismissive gesture at her.

"There's nothing to discuss, Claire. Two different RPs. Not our table. We shouldn't even go to the museum. Just a waste of time." Miriam stared at him, too baffled to say anything. "Let's go and tell Caesar we're dropping this one." Cyrus' voice was definitive, and he reached for the ignition key.

Miriam finally found her voice again. "Uh...? Cyrus? What made you come to that conclusion? You can't just make such a decision on your own."

45

He let go of the key and stared at her as if she was a five-year-old girl.

"It's obvious that they're not related. Even you should be able to see that."

She scoffed and scowled at him. "Even me? Why, thank you, Cyrus. Glad to hear your opinion about my intelligence." Cyrus rolled his eyes, and Miriam continued angrily, finding it hard to remain calm. "Since I'm so dumb, go on and tell me what's so obvious, 'cause I can't see it."

"All right. The Stevenson's is a lower class family. The professor's an academic. They move in different circles, and there's no connection at all between them, which means that he couldn't have known about them being exposed to the eels, even if he obviously have a specimen at work."

Silence fell for a second while Miriam stared unbelievingly at Cyrus.

"That's it?" she said eventually. "You want to drop the RP because of that? What's the matter with you, Cyrus?"

"Nothing," he said sullenly and looked out of the window. Miriam massaged her throbbing temple and gave up a frustrated sigh.

"I'm sorry, but this is silly. There's no logic at all in your reasoning. 'The professor's an academic and the Stevenson's is a lower class family'? And what does that prove? Nothing. You have no clue what his research area was. He might have contacted them and used them as his test subjects just because no one would connect them. Or they are distant relatives. Or he's an old friend to grandpa and served together with him in the war. Any connection is possible. Even Luce would be able to come up with something better than 'they move in different circles'."

There was a slight pause, angry and uncompromising as usual.

"Who's Luce?" Cyrus asked eventually, still stubbornly looking out of the window while frustration boiled in Miriam's body.

"The canary, Cyrus." When he didn't acknowledge her, she continued, while trying hard to calm down: "I named him Luce. That's *light* in Italian." Very aware that she babbled, she massaged her temple again and felt totally at loss. *How the hell am I supposed to handle this situation? This isn't Cyrus talking. I mean, dropping a project? Cyrus? Has he totally lost it?*

"What canary?" he asked eventually without showing any interest at all. Miriam felt a pang of irritation again.

"Come on, Cyrus! The professor's canary! The one we found in the kitchen."

Cyrus turned his head slowly towards her and squinted at her. "There wasn't any stupid bird in the house, Claire."

As she met his cold, inquisitive gaze, a chilly feeling grabbed her stomach tightly and made her breaths shorter and faster. Goosebumps appeared on her arms. Something was wrong. She knew that something was terribly wrong. With pounding heart she groped for the door handle.

"There was a bird in the kitchen, Cyrus," she said cautiously and tried desperately to reach the door handle without him noticing. "I decided to take it home and then Henr... Caesar brought it with him since you and I were supposed to go to the museum. You even helped carry the cage to his car."

Cyrus' eyes narrowed even more as he watched her intensely.

"Are you or I mad?" His low voice was on the edge of dangerous and Miriam swallowed nervously. "I never saw any bird, not in the kitchen, not anywhere. And... Wait a minute... We never went to the museum afterward, Claire."

Nervously she avoided his penetrating look. "No, you drove me home," she mumbled. "That's why we're supposed to go today."

Silence fell, hard and suspicious, in the car, while both of them glared at each other.

"I don't know what this is all about, Claire," he said eventually, still with that low, dangerous voice, "but I didn't

47

drive you home yesterday. You went with Caesar, and I went home and..." There was something stirring in his face. "... watched hockey?" He frowned confused. "I watched hockey? I don't even like hockey!"

Miriam's hand finally got a grip on the door handle. Cyrus moved uncomfortably on the car seat.

"Okay..." she said, trying to hide the distrust and slight sense of fear. "Something's really weird here, and it's not that you're a Canadian who don't like hockey. Tell me your name."

He glanced at her with that old humorless smile she recognized so well.

"Carl Hansen."

"Okay. Good. And what's my name?"

He gave up a sharp little laugh, never leaving her face with those watchful eyes of his. She had seen that intense gaze many times before, but never aimed at her.

"No way, Claire. I'm not that easily tricked. You tell me your name."

She hesitated, but gave in when mistrust rose in his face.

"Miriam Goldblum."

He still didn't ease off. They watched each other suspiciously. Miriam held her hand tightly on the door handle, ready to open and bolt out at the slightest sign of... of... something.

"That didn't prove a thing," Cyrus said finally.

"I know," Miriam agreed.

"When did you join the team?"

"Six years ago. And you?"

"January last year."

"Who did you replace?" she asked.

"Cecilia. And you?"

"Cedric, but you wouldn't know that anyway."

He shrugged. "Does it matter? What's the name of our team?

"FRT C2. What does GFS stand for?"

"Golden Fleece Society."

A short pause occurred. Then Cyrus relaxed and leaned back. With a pang in her stomach, Miriam saw his hand loosen the grip of his gun. *God, was he going to shoot me?* A thin layer of sweat covered her face, and her pulse raced. With great effort, she tried to calm down.

"This is silly," he exclaimed. "I believe you are you. What about you?" Miriam hesitated, far from being at ease. He glanced at her hand on the door handle. "You can relax," he said. "I'm not going to hurt you." A hot blush flashed over her face at the thought of how transparent she always was, and she loosened her hand and placed it on her lap. "Are you all right?" he asked and seemed genuinely concerned, and she nodded with a suspicious glance at him. Had he ever asked her something like that before?

"Yes, thanks... You just made me a bit nervous there," she mumbled and saw a faint blush on his cheeks.

"Sorry..." he muttered to her surprise. Cyrus apologizing? Really? Then he glanced at her. "Are you going to answer my question? I'm quite curious about what you have to say."

Once more she looked covertly at him, but then she shrugged.

"Well... To a certain point you seem to be yourself, but..."

"But what?" he asked when she hesitated.

"Well..." She puffed and frowned. "You've been acting so strangely lately."

He glanced at her. "Yeah? Since when?"

At his sincere tone and the calmer atmosphere in the car, Miriam started to relax too, and carefully she thought the question over.

"Since you came to the professor's house. It was like..."

"Like what?"

She shook her head. "Just a feeling that you weren't yourself, or that you were sick, or..." She hesitated, but decided to let the cat out of the bag. "Or that you were drunk."

Cyrus stared unbelievingly at her. "Drunk?" he repeated. "Claire, I'm a Field Researcher. I never drink."

She nodded. "Yes, that's what was so weird. You behaved completely erratically. Things you said. Things you did... Calling... calling me 'bitch.'" Anger flushed inside her again as she thought of it, but tried to let it go. He stared shocked at her and ran his hand through his hair.

"Claire, I... I would never say something like that. I mean, yeah, we don't really like each other, but... but that doesn't mean I'd be name-calling."

The sincerity in his voice and behavior made her believe him, but something had made him act weirdly yesterday nonetheless. With a deep breath, as if she was about to jump from a high cliff, she placed a concerned hand on his arm.

"Did something happen yesterday, Cy? I know we're not close, and as you say, don't really like each other, but if you need someone to talk to, I'm actually a good listener."

Cyrus looked down at her hand in surprise, and she let go of his arm, suddenly awkwardly blushing.

"That's... um... really kind of you, Claire..." He pulled a hand through his hair again, stealing a glance her way, and seemed to come to a decision. "You know, my memories of yesterday are really weird. Well, not weird weird, just not... you know..." He exhaled and started over again. "You know how it is with memory; it follows a straight line, like birds on a wire?" Miriam nodded. "Yeah. Well, my memories from after I left the professor's office yesterday are kind of foggy, like if three or four birds in a row have flown away, but those that are left behind appear much more vividly."

Miriam suddenly felt a strange expression appear on her face.

"Huh..."

Cyrus gave her a sharp look. "What?"

"Weird... You... you just described my own 'memories' from after you and I left the professor's house yesterday. I didn't realize how foggy they are until right now. That's... so weird..."

Cyrus' smile was devoid of humor. "I heard those quotation marks," he said. "You think someone messed with our brains?"

"As if you had much of a brain to mess with from the beginning," Miriam heard herself blurt out. Next second she felt her face burn with shame and she hid it in her hands. "Oh, God, I'm sorry... I'm... I'm sorry..."

Cyrus gave up an unexpected friendly laugh. "I deserved that."

It shocked her, hearing him say that, but then the sensation leveled out, and she couldn't help giving him the first genuine grin ever. When he grinned back at her, the tension in the air disappeared.

"So now what?" she asked as she leaned back in the seat, feeling more at ease with him than she'd ever done before. *Maybe because we finally admitted that we don't like each other. No need for pretense anymore.* "What's the plan? Museum or headquarters?"

"You know," Cyrus said thoughtfully, "you pointed out the craters in my 'logic', and I agree with you. The weirdest thing is that it doesn't even feel like my own way of thinking and it's so bizarre that I'm still completely convinced that we should drop the project. That's why I think we need to go to the museum, even though my whole being revolts against that idea, but we should also call Caesar. Have you heard from him today?"

A worried punch spread in her chest. "Well, I thought... well, not exactly... no, I haven't. You didn't see him this morning? I thought you would. He said you needed to talk about... about your behavior."

"The 'bitch'-thing, eh?" She nodded, and he grimaced disgustedly. "Can't believe it. No, no!" he exclaimed when she scowled at him. "I believe you; I... just can't believe that I

51

said that." When she looked at him without knowing what to think he shook his head and gave her a genuinely apologetic look. "I'm very sorry."

"Thank you," she said and felt both sincerely grateful and extremely surprised. How many used to apologize to her? She couldn't think of anyone, and then Cyrus did, of all people. Frowning she reached for her cell phone and dialed the familiar number. The first tone hadn't yet ended when Caesar answered.

"Mimi! Thank goodness!" To her surprise, she could hear his voice tremble on the edge of tears. "I thought something had happened when you didn't answer any of my calls."

"What?" she asked worriedly. "Have you tried to reach me?"

"Since ten p.m. Do you know where Cyrus is?"

"Yes, he's right here."

"That's a relief." Caesar's voice suddenly got angry. "What have you two been up to? I've been worried sick! I told you to call me!"

"Um... well... it's kind of strange..."

Cyrus suddenly started to wave his hand in a no-gesture. "Not over the phone! Not over the phone!" he whispered.

"Um... right..."

"What?" Caesar demanded. "Don't make anything up."

"What?" Miriam scowled, feeling insecure. "I'm not. It's just that... Well, it's kind of strange since I've been home all night and I don't think that Cy's been out partying either."

Cyrus gave up a short barking laugh. "No, I've been watching hockey. Yeah, right..."

"You haven't been home, Miriam. I've called you. You didn't pick up."

Miriam sighed soundlessly and avoided the whole situation. The last she needed right now was yet another

52

argument, especially with Cy sitting beside, listening to the whole thing.

"What about you?" she asked instead. "Has anything happened?"

He exhaled at the other end of the line, and when he started talking again, his voice sounded beaten, sounded old and sad.

"I'm at South Side Hospital. My mother suffered a stroke. The doctors don't give her much hope. In fact... she'll probably not live until tomorrow." Miriam's throat tightened. She knew how close he was to his mother.

"Oh, no! Oh, Henry, I'm so sorry!"

His sigh was more of a sob. "I don't know what you two are up to now, but if you can... would you mind coming over, Mimi? Just you? I... I'd like to have you here. Just for a short while?"

"I'd love to do that, Henry. I'll be there as soon as I can. It might take a couple of hours, though. There's something we need to do."

"Of course."

A thought struck her as she was about to hang up. "Have you been at the hospital all night, you said?"

"Yes, they called me at nine thirty p.m. Why? What's wrong?"

"Nothing. I just, you know... um... I just thought that you wanted me to bring you something real to eat."

"Oh... I don't think I'll be able to eat anything."

"Okay, I'll be over as soon as I can." She hung up and looked bewildered at Cyrus. "Someone's been at my place, Cy, someone who's not aware of my habits!"

He looked sharply back. "You're sure?" Somewhat apologetic he shook his head. "'Course you are." A slight pause occurred as he rubbed his chin and frowned. "What a damn mess..." Then he exhaled and counted on his fingers: "So, what've we got? A girl infested with eels, a fake professor knowledgeable about said eels, a searched office, probably stolen items, a ritualistically murdered professor, at

53

least two messed-up brains, a visit to your apartment, and C's at the hospital for some reason. And all this during a two-day span. Wonderful. I love being an FR sometimes."

Miriam couldn't help laughing. "It makes life more... interesting, I'd say. And Caesar's at the hospital because his mom had a stroke."

"Huh..." Cyrus got a thoughtful expression in his face. "That might be his luck, in a way," he said, and Miriam felt anger rise again.

"His luck? What do you mean? His mom is dying, Cy!"

Tugging at his hair, he exhaled. "Yeah, I didn't mean... I just... If he's been surrounded by people ever since yesterday, he might've escaped being messed with."

Miriam started to calm down. "Oh. Okay. But don't call it 'luck' in his presence."

A boyish smile appeared on his lips. "I hear you, boss."

She scoffed kindly and felt herself blush for some reason. "Okay, let's head for the museum then. We can check my apartment for prints and stuff later. They won't be coming back if they think they've succeeded in hiding their tracks."

"Good plan," Cyrus said and started the engine.

Chapter 5

Within ten minutes they were back at the museum. As they walked into the narrow vestibule where the tiny glassed-in security room was located, the security guard they met yesterday, a skinny, balding man in his sixties, greeted them with a friendly smile.

"Welcome back, sir, ma'am. I thought my colleague said you're all done here?"

"Well..." Miriam started, but Cyrus placed a discreet hand on her arm.

"The night shift guard, you mean?" he said casually.

"That's right, sir."

Cyrus nodded. "What was the name, now again?"

"Meille, sir. Annette Meille."

"Right. Yes, we're mostly done, but there are some things we need to get closure on."

"Absolutely. Just let me give you a pass and you can sign in here."

Cyrus wrote down the time and his name on the visitor record and left the pen to Miriam. The guard returned with two visitors' pass.

"Thank you, Mr. Swanson. We'll be as quick as possible."

"Ah, no need for that, sir. Take your time. There's no hurry. Professor Bruchheimer has not arrived yet, but he wouldn't disagree. Or if he did, he wouldn't let us know anyway."

Cyrus laughed together with the guard. "Nice fellow, Professor Bruchheimer, isn't he? I haven't had the chance to meet him myself."

"Oh, yes, very nice indeed. A little odd, of course, but nice."

"Odd?"

"Yes, you know how them Europeans are. Very polite, very friendly, but not really... not really American. It doesn't matter how long they live here."

"And how long had Professor Bruchheimer lived here?"

Mr. Swanson rubbed his chin thoughtfully. "You know, I'm not sure. Probably since the war. The big one, you know. My father served in it. A foot soldier he was. Liberated people like him."

"Like Professor Bruchheimer?"

"That's right. He used to say... my father, that is. He used to say: 'Never become a soldier, son. Anything else I can accept, but a soldier and you're not of my blood anymore'."

"That's pretty harsh."

"Well, I dunno. He saw some pretty bad things, and I know he had nightmares about it 'til the end."

"I see. His opinion was understandable then."

"I guess it was. Anyhow, you probably want to do your work. Shall I call someone to show you his room?"

"Thank you, but that shouldn't be necessary."

"All right, then."

"By the way," Cyrus turned to the guard again, "would you mind giving us a copy of the visitor record from yesterday? We need to give it to our boss. You know how meticulous they can be about your working time."

The guard laughed sympathetically. "No problem at all, sir. I'll have it ready for you when you leave."

"Thank you, Mr. Swanson. Much appreciated."

The guard hit the button and the security door opened. Miriam and Cyrus went through it and into the sterile corridor behind.

"Nicely done, Cy," Miriam said, finding it easier to say something pleasant to him than she thought.

"I know," he grinned and to her surprise she laughed, instead of being ticked off.

"No false humility from you, I hear."

"Of course not. I have no need for that."

She scoffed, but still in a friendly way. "How do you know when it's the right time to ask about things?" she asked with curiosity.

"Well..." He frowned thoughtfully. "I guess it's like music. You feel the tempo and the rhythm in people's talk. With that guard, for example; had I waited on asking him about the record until we're done, I wouldn't have gotten it. He's already started to regret his loquaciousness with an FBI agent and wonders if I'm going to question him about his participation in Vietnam."

Miriam looked surprised at him. "Vietnam? You think he cheated his way out of it?"

"Quite so."

"Huh..."

"And he wishes he hadn't promised us the record, and he's glad he can tell his boss that it was a 'request' from the FBI-agents, which of course includes you, since it's more intimidating with two agents than only one, even if one of them are female. His opinion, not mine," he said before she could glare at him, and instead of glaring Miriam found herself shaking her head admiringly.

"That's just amazing. I could never have done that."

"No. It's a matter of understanding people, Claire."

"And I don't, you say." She couldn't quite hide the hurt tone in her voice. He gave her an open look.

"You see things, objects, patterns, space between things. You take in every little detail with just one look. That's why you're so good at crime scenes. But you don't get people."

Miriam grumbled under her breath. "I hate to admit it, but you're probably right."

He grinned at her. "Of course, I am."

They turned around the corner to the corridor that led to Professor Bruchheimer's office.

"The tape's gone," commented Miriam. "Did you remove it?"

Cyrus' appearance was stern. "Not that I remember."
He hurried his steps. "I left it *in situ* because I wanted you to
investigate it," he said over his shoulder.

"Wait!" Miriam called out when Cyrus reached for the
door. "Let's check for prints first."

"Right," he agreed, and Miriam got to work.

"Could be interesting to see if we find other matches
with the professor's house than just his," he continued before
a slight frown appeared on his forehead. "Do you think that
I've actually been in that house, Claire, or are all my
memories from it someone else's?"

She looked up for a moment, disturbed by the
thought.

"I... don't know. Is it really possible to do that?"

"In *Blade Runner*, it's possible," he said with a smirk
devoid of humor.

"Yes, but *Blade Runner*'s a sci-fi movie. And you were
there, Cyrus. You weren't yourself, but you were there."
Cyrus shrugged and looked away. Miriam sensed the cold
barrier build up between them again. She rose and put a
gentle hand on his arm. "I don't know what's possible or not.
I have the same memory failure as you do. I guess I just don't
want to accept that someone could have the ability to mess
with my brain in that way. God knows I've seen so many
strange things these past years that this one would be one of
the mildest."

Cyrus' laugh was like a short bark when he looked
back at her.

"Yeah... come on, let's get this thing moving."

It was a strange sensation, Miriam thought, coming
into the neatly cleaned-up office. She looked around,
wondering what felt wrong. She turned and gazed at Cyrus,
who stood leaning towards the doorpost, watching her
intently. She turned back into the room again. There was
another picture of it that struggled to come up to the surface,
a picture that didn't match either this tidy room or the chaotic
order she had seen the first time they were there. Miriam

closed her eyes and took a deep breath, and then another one, concentrating on nothing. Something stirred. She faced the bookcase, still with her eyes shut.

"There's a row of books, right here..." she said, slowly and pointed, seeing it with her mind's eye. "All the other books are lying on the floor..." A shadow appeared on the outskirts of her mind. She turned to face it. "Someone's standing there... Her face is covered by a... a veil... or something, but she is a woman. It feels like she is staring right into my soul..." Miriam shuddered violently at the memory, but inhaled and concentrated on the images that wanted to come through. "These books... they are important... You... you are leading me here, Cyrus, and you're standing right behind me, holding my shoulder securely. It hurts." Now when she thought about it, she remembered seeing bruises on her shoulder this morning. She frowned and let the thought go. It wasn't important. "They want something from me... What is it?" Miriam turned towards the office table, keeping her eyes closed, afraid that the picture she saw in her head would disappear if she opened them, and took the few short steps until she could touch the solid wood under her fingers. "A man stands behind the table... He... he asks me... something... I can't remember what. I know that I'm in danger, and I need to get away. I... I grab your arm, Cyrus, and throw you over, rushing for the door..." She opened her eyes and looked at him. He was still leaning towards the doorpost, attentively listening to her. "Apparently I didn't get very far."

"Apparently."

Miriam walked up to the bookcase. The shelf she remembered had books on it now too, books on Antarctic flora and fauna. She had a strong impression that the books in her memories held another subject.

"What happened then?" Cyrus' voice was low.

"I don't know. There's only one other thing that stands out in my memories..."

"What's that?"

She turned around, looking at him. "It's you, Cyrus, lying on the floor, face down, with dark-brown hair."

"Dark-brown hair?"

She nodded. "I can't say for sure, but I think that this man, 'you,' was quite chubby too, and very young, more like a teenager than an adult."

Cyrus looked utterly surprised. "So it wasn't me! It can't have been me!" A deep, relieved sigh heaved from his chest, and suddenly he smiled. "I was afraid that... that whoever they were... did something to force me to do things..."

"Yeah..." Miriam felt tired.

"What? What's wrong?"

She made a frustrated, troubled gesture with her hands.

"Who can we trust, Cyrus? Who can we trust if they can take on our appearances? Can we trust that you'll be you tomorrow morning? That I'm me? Can we trust that Caesar is Caesar when I meet him tonight? He wanted me to come alone."

The sudden silence was so heavy that she was physically aware of it. Cyrus exhaled and pulled a hand through his copper-red hair.

"I don't know, Claire," he said eventually. "I have no clue who we can trust, but I'm not letting you see C alone tonight. We can't risk that. Let's go through the room and then... get the hell out of here. I need something to eat anyway."

Miriam nodded. It felt important to leave the office as soon as possible, to just get away from the powerlessness and the fear it represented. She had a feeling that both of them hastened through the room with less meticulousness than they usually would. Caesar wouldn't be happy if he knew, but to her own surprise that didn't bother her much. During her years in FRT C2, she'd learned to trust her instincts, and they told her that they wouldn't find anything here. After only fifteen minutes they agreed that this was enough and headed out to Cyrus' car. They both seemed to breathe easier as soon as they drove away, leaving the museum behind.

Cyrus took her to a small Arabian restaurant, hidden away on the outskirts of the dock district. Going in there was like being transferred directly to a market somewhere in Bahrain. Cyrus surprised her by being able to read the Arabian menu and order their food in, what at least to her, sounded like perfect Arabic.

She really enjoyed the whole place; the atmosphere and the exotic smell, the clientele, the delicious food, and the fantastic service. They didn't talk much, but Miriam didn't know what to say anyway. She wanted to ask him how and when he learned Arabic, not talking about work or the weather, but Cyrus seemed to be far away in his thoughts and too unreachable. His closed face would not let her in. She sighed soundlessly. It had been nice not tipping around on her toes for once, but... She shrugged, feeling disappointed.

The lunch was mostly consumed in silence, even though it wasn't as awkward as it used to be. In spite of that, one hour later she was refreshed enough to continue with the work. They left the docks, avoided the high traffic areas, and thus arrived at her building complex just half an hour later.

"All right," Cyrus said when they stood outside her apartment door on the fifteenth floor. "You're the expert. You tell me what to do."

"Okay. I want us to start looking for fingerprints. There shouldn't be more than... um... five different ones that I'm aware of, mine included. I'd be surprised if we found any others. I mean, if they can copy our appearances, then they're probably smart enough to wear gloves." Miriam shunned away from the thought of how, exactly, other people's looks could be duplicated and if that included fingerprints and DNA, and stared sternly at the naked facts. "Let's also check for dust-covered shoe prints in any other size than mine."

Cyrus looked down at her small feet. "That shouldn't be hard."

"There might be traces from Caesar, though, since he got the bird cage here yesterday." It was a relief having an excuse for Henry's presence in her apartment, even though Cyrus probably knew about them having a relationship.

As Miriam suspected there were no recent fingerprints on the doorknob other than two different pairs, probably her own and Henry's. She collected them and opened the door. A happy chirp greeted them.

"The canary?" asked Cyrus while checking the floor for prints.

"Mhm."

"I wouldn't mind checking him out in a moment, just to see if there are any memories flashing back."

"Go ahead. He's in the living room. To the left."

"Let's do the prints first."

They worked in silence on each end of the hallway, but it didn't take more than five minutes before Cyrus called out to her. Miriam walked over to take a look. Cyrus stood pointing at a practically invisible trace of a right shoe, clearly about four sizes bigger than Miriam's.

"Do you think this is C's print or some mystic other guy's?"

Miriam frowned concernedly. "I don't know. I can't say I've paid much attention to Caesar's shoe prints lately."

Cyrus gave up a friendly laugh while taking a photograph of the print and a ruler.

"Not me either. It shouldn't be any problem borrowing the shoes he used yesterday, just to check them."

They worked for another twenty minutes, but as Miriam had suspected, they didn't find anything that stuck out in any way: just a couple of other fingerprints, probably from her sister and parents, but that would be easy to check as soon as they got them to the lab. At last, Cyrus got the chance to see Luce. He stood in front of the cage, staring at the canary for several minutes, before turning to her.

"Can't say I recognize it. Probably never seen it. There are no memories at all popping up."

"I don't think it proves very much, Cy, but it's certainly an indicator that you might not have been in the professor's house."

He nodded and suddenly that old, reserved air returned to him.

"What?" she asked uneasily.

"Do you mind taking a detour to my apartment, as well, or do you want to go directly to the hospital?" He paused before continuing: "It would be good to be able to eliminate my place too."

Miriam felt unexpectedly torn. Henry needed her badly, she knew that, but Cyrus needed her too, and she had a strong sense that their new, fragile companionship depended on her answer. She gave him a quick glance, but he was sternly concentrated on the little bird. A second went by as she tried to decide, then she shrugged.

"Why not? It's a good suggestion."

Cyrus put his finger into the cage and Luce hopped away a couple of steps.

"Cute little fellow, this one." He looked back at her. "Don't worry, Claire, it's a small place. It won't take long."

He was right. The whole apartment would easily have fit into two of her three rooms, but it was neatly cleaned, not unexpected for a former Star Student, and surprisingly comfortable and inviting with lots of warm, red hues and Arabic patterns. The lingering smell of often used incense made Miriam take a couple of deep breaths and relax. Both the living room and the minuscule bedroom had a wall full of bookshelves with novels by old classical Russian and English authors, as well as quite a few written in Arabic. The DVD-rack contained romantic comedies. He caught her looking at the sleeve to *Music and Lyrics*.

"Yeah, I guess I'm one of the few guys who actually like that one," he commented without seeming ashamed of it, which was extremely refreshing, Miriam thought.

"It's sweet. I've seen it."

"Yeah…"

He left her for the kitchen, and she continued her search for prints in the living room, but as in her apartment, there wasn't anything particular to collect. What she did find, though, almost hidden on one of the bookshelves, was a photograph of a little girl, maybe seven years old. Her copper-red hair in two thick braids framed her slender face with gray eyes and a sensitive mouth.

"That's Sarah. My daughter," Cyrus said behind her. "Best mistake I've ever made."

When Miriam surprised studied the serious-looking child, she immediately saw the resemblance.

"She looks very much like you," she said and smiled at the picture.

"Yeah. Poor girl. Wants to become a police officer too, 'just like daddy'." Cyrus scoffed. "Most kids want to become dancers or horse trainers, heck, even circus princesses or fairies, but not her. 'Police'? I wish she'd change her mind before she applies for the academy."

"What does her mom do?"

"Manda's a Ph.D. Philosophy. Very clever woman."

"They don't live here, do they?"

"With our job? No way! I wouldn't risk that. Not that I have any say in where they live" He hesitated, but shrugged and continued: "We're not married anymore." There was another pause, longer this time, before he said with a lower voice, clearly avoiding her gaze: "Sometimes, you know, you grow into loving each other as a sister and brother. We're still best friends, though."

Miriam nodded, even though she was astonished at the unexpected confidence, and gave him a friendly look.

"You're very lucky, Cy."

"Yeah, I know…" His expression became just slightly concerned. "They're not easy to find, and I've been thinking so many times that I should put away that picture, but I want something… you know…" His voice trailed away, and he turned his back to her. "I think we're finished here. Let's go and see C."

Miriam shot a last glance at the girl and at Cyrus' suddenly tensed back before she followed him out of the apartment.

Ten minutes later they were finally heading toward the hospital to Miriam's great relief. Now when she had a moment to think she couldn't help worrying. The city skyline rushed by outside the window, trying to keep up with those anxious thoughts rushing through her mind. What had happened yesterday? What had the man behind the table at Professor Bruchheimer's office asked her? What had she answered? What had they done to her after her failed escape attempt? The investigation of the actual office hadn't given much: only thirty-seven different fingerprints. Miriam suspected that none of them would match any fingerprints in either the Professor's house or in her or Cyrus' apartments. Nor did she think they would find any prints other than the expected. The next step was to identify the ones they had found. Most likely they would belong to completely innocent students or, if not innocent, at least not involved in this project. None of the encrypted pages she had seen yesterday had been found either. The important question now was of course who had them: the fake professor or the people who had changed her and Cyrus' memories? In what way did these two apparently different factions connect to each other? Did the pages have anything to do with this case at all? Did the murder have any relevance to them or was it just an unlucky coincidence? No, she didn't believe that. Her instincts told her that they were connected in a way she couldn't yet figure out. And then what? What about Henry? They were heading towards the hospital as if driving blindly. What if he wasn't Henry? Would she be able to see the difference? She truly thought so, especially since she had been able to see that it was something wrong with Cyrus yesterday, but then again, who knew how good these people could be at disguising themselves? *Never underestimate your enemies*; she thought grimly and shied away from the memories of when she did just that and how that mistake had killed Conrad. For a moment, it was hard to breathe when the image of Conrad's dead body appeared in her mind, and she closed her eyes and concentrated on the neutral sound of the engine. No one knew it was her fault. She couldn't even bear telling Caesar about it. Just thinking about the anger and disappointment he would show her made her stiff. *No, let it go. Don't think about it. You know you can let it go.* After some calm breathing, she could sternly steer the line of thought back to the present. *Okay, think about this now, about Henry.* They had been a couple for almost four years, and surely she must know him well enough to see if there was a difference. But if she didn't? If he looked, sounded and acted so well that he'd trick her? What if she made yet another mistake? What if... Miriam suddenly looked at Cyrus.

"Cy! Stop the car!"

"What?"

"Just stop somewhere!"

Without questioning her, he checked the mirrors and the blind spots before turning left into a McDonald's parking lot. Miriam was surprised, but grateful, and grabbed her cell phone. Her cheeks blossomed red as they always did when she got excited. Decisively, she dialed the well-known number of Henry's cell phone.

"Yes?" Henry's deep voice caressed her.

"Hi, it's me. I just wanted to say that we're on our way."

Henry gave up a gentle sigh. "Thank you, Mimi."

"Is she...?"

"She's still alive."

"We'll be there shortly."

Miriam hung up and met Cyrus' intense gaze.

"That's phone call number one," she said firmly and started to dial the well-known number to Henry's small house on the outskirts of the city. One signal went through, two signals...

"Yes?" Henry's deep voice caressed her.

Miriam swallowed nervously while her hands became all warm and sweaty.

"Hi, it's me."

There was a short pause.

"Miriam?"

"Yes."

"Where are you? You've not been in today."

"I know. I got a tip. I've been in the docks. Are you coming down to HQ?"

"Not today. I'm... I'm working from home."

"Okay. Anything specific you want me to do?"

"Uh... No. Just the regular stuff, you know."

"Sure. I'll see you tomorrow then."

"Yeah."

Miriam hung up and let the cell phone in her shaking hand fall down in her lap. She leaned back in the seat and covered her eyes while drawing deep breaths to calm herself down.

"If I didn't know what I do know... I'd be losing it by now..." She rubbed her face and looked at Cyrus. "He's both at the hospital and at home. His voice... it sounds just the same... I'm quite sure that the Caesar at home is waiting for the Caesar at the hospital to give him a surprise."

Cyrus looked severely at her.

"Let's try to keep it that way. I would regret it if we ruined his expectations."

Chapter 6

Cyrus had parked the car at the far end of the hospital's parking lot. Now, they sat silently and watched the big gray building, both deep in thought. The merciless heat of the afternoon sun made the car into a sauna and the air hard to breathe. Miriam wiped away the sweat from her forehead and wished that she could open the window to let a draft in. Cyrus played absentmindedly with the car keys, making them jingle with a dull metallic sound.

"I don't know," he finally said. "Either we can hope that they don't have him under surveillance, and go right through the main door, or we could figure out a way to sneak in. The last option seems a little bit over the top, but the first seems a little bit too reckless."

"Mm…" Miriam agreed.

"Question is," Cyrus continued, "how paranoid do we want to be? I mean, if we want to run down that alley, then we can assume that we're under surveillance right now too and that they have all our phones and cell phones and maybe even the car bugged. If that's the case, then they already know that we know."

"How about just a little paranoid?"

Cyrus laughed. "Sure. I'm all for it. Just enlighten me."

"Well… what we could do is have HQ call Caesar and demand his presence and then we can wait for him at his car."

He gave her an appreciative look. "Not a bad idea, Claire. And then we just assume that they're not bugging us?"

She shrugged. "If they did, why did the other Caesar answer at home?"

"Now you're just presuming that he's the false one, you know."

She gave him a quick, surprised peek from the side, ready to argue against that, but at a second thought, she swallowed the angry words that wanted to spill out, sighed, and continued to monitor the parking lot instead. Silence fell in the car again. The metallic jingle of the keys sounded nervous. Then Cyrus abruptly dropped them in his pocket.

"C'mon. Let's go in. There are two of us and a whole hospital full of people. We should be safer in there than out here anyway." He opened the door and let his tall, lanky body out of the car. Miriam looked his back in surprise for a second, before hastening out into the slightly cooler breeze. He gave her a humorless smile. "Just check your gun first, will you."

She nodded and loosened it from her holster. It was as ready as she could ask for. She put it down again and glanced at Cyrus.

"You're sure?"

"No, but we can't sit here all day."

They shared a smile and headed towards the main entrance.

It was blessedly cool inside the dull building. The low buzzing sound from the air conditioning was like music to Miriam's ears as she walked to the reception desk.

"We're here to see Daisy Wittinger. Is she here?"

"Daisy Wittinger? Yes, that's correct; she came in with a stroke yesterday evening. Are you relatives?" The elderly blond nurse behind the desk watched them disapprovingly.

"No, co-workers of her son, Henry Wittinger," Miriam answered. As if that answer pleased her, she turned to her computer again, dismissing them with her back. "I'm sorry, only relatives are permitted into the room."

Cyrus' face went blank. "We'd like to talk to Mr. Wittinger. Could you send someone to get him for us, please?" he interposed.

The nurse looked up with a frown. "That's not really…" she began.

Attested by Cyrus' stubbornness, Miriam opened her mouth again.

"He did call for us," she said urgently. "Please let him know that we're here."

The nurse hesitated, but reached for the intercom. "Susan, can you let Mr. Wittinger in room seven ten know that he has visitors? Thank you." She turned to them again. "Please sit down in the waiting room. Someone will be with you shortly."

Instead of doing as he was told, Cyrus casually leaned on the desk.

"Has Mr. Wittinger had many visitors since he arrived yesterday?" he asked the nurse. She scowled at him.

"I don't know," she said somewhat content. "I haven't been here more than six hours."

Cyrus didn't let that stop him. "Could you look it up for me, please?" The way Cyrus spoke made it clear that he wasn't asking for a favor. The nurse frowned even more.

"It's restricted..." she began.

"Please don't make me flash my badge," he interrupted.

She glared at him a couple of seconds longer than necessary.

"Police?" she asked doubtfully.

"FBI."

"Really?" The nurse sounded skeptical. Cyrus gave her a stern stare and flashed his badge. Two red spots started to show on the nurse's cheeks, and she gave him a glance that Miriam found hard to interpret, but Cyrus put his badge down, and the nurse reached for the visitor records. With her eyes still on the records, she said to no one in particular: "It's not customary for mourners to have visitors in a situation like this."

"And that's a no, I take it?"

She looked up, still red-cheeked and clearly annoyed. "Yes, that's correct; he hasn't had any visitors at all. If you

70

could please go to the waiting area now, I'm quite sure that Mr. Wittinger will be with you shortly."

She folded the records demonstratively. Cyrus took the few steps into the light blue waiting room and sat down.

"All right, that doesn't prove anything," he said in a low voice as she sat down beside him, "but it makes things look a little brighter."

Just a couple of minutes later, a sweet-smiling young nurse approached them and turned to Miriam.

"Are you Miriam?" she asked with a low, gentle voice, perfectly suited for mourning relatives.

"I am."

"Mr. Wittinger does not want to leave his mother, but he asked you to come to Mrs. Wittinger's room."

Miriam got up immediately and glanced down at Cyrus, who nodded almost unnoticeably and rose from his seat as well. He gave the young nurse a warm, reassuring smile and put his hand under Miriam's arm. After the initial shock, she found that she didn't mind since it was just for show. The nurse smiled back and led the way to an elevator.

"How is Mrs. Wittinger doing?" Miriam asked concerned while the doors closed.

"She has an iron will," the nurse said admiringly. "No one thought she'd live through the night, and though she's in a coma, she still fights for her life."

Miriam felt warm inside. "She's like that. A fighter."

"Has anyone else been here to support Henry?" Cyrus' tone was an imitation of the young nurse's. Miriam couldn't help admiring his chameleon-like ability to adjust to any kind of situation. The nurse looked up at him with a thoughtful frown.

"Not that I can recall, but she had already come in when I started my shift. As I understand it, Mr. Wittinger is the only child, and in situations like this, you know, it's unusual that other than parents and children care to be present."

71

Cyrus nodded understandingly. The elevator stopped at the seventh floor, and the nurse headed out with silent steps, while they lingered behind, scrutinizing the empty corridor in front of them. The nurse turned left and continued down a dimly lit corridor where no one else was in sight. As they followed her, Cyrus let go of Miriam's arm and put his hand in his pocket, suddenly on his guard. Miriam's heart began to race, and she looked cautiously over her shoulder, prepared to raise her gun. She couldn't see anyone behind them. Just then the nurse stopped at a closed door. She turned to them with another sympathetic appearance, but all at once she picked up the different mood and frowned uneasily.

"Is... um... is something wrong?"

Cyrus shook his head and put on a warm smile again, still with his hand in his pocket.

"Just... you know... it's hard coming to a friend when his mother is dying. It's... hard. I mean, what do you say?"

"Oh... of course..." The sympathetic smile returned. "Just try to be natural. I think he'll appreciate that."

She opened the door, and the small room behind it smelled like it had been abandoned for years. In the middle of it stood a hospital bed. Daisy Wittinger laid on her back, barely breathing, her eyes closed. If she hadn't known that it was Daisy, she would never have recognized her, Miriam thought. Not with that thin, bluish-tinted skin, plastered so tightly to the bones. Not that she'd met her often, Miriam thought. Henry hadn't been keen on it, for some reason.

The green line on the monitor ticked slowly. Henry sat at her side, holding her hand. He looked up with a face more accentuated with wrinkles than usual. A tired smile showed when he saw her behind the nurse.

"Here she is, Mr. Wittinger," the young nurse said with a comforting tone, before turning to Miriam. "Please let us know when you leave."

"I will. Thank you."

As soon as the nurse left, Henry got up from his seat and enclosed her in a warm embrace. She could feel his shoulders relax and his breath gently touching her hair. The light smell of his sweat was so familiar that Miriam involuntarily took a deep breath of relief. He held her for a minute before sighing and letting her go, smiling down at her. Then he looked at Cyrus, who was still at the door, watching the corridor.

"Cyrus," he greeted the younger man.

"C," Cyrus acknowledged him and came into the room, closing the door behind him.

"All clear?" Miriam asked.

"All clear."

"Good."

He nodded and eyed Henry with that blank expression of his, which she had seen numerous times on his face when he questioned suspects. Henry's eyes narrowed, and he watched both of them with a slight frown. She noticed that his eyes were red and tired with dark bags underneath, but the expression and the stance were so much like him that she didn't have any doubts left that he really was himself. Apparently Cyrus had come to the same conclusion, because he stopped staring at the older man and casually strolled to the windowsill and sat down, taking in the scenery of the parking lot with one quick look.

Miriam went to the old lady's side. Her paper-thin skin was accentuated and bluish-white in color and Miriam was amazed that someone who looked so dead still breathed. She turned to Henry.

"How is she?"

He shook his head and sighed. "Not good. I just wish it would be over. She's just... just struggling for... I don't know what. Something. It's over, but she doesn't want to admit it. She's always been like that." A shadow of a smile played on his lips. Miriam took his hand and squeezed it. His smile deepened slightly, and he patted her shoulder gently. Then, half-turning towards Cyrus, he included him in the conversation. "So you're here, even though I asked Claire to come alone, and you both share that gritty face. What's gone wrong?"

Cyrus glanced at her.

"He's good," she answered the implied question.

"Yeah, I thought so." His gaze wandered out through the window again.

"It's good that I'm good, so can you please enlighten me?" Henry's tone was just slightly irritated. Miriam glanced at Cyrus, who was still watching the parking lot. She groaned silently when she realized that he wanted her to tell Henry about the unlikely events that had happened.

"Um…" she begun, and walked over to the other chair in the room and sat down to save some time. "Well… you know yesterday when we were at Professor Bruchheimer's house?" Henry nodded impatiently. "Yes, well… you remember Cyrus behaving strangely, right?" Henry raised his eyebrows, but didn't say anything. "Um… well, that man wasn't Cyrus. He just looked like Cyrus, and afterward, when he took me to the museum… something… happened… I'm not really sure what, since they erased my memories, and they've erased Cy's memories too. But earlier, when we went back today I remembered some things, like Cy changing his appearance after I tried to escape, and a woman with a veil, and an elderly man wanting to learn something important from me. I don't know what and I don't know if I told them anything, and now someone's waiting for you at your house, someone who sounds exact like you, and who tries to act like you, and we weren't sure if you were you until just now…" Silence fell in the room while both men stared at her. She looked away with heated and blossoming cheeks, feeling embarrassed. "Um… that wasn't very clear, was it?" she asked no one in particular.

Cyrus laughed in a friendly way, but hushed so as not to show disrespect for the old woman.

"No, not very," he smiled at her.

74

She gave him a pleading glance. "Please, can't you tell him?"

The smile disappeared and for some reason, she felt as if he was disappointed with her. Awkwardly she squirmed on the chair and thought about trying again, but Cyrus had just begun talking.

"C," he said, "I went to the museum by myself yesterday... yes, yes, I know. I know it was stupid," he said with his hand up in the air as if he wanted to silence Caesar's raised eyebrows. "I paid for it too," he muttered annoyed. When Miriam glanced at Caesar, she wondered if his eyebrows could get any higher up on his forehead. Cyrus looked the older man straight in the eyes. "Next time, I'll bring Claire with me. Pinkie promise. Scout's honor." Caesar just folded his arms and continued to stare at him. Cyrus cleared his throat and eyed his shoes like a berated child. "Anyway. I wanted to check some details about the professor because we... well, we started to suspect that he might not be who we thought he was... He wasn't there anymore of course, and the whole room was just a mess. I sealed it and called Claire, and we decided to meet at Professor Bruchheimer's home together with you, and then I left... and some time after my departure from his office, my memories are... strange." He glanced up at the silent man and then continued to examine his shoes. "Strange... weird... like... blurry... but accentuated... highlighted, so to say... here and there..." He cleared his throat again. "I do have memories of the professor's house, but just three very clear pieces: the entrance, a door inside the house, and the bed with someone lying brutally murdered. Just enough to not question my presence there had no one asked, but Claire started to talk about a bird that I still don't have one single memory of, and that's how we started to figure the whole thing out."

Henry kept staring at them for a moment, before sighing and rubbing his eyes.

"I need to sit down," he said and sat down heavily in the chair beside the hospital bed. He sat in silent thoughts for a couple of minutes before turning to them again, clearly the professional agent. "First of all, Cyrus; never ever go somewhere on your own again. I thought we've talked about it before, quite thoroughly, and you still do it?" He shook his head, and Cyrus was red as a beet in the face.

"Last time, I promise," he mumbled. Miriam felt sorry for him.

"We did have phone contact, Caesar. It wasn't as if I didn't know where he was this time."

When he turned his disappointed stare to her, it felt as if she shrunk inside, and she looked away.

"Maybe you both should think about what could happen next time before you make such a mistake again." The silence stretched out and eventually Caesar sighed. "Let's not talk about it anymore." He paused and looked at Cyrus again. "You're sure about this? You don't think that you were in Professor Bruchheimer's house, Cyrus?"

Apparently feeling relatively secure again, he looked up. "No, I wasn't. They made a mistake, C. They implanted a memory in me of you driving Claire home and of me driving home alone and spending the evening watching hockey, something I would never do, and they implanted a memory in Claire of me driving her home without that trip to the museum that apparently was planned."

"And someone's been at my apartment, Caesar, when I was asleep," Miriam added. "There were a lot of things changed at home that I wouldn't have done. And when we came to the museum today I had lots of memory pieces flashing back to me, as I said. For example, one where I get Cyrus down on the floor in an attempt to escape and his appearance changes from Cyrus to a chubby, brown-haired teenager."

They both watched Caesar attentively while he rubbed his chin and sat in thoughts for a moment, absentmindedly stroking his mother's unmoving hand.

"So we're dealing with something even more dangerous than we thought at the beginning. Not only do they deal with ritualistic murders and creatures that shouldn't exist, but they also have the ability to alter and erase memories." He shook his head. "We have to assume that it all is connected, even if I, at this point, can't see what the connection is. It would be dangerous and stupid to treat it as three different cases." Miriam tried to hide her side-glance at Cyrus and saw him blushing heavily again. "One thing has led to another, and at this point, I can only see that we need to sit down with the facts we have and discuss them in this new light. We probably need to go back to the Stevenson apartment, as well as to Professor Bruchheimer's house and office, and even our own places, to check for details that we might have missed earlier."

Cyrus nodded, composed again. "We did check the office and Claire's and my places before we arrived today. We didn't find anything strange."

"Very good work, you two," he praised them, and they both started to shine like children at Christmas. "I can't say that I'm surprised," he continued. "It's quite clear that they're no beginners, even with the mistakes with your memories. It must be very hard accomplishing something like memory-change perfectly. And you did say that someone is waiting at my home?"

Miriam nodded eagerly. "Yes, I called both your cell and your home phone within the minute, and you answered both."

Caesar raised his eyebrows again. "Interesting. We really need to investigate that." He looked down at his mother, clearly torn apart. Miriam glanced at Cyrus, who gave her an encouraging smile. She turned to Caesar again.

"We can wait, Henry. They've probably been waiting for you since yesterday. They won't leave."

His expression varied between relief and professional impatience.

"It's okay, C. Claire's right. They won't leave. We're staying here with you and then we'll go together."

Caesar looked surprised at them both and then he smiled. "You've really become a team, haven't you? I'm glad. Very glad. It was about time, don't you think?" A light blush colored Miriam's cheeks and when she glanced at Cyrus, he looked as embarrassed and pleased as she felt. *Weird... Just so... weird... We told each other that we don't like each other, and suddenly we're a team. We should have admitted that months ago.* She smiled broadly and shook her head slightly. Henry continued to watch his mother and hold her hand in a gentle grasp. "Fine. Let's do as you suggest." He paused a second as his fingers continued to stroke Daisy's hand. "Thank you."

Five hours later, Daisy Wittinger died without ever waking up from her coma. Henry held her hand as he watched her go. Her breaths became even shorter and lighter than before and with longer intervals. Then they stopped entirely, and she was gone. Henry watched her old, tired face as if to imprint the memory of her before he bent over and kissed her wrinkled cheek. Miriam could see his lips pronounce words she couldn't hear, as she and Cyrus sat silently still, giving Henry the privacy he needed for his last moments with his mother. He looked her solemnly in the face while gently stroking her hand. Miriam started to wonder why no nurse showed up, but was grateful that no stranger disturbed the moment. He lingered a little longer before turning to them with moist eyes.

"She's gone," he said with a gentle voice. "Ninety-seven years... all her memories, experiences... emotions... gone with her... It feels strange..." His voice trailed away. Cyrus got up and put a compassionate hand on his shoulder. Henry laid his hand over Cyrus' and clasped it. Miriam got up too and flew into his arms. Together the three of them stood in sympathetic silence until Henry patted them both. "Thanks," he said with low voice. He cleared his throat while extracting himself from their embrace and said in a louder voice: "I guess we need to go. There's nothing more we can do here." He gave his motionless mother another glance, but turned away from her as definitely as if he was closing a door, his face all Field Researcher Caesar again. "I know it's late and that we've been here all day, but someone's waiting at my house, and I'd really like to catch that other me. I think that we need to do that a.s.a.p. before they find out where we are. Let's grab a burger on the way. We can't act on empty stomachs."

"I'm all with you, C."

"Me too," Miriam said.

Caesar nodded firmly, opened the door and stepped out into the dimly lit corridor where a nurse finally came hasting towards the room. As the door closed behind her and shut Daisy Wittinger in, Miriam felt a cold chill running down her spine. Something new was about to begin, something that they had set in motion. Even if they might not yet be in control of the situation, they had clearly taken the initiative this time.

Part Two

searching and finding

Chapter 7

The soft summer darkness had already fallen when they parked the car four blocks away from Caesar's house. They had changed into black comfortable clothes and sneakers to be able to move as invisibly and silently as possible. As she walked between the two silent and stern men in the back alleys, and the warm night air tried to untidy her hair, Miriam felt uncertain and insecure. She hated not having enough information about a project; just enough to know that she might be walking into a trap. Of course, she admitted, it was better than to be caught in a trap unawares, but it still made her uneasy, as if she had nettles inside her shirt.

Soon enough, they saw Caesar's small brick house at the end of the street, the forest-like park closing in on two sides and the only neighbor about fifty yards down the road. Caesar stopped at the corner of the last house on the parallel street. There were no lights on in his home and no cars parked on the street. It looked empty.

"Let's go round Mrs. Nelson's house and close in from the park-side," he said.

Cyrus and Miriam nodded their agreement. He led them back and took another route down towards the park far from any possible watchful eyes. The park was silent and dark. Only the mild wind rustling through the leaves was heard over the faint sound their feet made on the gravel-clad path. It didn't take long before the trees thinned out and met the dark-brown wooden fence that surrounded Caesar's yard. They stopped just before the tree line and watched the house. Nothing seemed to be out of the ordinary.

"All right, team," Caesar said in a low voice. "We need to get close to the windows. Cyrus, you're the best shot. You're staying here, covering our backs. Claire and I are going to take a closer look. If nothing happens, we'll need to get in and then we'll need you with us. Clear?"

"Clear." Cyrus let the bag containing the hunting rifle down from his shoulder. They had picked it up from his place on the way. While Cyrus assembled the rifle and the scope, Caesar and Miriam studied the house. Nothing seemed to move inside: no lights, not one thing out of the ordinary that could give any intruder away. The usual feeling of insecurity started to nag her at the back of her head. What if she was wrong, if there wasn't anyone there? She would never be able to look the other two in the eye again. Even at the thought of messing up she felt her cheeks heat with embarrassment.

"Ready," Cyrus said and stood up with the mounted rifle in his hand. Caesar nodded.

"Claire, we move together. Let's start from the left side of the house and move towards the right: me on the left side of every window and you on the right. You're the one looking into the rooms. If you see something out of the ordinary, we just make note of it and continue. There might be more than one in there, and we don't want to make any mistakes. Clear?"

Miriam swallowed and nodded, feeling her cheeks heat at the admittance of how often she spent time at his place, often enough to be able to see if something was out of the ordinary. Cyrus didn't seem to notice, she saw when she covertly glanced at him. *That doesn't mean a damn thing,* she thought dryly. She knew how much he observed.

"Clear," she mumbled.

"All right, let's get going. Cyrus?"

"I'm all prepared."

"Good."

They all went to the far left side of the fence and followed it down where it turned. They left Cyrus where the angle at the front of the house made it difficult for someone inside to see, and snuck over the fence, crouched and hurried towards the house's corner. Nothing happened. Caesar gave Miriam a nod, and she peeked around the wall. When she didn't see anything, she loosened her gun in the holster, hurried past the first window, remained crouched, and waited for Caesar to get into position. As soon as he did, she snuck a peek inside the dark room. The office. The computer was turned off, and the chair was neatly placed at the desk. She could see the edge of the bookcase containing Caesar's work material. The door to the corridor behind was open and showed nothing but darkness. She bent down again, gestured to Caesar and hurried past the next window, which showed the bedroom. The bed was made, clothes hung on a coat hanger, and the closet was closed. The open door showed part of the dark corridor outside. It was empty.

She stopped at the next corner, waiting for Caesar before peeking around. When she saw nothing out of the ordinary there, she hurried past the first window on the back of the house, trusting that Cyrus would follow them around along the tree line. Another quick peek showed her the bathroom. Shaving tools stood on the sink, the shower curtain revealed the empty bathtub; the top of the toilet's lid was open... She ducked down, took a step to the side and gestured towards Caesar, who immediately came to her side.

"The toilet lid is open," she breathed in his ear. He raised his eyebrows at this oddity and nodded, gesturing her to move on.

The next window was the living room. The armchairs stood as they always did, grouped opposite the fireplace with the end table in between. The crammed bookcases filled every wall and made the room seem even smaller and darker than it was. It was as empty as the other rooms. She crouched, hurried past the veranda and the back door to the opposite corner of the house, and snuck around it. Another window opened to the living room. A quick glance showed her nothing new. The two following windows before the next corner that led to the front of the house showed her the kitchen. The small kitchen table was bare except for the newspaper. The sink was clean, no dirty dishes anywhere. Nothing seemed to be out of the ordinary.

Caesar watched her when she turned towards him. She shook her head. He gave the thumbs-up in return and led her to the corner at the back of the house, turning towards the park and waving. A minute later Cyrus jumped over the fence and hurried up to them, still with the rifle in his hand. Miriam could barely hear Caesar's low voice when he turned to Cyrus.

"No direct sign of any intruder, just one small thing out of the ordinary. We need to go in."

Cyrus nodded, and his grip on the rifle hardened. Caesar turned to both of them.

"Let's go through the back door. Cyrus, you cover my back when I open the door, but when we get in, we need to stay close together. No one strolls off by himself or herself."

He pulled out a key chain and silenced it with another checkered handkerchief, took out his gun, and looked inquiringly at Cyrus and Miriam.

"Any questions?" They both shook their heads. "Good. Let's go."

Miriam pulled out her gun and heard the low click from the spring bolt when Caesar turned the key and opened the door. Then he waited, listened. Nothing moved inside. He squeezed himself in, followed by Cyrus. After a quick, thorough glance around the garden and the park, Miriam took the few steps into the living room, gun prepared, without closing the door fully, just in case they needed to get out quickly. The two men already stood at the doorway leading to the kitchen, tense, listening. Miriam hurried to Caesar's side. He held up his hand, and all of them stood agitatedly quiet. Still nothing.

Cyrus and Miriam watched Caesar as he beckoned to them and stepped into the kitchen with his gun raised while the other two covered his back. From the kitchen, they went to the hallway and the front door, checked the office, the bedroom, and the bathroom before coming back to the dark and empty living room, a little more relaxed than when they had left it. Still, Miriam couldn't help feeling disappointed,

84

which was silly, she berated herself, but she had been so sure that someone was waiting here. Had they tired and left? Had she totally misunderstood things? That thought made her uncomfortably hot in her face, and embarrassed.

Caesar turned to them. "Well," he said, "it seems as we've missed them."

Cyrus drew his hand through his hair. "It doesn't look better."

Miriam didn't say anything. She was so embarrassed that she couldn't look the two men in the face.

"So, now that we're here, you might as well stay for a late dinner," Caesar said with a smile and took a step towards the kitchen. That was when the light came on.

"Well, well, well..." said a deep, caressing voice behind them, way too familiar. A cold shiver ran down Miriam's spine when they spun around and saw themselves standing just inside the back door. She felt sick. The three others aimed at them with something that looked similar to pistols. The other Caesar watched them with a friendly expression on his face.

"Henry, Carl, and Miriam, together, here. That wasn't really what I expected." Jovially, he turned his head and looked at the other Miriam, who got visibly pale and swallowed hard. He looked back at them. "Please, drop your weapons. We're all friends here." Miriam fought down a hysterical urge to laugh, but didn't move. Cyrus and Caesar stood still as statues on each side of her. "Now, it's easier, and less painful, for all of us if you cooperate." None of them moved, but Miriam could sense the tension that emanated from the two men as almost physical. The other Caesar sighed somewhat regretful. "It's your choice, of course."

He straightened his pistol, but suddenly Cyrus moved beside her.

"Wait!" he exclaimed. "I'm not going to cause any trouble."

Content, the other Caesar said: "Very well, Carl. You can put the rifle there and come over to us."

85

Miriam stared unbelievingly at him as he started to put down his rifle on the floor.

"You can't do that! You just can't!" she burst out.

Cyrus gave her a cold look as he crouched. "Yes, I can. It's very simple."

Something inside her died, the growing friendship she'd experienced with him crushed under his cold stare. The other Caesar watched them with a pleased little smile. The rifle was down on the floor. Caesar moved slightly and nearly unnoticeable beside her as Cyrus rose up and with one smooth move shot the double Caesar in the stomach with his gun. Another shot sounded, and the other Cyrus stumbled and fell, blood gushing from his leg. As he cried out in pain, his appearance started to change to the chubby, brown-haired teenager she almost remembered from yesterday. Just as Miriam began to get a grip of her own confusion, something bit her on her cheek. Fire drenched her face, and she pulled the trigger on her gun, not even being able to see, just shooting blindly before everything started to spin around her and her legs collapsed. She fell down into darkness.

When she woke up, she lay in Caesar's bedroom with the night-lamp shining gently on the bedside table. A duvet covered her, making her uncomfortably warm and feverish, and her left cheek hurt. She wondered what time it was and how long she had been unconscious.

"How are you feeling?" Cyrus' soft voice came from the corner of the room. She turned her head and met his concerned gaze.

"My cheek hurts, and I'm warm."

She removed the duvet from her fully dressed body to get a chance to breathe. Cyrus took a step towards the bed, leaned over her and touched her cheek and forehead carefully. A painfully burning sensation spread over her face, and she grimaced. Immediately, he removed his hand.

"You're red and a little warm, but not much else."

"I thought she shot me," Miriam said surprised.

"She did, but we're not really sure what she hit you with. Some sort of sleeping fluid is my guess."

"Sleeping fluid?" Miriam frowned. Cyrus nodded and pointed at the bedside table. In a large evidence bag lay a big black water-pistol. She stared at it, baffled.

"You're kidding me? It was a water-pistol?"

He scoffed in a friendly way and fell silent for a moment. Then he cleared his throat and looked a little embarrassed.

"I'm sorry that I fooled you," he said, "but I really needed them to believe me. It was the only chance I had."

She gave him a friendly, but regretful smile. "I should've trusted you."

"Actually, it was very good that you didn't. It helped my little show. I'm not sure Caesar number two would've believed me otherwise."

"Where is he?"

"He's dead. C's out there with the ambulance guys, filing a report."

Miriam hesitated, but she really needed to know. "Does he still look like him?" Cyrus shook his head, and a great relief filled her, made her heart lighter. "Good," she said.

"When you're able, I'd like you to take a look at him to see if you recognize him from your memories at the museum."

"Ah, of course!" she exclaimed enthusiastically and sat up on the bed. Everything started to spin, and she had to stabilize herself, but just a couple of seconds later she could see clearly again. "You're right! It must've been those three at the museum. This is our lucky day, Cy! We can question them about everything!" Cyrus looked away. "What?" she asked, enthusiasm slowly giving way for concern.

"She's dead too." He looked at her again. "You managed to hit her in the eye when you fell."

Miriam felt speechless and stared at him. Then she fell back on the bed again and sighed as she rubbed her eyes to get rid of the dizziness.

"And what about the third guy? Is he also dead?"

"No, but he's in some sort of coma."

"Coma?" she repeated unbelievingly. "But... I thought... Didn't Caesar hit him in the leg? How can he be in a coma?"

Cyrus shrugged. "I don't know. He had some kind of seizure and then just fell unconscious and hasn't woken up since. The ambulance guys say he's in a coma. They're taking him to the South Side Hospital."

Miriam let out a frustrated sound and tried to sit up again. A little dizziness came and went, but nothing serious.

"So we won, but lost at the same time. We still don't have a clue about what's going on. Damn it!"

Cyrus' laugh was more of a short bark. "Totally my reaction too." Then he fell silent, and his gaze shied away. "There's something else you probably need know..."

"Yes?" she said when he hesitated.

"Well... when she died... she changed from looking like you..." Cyrus' already pale cheeks got even whiter, making him look wax-like in the dim light. Butterflies started to stir in Miriam's stomach, and she had a distinct feeling that she didn't want to hear what he was about to tell her. "Uh... I don't really know where to start..." The butterflies grew bigger. When Cyrus hesitated and didn't know where to start, it had to be really bad. She couldn't stand it any longer.

"Did she turn into a blob? Or did she burn and become ashes?"

"No... no... She's dead, alright, and most likely human, but... She doesn't have eyes. The sockets are all empty. Caesar said that it looked like they'd been carved out by a knife. Her tongue has been cut off too, and her face... Well... the whole face has been carved into some kind of... spell... also with a knife. I think it's that amnesia sleep spell, but when the bullet went into her eye... socket... it disrupted the spell. Now when you look at her face you get dizzy, you faint for a short period of time, and you don't remember what happened just before you fainted. Everyone did it; me, Caesar, the ambulance crew…"

Miriam felt weak and nauseous. "Um… I… don't know what to say… It's… I don't know… sickening…?" She tried to gather herself from the repulsive images that forced their way into her mind. With a struggle, she opened her mouth to say something, anything. "So where are we going from here? Has Caesar said anything?"

"Caesar said we should sleep on it tonight," Caesar said with a tired smile as he came into the room. "How are you feeling? You look a little flushed."

"I am a little flushed. Nothing I can't handle, though."

"I'm glad. I got a little worried when you just went down." His look caressed her, and she was thankful that she apparently had red cheeks already, or they would have noticed her blushing. She looked down like a shy schoolgirl, but not fast enough to miss Cyrus' amused expression. It disappeared as quickly as it had come, and he stood up and stretched.

"I should be getting home," he said. "It'll be dawn soon, and I wouldn't mind getting some sleep before our briefing tomorrow."

Caesar nodded. "Let's say ten a.m. Just a couple of hours extra to get proper rest. We certainly need it." He paused and frowned. "I think it's safe for us to part, but just in case, I'd like us to have some sort of code word for tomorrow. I know it's a little bit silly, but rather silly than infiltrated again."

"Sure. What kind of word?"

Caesar shrugged. "What about… *emerald*?"

"Whatever. Sounds good enough. Nah, don't worry about me," he continued when Caesar rose. "I'll find my way out. See y'all in the morning."

He turned around, but Caesar put a hand on his shoulder and stopped him.

"Cyrus, you did really well tonight. Really well."

To Miriam's great surprise Cyrus blushed intensely.

"Thanks."

And with that, he briskly stepped out of the room. Caesar listened to his disappearing footsteps and the front door opening and closing, before turning to her with a kind, warm smile, being all Henry again. He came to her side, sat down on the bed, and took her hand. Then he embraced her powerfully. With his mouth to her head, he mumbled: "Mimi... When you went down... I thought you'd died... I was so scared."

His hands found their way to her aching face; they held her gently while he looked lovingly into her eyes for a moment before kissing her – so sweet, so tender. Her heart beat faster, she cling to him, deepened the kiss urgently while her body reacted forcefully to his touch. With impatient movements, she undressed and pulled him down on the bed. He smiled at her, hindered her hands as they tried to open up his shirt.

"Easy now, Mimi, easy..."

A disappointed sigh broke free, and she lay down the way he wanted and let him take her at his own pace.

Chapter 8

The morning sun shone through the curtain-less windows in Henry's kitchen while Miriam put their breakfast on the table: hot tea and whole grain bread with butter, cooked ham and Swiss cheese, topped with sliced cherry tomatoes, deep red in color, and creamy Greek yogurt. It looked so tasty that Miriam's stomach started to rumble. She usually wasn't this hungry in the morning, but the night had been exceptionally full of adrenaline, so she wasn't surprised that her body needed the energy. She placed the chocolate-brown ceramic tea cups on the table together with the matching plates for the bread and admired the result.

"Henry! Breakfast's ready!" There was no answer, so she went to the bedroom where she found Henry kneeling on the floor at his closet. "Breakfast's ready," she repeated.

He looked up at her with a smile. "There's a camera on my office table. Could you get it for me?"

She almost pouted. Almost. Then she repressed a sigh and went to get the camera. When she came back, he was still kneeling at the closet, a concerned frown showing on his forehead.

"What's wrong?"

"I don't know yet, but this bag here isn't mine."

Miriam peeked in. A big black leather bag lay neatly on the floor. He turned on the camera and took a couple of pictures.

"Do you think it belongs to the other Caesar?" she asked and kneeled beside him, breakfast nearly, but not quite, forgotten.

"I hope so. Here, take a couple of gloves." He picked up a pair of latex gloves from his FBI jacket, gave them to her, and put on another pair himself. Then he dusted the handle and checked it for fingerprints, but no prints were to be seen. He frowned again. "Open it," he said and grabbed the camera once more.

Miriam reached in, took a firm grip on the handle and pulled it out. It was quite heavy. Henry moved a couple of inches to give it plenty of room. She unzipped it and opened it. The bag seemed to contain things wrapped in black fabric. The camera flashed again. Miriam leaned over the bag, examined it closer, and drew a fabric-covered item from it.

"Black velvet," she said. "And expensive," she added while unwrapping it.

The daylight glimmered on a plain silver candleholder. She frowned and glanced at Henry, puzzled. His expression was slightly concerned, and he beckoned her to continue. She put the candleholder on the floor. The camera flashed while she took out the next item, also wrapped in black velvet. Another silver candleholder. The next items were two black candles and two small vases, both in silver. As she grabbed yet another object from the bag, a cold shiver ran down her spine. It had a too familiar shape to not be recognized through the velvet. The arm length silver knife was heavy and made in one piece. She let it slip down to the floor, and it landed with a muffled sound, shining dimly in the sun. They looked at each other in silence. Then Henry cleared his throat.

"Is there anything else in there?"

Miriam bent over the bag and took out two bouquets of forget-me-nots with their stems wrapped in wet paper and covered with plastic bags. She studied them with something that bordered on horror and hurriedly put them down beside the knife with hands that were so cold that they had nearly lost their feeling. The last thing in the bag was an ordinary paintbrush, ordinary had it not had some traces of a rust-red color at the base.

Henry cleared his throat again. "We need to take that to the lab."

Miriam nodded. Then she looked at Henry. His face had a slightly gray nuance.

"They were going to murder us, Henry."

He shook his head, and a deep sigh heaved in his chest.

"You forget what he said, Mimi." Henry's voice was slightly disapproving, and she blushed. "He said: 'Henry, Carl, and Miriam, together here. That was not what I expected'."

As the words came out of his mouth, she stared at him with horror.

"They were going to murder you! They were…" She swallowed. "They were going to murder you!" She flung herself around his neck, and when she felt Henry's strong arms around her, the tears started to trickle down her cheeks. The image of Professor Bruchheimer's brutally mutilated body flashed before her eyes, but the face was Henry's. Deep sobs found their way out of her chest. Henry rocked her gently and stroked her over her hair.

"Shush, shush, it's fine, it's fine." Finally, she could stop crying, and she sat up, drying her cheeks and eyes. Henry lent her the old checkered handkerchief with a kind little smile. "You might just keep it, Mimi. You seem to need it more than I do." At that, she managed to laugh, even though it sounded hollow and weak. "Let me just photograph these things and put them back into the bag. We need to eat and get to the office."

"I don't know if I can eat. I feel nauseous."

"I know, but you'll feel better after some bread and tea. I promise you that."

"Okay…"

She watched him folding up all the objects in their velvet wrappings and putting them back down in the bag. If she could avoid touching those horrible things again, she would be more than happy. Just the thought that they had made love in the same room as the items used in that gruesome ritualistic murder she had seen two days before made her feel sick and unclean.

Suddenly, a wave of nausea washed over her body, and her face became cold and sweaty. She got up to her feet, ran to the bathroom, opened the toilet lid and let it all out.

Afterward, she dropped to the floor, leaning her forehead towards the cold porcelain, breathing hard. Her stomach hurt, and she had a disgusting taste in her mouth. She heard Henry moving outside the closed door.

"Mimi, how are you feeling? Can I come in?"

"Wait... wait, I'm coming out..."

She flushed the toilet twice, washed her face with cold water and soap, and rinsed her mouth. The mirror showed her a dead white face with two dark holes for eyes. She washed her face again and rubbed it hard with the towel. She grimaced when her cheek went from sore to outright throbbing, but it was only one extra unpleasant sensation on top of all the other ones. Shivering she opened the door and got out. Henry took her face between his hands and watched her closely and concernedly.

"Maybe you should stay here today, just relaxing. You don't need to be with us if you're sick, you know. I can brief you on what happened when I get home."

She shook her head, still feeling her body trembling. "No, no. If I stay here, I'll go crazy. I need to focus on something."

He gave her a long, worried look. "If you say so..." He hesitated.

"I'm fine, Henry, I really am. I just need something to do, you know, to keep my mind occupied. Let's go eat breakfast. I think you're right. I probably need it."

She realized that she tried to convince herself as much as him, but a cup of tea and a slice of bread later, she actually felt relatively fine and prepared enough to go to the office. They stopped at the coffee shop at the corner of the FBI headquarters and bought muffins and Jamaican coffee before heading up to their room. Cyrus was already there. He looked amazingly fresh and well rested as he sat on the chair, tilting it on its back legs, with some papers in his lap, and chewing away on a pen. He looked up when they came in with their hands full of goodies and smiled.

"Ah, there you are. I was just about to call you."

94

"We got a little occupied," Caesar said.

Cyrus' face turned unreadable for some reason, and he viewed the park at the opposite side of the street from the window.

"Lovely day today, isn't it? Wouldn't it be nice to take the day off and just relax in the park, dozing off in the amazingly emerald-green grass?"

Caesar stared unbelievingly at Cyrus a moment before he suddenly burst out laughing.

"Sorry, I had forgotten about that little deal we came up with tonight, but apparently you're as green as the emerald grass out there." He put up the black bag on the table. "Here, take a look. We found it in my closet this morning."

Cyrus put away his pen and papers and got up from the chair, putting on a pair of latex gloves before opening it. Miriam busied herself with arranging the muffins and the coffee at the window table, carefully turning her back on the bag and its contents. She could hear the dull clang when the knife was put down on the table, and the very sound made her shiver. She took a sip of the coffee and felt the warm liquid heat up her stomach.

After what seemed like an hour, Cyrus finally said: "So they were our ritualistic murderers, eh?"

"That seems very likely, yes, but we need to get that paintbrush to the lab and see if the blood will match Professor Bruchheimer's."

There was a slight pause.

"And I take it you were the next in line, C?"

"I can't really see why they would have placed it in my bedroom closet otherwise."

"Mhm…" Miriam could hear the drumming of Cyrus' fingers at the table and took another sip of her coffee. "I wonder what they thought they would achieve with that," he said at last. "Split our team, most probably, not that they seemed to be aware of us being a team, mind you, but at least make us disoriented and lose our focus with our P.I. dead. It could of course also be a sign of their preferences of murder victims."

"Elderly, white males?" Caesar asked dryly.

"With an academic profession or background, yes," Cyrus responded calmly.

"It's a possibility," Caesar said, and to Miriam's ears, his voice sounded grumpy. "Let's put everything in e-bags and hand them over to the lab."

"Right. By the way, here's some juicy news for you: neither one of the other us have fingerprints."

"What?" Miriam turned around.

Cyrus gave her a wry smile. "No fingerprints whatsoever. According to the lab, their fingertips are as blank as a mirror."

"How can that be?" She felt almost angry: mad and powerless and scared. How many times had they been in her apartment? How many times had they watched her sleep without her knowing? How many times had *she* been there, staring at her with her eyeless sockets? There was a memory of a memory stirring somewhere in Miriam's mind, but as Cyrus shrugged, it vanished. She drew an inaudible sigh of relief and immediately felt ashamed of her cowardice.

"If they can manipulate their bodies, why wouldn't they be able to manipulate their fingerprints?" He paused and gave her a penetrating look, but his voice only showed concern when he said: "By the way, how are you? You look a little pale."

She turned halfway around, flushing again with anger. It was none of his business how she felt.

"I'm okay," she said gruffly. He studied her a little longer than she thought necessary and that old, familiar awkwardness in his presence awoke again. She turned her back completely on him. "We brought muffins and coffee if you'd like."

"Thanks." Miriam heard him fiddling with the cups while he said with an unreadable tone: "Do you want to hear the other juicy part?"

"I don't know," she said in a snappy voice. "Do I?"

He gave up a short, humorless laugh. "Probably not. I'll give it to you anyway. Neither of them had genitals."

Miriam swung around and stared at him.

"What do you mean, Cyrus?" Caesar asked demandingly. Cyrus suddenly looked uncomfortable.

"The woman had apparently been burned with a hot iron, and there was nothing left. Her breasts were carved away, as well."

Miriam felt herself get cold and sweaty again. "That's horrible!" she burst out. "She didn't have anything left, no eyes, no tongue, no face, no breasts and no genitals. What was she? A shell?"

Cyrus just shook his head. "A mirror, perhaps?"

Miriam gave him a surprised glance, her apprehension forgotten. "A mirror? That's an interesting angle."

"And the men?" Caesar asked impatiently with a scowl.

"The other you had neither testicles nor penis. The other me has no testicles." They both stared at Cyrus, who shrugged uncomfortably. "I know," he said. "It's nuts."

Caesar shook his head unbelievingly and put the last ritual objects in evidence bags. "Have you heard anything about the third member?" he asked.

Cyrus nodded while taking a big gulp of the coffee. "Yeah, he's still in a coma. They don't know why. According to the doctors, he's as healthy as an elephant. Could be running the triathlon if he'd like to."

Caesar frowned again and put his regular FBI bag on the table.

"So," he said while taking out the other evidence that he and Cyrus had gathered last night when she had still been unconscious, "if we leave the really strange things out of the account, the whole case actually makes a little bit more sense now. What I wonder is what connection they have to the Stevenson family."

"And what I'd like to know," Miriam burst out, "is if there are more of them out there!" The two men stared at her. "Oh, come on!" she said with just the slightest twitch of irritation in her voice. "You both know that they very well could belong to a smaller faction or maybe even a whole organization. They've been doing enough strange things for that. Or do you really think that three single individuals would be able to carry out all of this?" Cyrus drew a hand through his hair, and Caesar frowned and looked out of the window. None of them said anything. Miriam stared angrily at them and continued: "Three individuals have accidently found out how to use mind-control, appearance-changing, and fingerprint-removal, and enjoy ritualistic murder, burning their genitals with hot iron and breeding sci-fi animals in their spare-time? Seriously!"

"Well…" Cyrus said after a moment of silence. "You do have a point… C?"

Caesar sighed and looked back at them. "Unfortunately, I think we have to take that into consideration." He sighed again and sank heavily into a chair. "I feel too old for this."

"C…?" Cyrus' voice was concerned.

Caesar waved him away. "I just need a minute." He sighed once more and rubbed his eyes. "It's been a little bit too much with my mother and all. I'm just tired."

Miriam watched him anxiously. His face had a slightly grayish tinge, not very apparent, but when she studied him closely, she could see it.

"Do you want to go home?" she asked.

He shook his head. "No, there's too much to do. We can't let go now, can't let the trail grow cold." There was a new pause and, then he looked up at them. "Let's drink that coffee and eat those muffins while we decide where to go from here, and after today's work, I'm going to indulge myself in a spa. Does that sound good enough to you?"

"Sure thing," Cyrus said with a trace of a smile. "To tell the truth, I think we all could make good use of a spa session this evening."

Miriam tried to smile as well. "I'll see to it that you get a nice color on your toenails, guys."

Cyrus chuckled, but Caesar just frowned and sat down at the table.

"We need to start from the top again," he said when she and Cyrus gathered around him. "We need to find what links these people to the Stevenson family. This means that we have lots to do right now."

He rose, went to the whiteboard beside the crime map, fetched a black pen, and started to scribble.

Emilia Stevenson — why was she targeted?

The disappearance of Robert and Stella Stevenson — did they leave voluntarily or have they been captured/murdered?

R and S Stevenson — any connection to the other us?

The eels — where do they come from — who breeds them — who plants them?

Professor Bruchheimer — what's his connection to the Stevenson family and the possible faction?

P. B. — did he breed the eels?

The false P. B. — see above: connection + eels

The other us — who are they — where do they come from — do they belong to a faction?

Possible larger faction — need to find out a.s.a.p. and if possible take them down

Checking lab results a.s.a.p.

He looked at Cyrus and Miriam, his face slightly grayish still, and his voice had a tired tone when he began to speak.

"This afternoon we're going to do something different. I'm going to check Emilia Stevenson's body once more and see if I can find any clues to as why she was targeted." With an unreadable glance at her he continued:

99

"Claire, you'll have to take a look at the other Caesar and see if he resembles that man in your memories from the museum and then do a background check on Professor Bruchheimer." With another unreadable glance, but aimed at Cyrus this time, he said: "Cyrus, I need you to check on the eels again to see if they're still alive and inquire if the lab reports are available yet. There should be some. When you've done that, I want you and Claire to watch the security cameras at the museum, beginning with Tuesday's surveillance films." Turning half away, he pointed towards the whiteboard. "We also need to find out the identity of the false Professor Bruchheimer and see if we can figure out if he's a part of the probable faction the other us might have belonged to. That's a question for tomorrow, though, if we can't get to it today." Once again he pointed at the whiteboard. "Another thing we need to check out is the FBI files on Mr. and Mrs. Stevenson since you didn't find anything in the regular files, Claire. I'll do that during the afternoon." He fell silent, clearly thinking the day through, but then he scowled. "Oh, and yet another thing I'll look into is if there's any information in the GFS files about a possible faction or organization that matches what we know so far about the behavior of the other us. Hopefully, we'll have a clearer picture of this project by tomorrow." This time, when he looked at them, they could see that he was done, and they both nodded their agreement. "And speaking of tomorrow, we need to go back to the Stevenson's apartment to check for traces of evidence that we might have missed the first time. Any questions?" They both shook their heads. "Well, let's get started then."

He folded his notebook, took it under his arm, and with an emotionless nod towards them he left the room with determined steps, heading for the morgue. Cyrus bounced up from the chair and began to clean up the leftover muffins from the table. Miriam got up a little slower, looking at the door as it closed, wondering why it felt like Caesar abandoned her.

"So, how are you feeling?" Cyrus asked over the shoulder.

"Hm?"

"I said, 'how are you feeling?' Your 'I'm okay' back there didn't sound very convincing to me. Not quite recovered from that sleeping fluid, are you?"

"Oh... Well... I don't know." She frowned.

"No side-effects?"

Miriam turned towards him, raising her eyebrows. "What?"

"I said, 'no side-effects?'"

"I did hear you. I just wondered what the hell you're up to, Cy? Worried about me? That's not like you."

Cyrus stopped wrapping the muffins in plastic and glanced at her. Then he came back to the table and leaned casually on it.

"I could say that I'm just concerned about you, you know."

"You could."

"But?"

She sighed wearily and sat down again. "What's wrong, Cy? Can you spit it out so we can get to work?"

Cyrus drew his hand through his hair and sat himself down on the table, avoiding her gaze.

"You're quite bothersome, Claire. Why not just tell me exactly how you're feeling?"

The irritation she had tried so hard to hide suddenly rose to the surface.

"Okay. I'm nauseous and sweaty and dizzy and have stomach pain. Satisfied?" she snubbed, but instead of shrugging, as she had expected, he met her irritated stare with an open, concerned look. All her annoyance melted away by this unexpected sight, just to immediately be replaced by a worried pang. "What?"

He looked away. "I don't know. I'm not sure."

"Not sure about what?" She stared anxiously at him. "You think there was something more in that sleeping fluid?

Like what? You think that I'm sick in some way, or spreading something, or…" She stopped abruptly as the thought hit her like a bullet. Her breaths hardened, rasped in her throat. The cold sinking in her stomach dug its fingers hard and deep inside her, crept, and crawled out to every limb until she couldn't move. Cyrus' voice sounded as if it came from far away, muffled by the buzzing in her ears. She couldn't move or talk or see. The only thing she could do was to give herself up to that sinking drowning feeling inside her. Suddenly, she felt something warm on her hand. Cyrus was holding her hand in his. When did he get so close to her? The buzzing in her ears went away, and she could hear his voice. It sounded alarmed when he said her name.

"Claire? Claire? Miriam?"

She managed to come back to life and looked at him with pure terror. "Am I…" Her voice cracked. She swallowed hard and tried again. "Am… I… infected?"

His hand tightened the grip on hers. He hesitated and the silence in the room grew thick. The blue eyes that watched her so closely had a look that she had never seen before. They looked vulnerable.

"You just need a simple x-ray, Miriam. Nothing more than that. If we do it today, we can remove them immediately if you have them. We'll let Dr. Bernard look at it. It won't take more than a couple of hours. You'll be able to work again tomorrow or maybe even this afternoon." She couldn't stop the hysterical laughter that burst out of her. When he awkwardly patted her on her shoulder, hot, aching tears started to trickle down her cheeks, but she still laughed. "Miriam, Miriam… Keep it together. You have to keep it together. Will you let these bastards win over you? Have them walk away with the victory even in death? You're stronger than that, Miriam."

She bit her lip hard, letting the pain calm her down. Finally, she managed to get control over herself.

"I'm sorry."

He shook his head and gave her hand a friendly squeeze.

"Come. I'll take you to Bernard. It's no use waiting. If it makes you feel better, I need to go through one as well."

She stared at him. Then she took a deep breath and helped herself up from the chair.

"I want to look... I want to look at him first. At the morgue."

Cyrus raised his eyebrows. "If you're sure." was all he said, but he gave her hand a final squeeze before letting it go.

Chapter 9

"Carl! What a pleasant surprise! I haven't seen you since I stitched those claw marks on your back together last summer."

The wrinkles in the corners of Dr. Bernard's eyes deepened when he smiled mischievously. For the second day in a row Miriam had the pleasure of seeing Cyrus blush, this time awkwardly at the memory of the project he had failed.

Dr. Bernard turned to Miriam. The salt-and-pepper in his hair had become more accentuated, and his warm brown skin tone had developed gray shadows of tiredness. She had known him briefly for six years and had had numerous wounds treated by him, wounds that no one wanted to have written down in official hospital records. Both Dr. Bernard and his nurses, Banafshe and Blaise, were members of the society and treated all unnatural injuries that former Star Students suffered from. Rumors had it that he and Caesar had known each other since they both were students themselves, but for some reason, she'd never asked Henry about it.

"How's your shoulder, Miriam? Does it hurt?"

"Only during winter."

He nodded. "You'll probably experience that during the rest of your life if you stay here. It's too damp here. Move to Arizona. That'll do it. Or you can come visit me when it's getting cold, and I'll give you something for the pain." He paused and scrutinized them thoroughly. "So, what brings you here today? Apparently you can walk, so there's nothing broken or wounded."

Miriam glanced at Cyrus to let him do the talking.

"We need an x-ray each of our stomachs, Dr. Bernard. We might have something… some kind of living creatures there." He opened his bag and brought out a small glass jar with one of the dead eels in it, which they had picked up before they left headquarters. "This is a fully grown example of the species. We have reason to believe that if we're carrying this kind, they're still in the larvae state."

Dr. Bernard held out his hand and reached for the jar. Nothing but a mild curiosity showed in his face while he studied it. Still with his gaze fixed at the eel he said: "If you have anything like this in you, we'll have it out before noon." He looked up. "Who wants to start? Ladies first?"

Miriam felt a pang of fear, but she managed to smile and nod. "Sure. Why not? Carl?"

"Go ahead."

Dr. Bernard brought her into the small, gray examination room and waved at her to take a seat on the bunk. He took his place in the swirling chair and turned on the computer.

"So, Miriam, an x-ray wouldn't do any good. We need to do an ultrasound instead."

"Okay."

He studied the screen and wrote something down.

"I take it that the species have some kind of teeth or another way to fasten them to the stomach. Otherwise, they would enjoy the exotic sight of the drainage instead of your abdomen, if not now then at least after your next visit to the washroom."

Miriam blushed. "Um… I've seen the results of them, and it wasn't pretty. They hadn't been flushed down in a toilet, that's for sure. I can't tell you more than that, I think, since it's part of our ongoing investigation."

"Mhm." Dr. Bernard swirled around and patted on the bunk. "Take off that shirt of yours and lay down, please. Here's a gown you can put on. Ribbons at the front." She took the offered blue-flowered hospital gown and did as he asked while he occupied himself with preparing the ultrasound. "Have you had an ultrasound done before, Miriam?" She shook her head. "No? Okay. It doesn't hurt. You might feel a warm sensation from the sound waves and the gel I'm using is cold at first touch, but other than that you won't feel a thing."

105

She inhaled sharply when the gel touched her skin. "Yes, cold indeed."

Dr. Bernard nodded and put the probe on her stomach. He moved it calmly over her skin while he watched the screen, which was placed at such an angle that Miriam couldn't get even one glimpse of what was going on. The humming of the machine was the only sound in the room. Time ticked on without anything happening. Since she couldn't read anything from Dr. Bernard's calm facial expression, her thoughts started to wander.

She was happy that the man at the morgue indeed was the same elderly man from her memories. That made them more reliable. It had been hard not knowing if what she thought had happened had actually occurred or if it had been some sort of hallucination invoked by whatever had been used to create the amnesia. It was also a relief that he was dead.

"You do know that you're pregnant, right?" Dr. Bernard suddenly said.

Miriam's head turned violently towards him.

"What?" she burst out. He looked at her and blinked mischievously. What?" she said again, without finding anything more intelligent to come up with. Dr. Bernard burst out laughing.

"Just kidding. Sorry, it was just too tempting."

Finally, she managed to grasp the joke, and she frowned at him.

"Thanks a lot. It's not that I have nothing else to worry about."

He laughed again and didn't seem regretful at all. "You should have seen your face, Miriam. It was just too funny."

"Very funny…" she grunted.

"Do you think Carl will be happy when I tell him the same thing?" Dr. Bernard said with a grin. Miriam tried not to smile, and he blinked at her. "But," he continued with more seriousness in his voice, "I'd like to show you something." He started to turn the screen towards her with one hand, while the other held the probe in its position slightly below her solar plexus. A black screen with white-ish patterns became visible for her. He pointed out some small dots on the screen. "This is probably what we're looking for."

The familiar sinking feeling came over her again. She closed her eyes and took some deep breaths before managing to look at the dots again.

"Are they…" She swallowed hard. "Are they moving?"

Dr. Bernard nodded.

"Mhm. They don't seem to like the sound waves."

She looked at him with terror. "You mean that they react to the ultrasound?"

"Yes." He pointed at one of the dots. "This seems to be the head."

"How can you tell?"

He glanced at her. "It has teeth at this end."

Miriam felt sick. She put an arm over her eyes, trying to close off the world. Dr. Bernard took away the probe and started to wipe the gel off her stomach. Then the warmth of a blanket over her body comforted her, and she realized that she had started to shiver. Silence fell in the room while she tried to gain control over her terror. Dr. Bernard's sympathetic, but professional voice managed to calm her down enough to take her arm away from her face.

"You have two options as I see it. The difficult way is to do a surgery. Not the most optimal choice if you need to get back to work immediately. The other way is easier, but it takes a lot out of you. Gastroscopy. We can do it with you either sleeping or awake. You need to fast for at least six hours before we can give you the anesthesia, but you won't feel anything. If you're awake, we need to anesthetize the throat while you're biting onto a block so you don't bite off the gastroscopy tube. During that time, I will have to lead clutching-tongs down your throat into your stomach to remove the eels. I counted to six eels, which means that we will have to do the procedure six times to get them all out."

She simply looked at him, finding it hard to speak.

"No surgery," she said finally. "Can I think about the other options for a while?"

"Absolutely," Dr. Bernard said and rose. "You can have this room, and I'll take Carl into another while you think."

It was two sore agents who, one and a half hour later, stepped into Cyrus' car and drove to the museum. Miriam decided that this episode was going to be one that she would force herself to forget as soon as possible. It was such a relief to have the eels removed safely from her stomach that she had cried like a baby afterward. During the whole procedure, the image of Emilia Stevenson being eaten alive from her inside danced in front of her eyes, giving her the strength to endure it, but even the memory of the procedure made her shiver, making those traitorous tears spill. She wiped them away while looking out of the window. Cyrus sat silently beside her, a little pale, but otherwise, he didn't seem to have gone through anything worse than a car wash. She gave him a sour eye from the side, but he didn't seem to notice.

At the museum, Mr. Swanson greeted them with a little less enthusiasm than the last time they had seen him. Miriam stood quiet and let Cyrus do the talking.

"Mr. Swanson," he greeted the guard, a tad hoarsely. "How are you doing?"

"Huh." The guard snorted. "I didn't think you'd remember my name, but then again, you policemen always have things like that written down, right."

Cyrus looked a little embarrassed, but Miriam had a feeling that it wasn't sincere.

"That's right, but I do remember your name nevertheless. I'm good with names and faces."

"Yeah, right. So what do you want? Professor Bruchheimer ain't in today and will never be so you can do whatever you want with his room, I guess."

"We're actually here to watch the surveillance films from Monday and on."

"The surveillance films...?"

Miriam could see how the security guard's curiosity awakened.

"Yes, please. And a copy of an updated employee list included with photos, if you'd be so kind."

"Hmm..." He turned around, reaching for a key box. "May I ask why?" he asked over his shoulder.

"You may, but unfortunately, I can't tell you more than that it has to do with Professor Bruchheimer's death." Cyrus sounded apologetic, and the guard nodded when he came back to the desk with a key in his hand.

"You'll have to wait here while I get them for you, but let me say this much to you: we all liked the old man, and if you can get the bastard who killed him and get him fried, I'll help you as much as I can."

He stared defiantly at Cyrus and Cyrus acknowledged him respectfully. "Thank you, Mr. Swanson. I really appreciate that. We will need as much help as you can give us."

The guard seemed to relax and turned around to unlock the security door. "I'll be back," he said over his shoulder in a frightening likeness of Arnold Schwarzenegger and let the door slam shut behind him. Cyrus looked down at Miriam with a warning gaze.

"Don't giggle."

She suppressed the smile and the giggle that wanted to break free, and they waited for the guard in silence. It didn't take long until he came back with six tapes under his arm and a binder.

"Right," he said. "Here are all the films from Tuesday morning until eight o'clock this morning, as well as the list." He gave Cyrus an apologetic look. "I will need your ID, sir, and your signature on this paper, please. It's a loan form for security devices."

109

"But of course," Cyrus said obligingly and signed the form with his unusually beautiful signature before providing the guard his FBI card.

"The loan is for seven days. After that we will need to sign a new application," the guard said while writing down the information on the loan form. He gave the card back to Cyrus, who flashed him a friendly smile.

"No problems at all, Mr. Swanson. We will most likely be back with them within the next couple of days."

"You have a good day then, sir." His gaze wandered unwillingly towards Miriam. "And you too, ma'am."

The smile she gave him was as thin as it could be and still be called a smile. She had a strong impression that Cyrus was amused when he turned away from the guard and followed her out to the car. He threw the binder and the films in the back seat. Miriam, still annoyed of the guard's behavior, raised her eyebrows.

"That's an interesting way of handling possible evidence," she said sarcastically.

He jingled restlessly with his car keys without looking at her.

"Let's go back to HQ. We've lots to go through before the spa tonight."

She turned silent for a moment, startled by his sudden defensive tone.

"Okay."

Cyrus started the car and backed out of the parking spot. The rest of the way was driven in uncomfortable silence, but even if it was something to which Miriam was accustomed, she had the distinct feeling that it was her fault this time, that Cyrus had started to open up towards her, and she had slammed the door shut in his face.

She moved uneasily on her seat and threw a discreet glance at Cyrus' blank, emotionless face. Telling him that she was sorry was totally out of the question. She couldn't make that kind of admittance, not to him. She looked out of the side window again, watching the moving traffic without really seeing it.

Fifteen minutes later, they finally reached the garage underneath the FBI headquarter and Cyrus parked at his designated spot. Just as he reached for the door, Miriam put a light hand on his arm. Clearly caught off guard he looked down at her hand before meeting her eyes.

"Thanks, Cy," she said bashfully and felt her cheeks blossom.

"For what?"

"For being there when I didn't even realize that I needed you."

"Oh..." The smile he gave her was surprisingly shy. "Nothing to talk about." He opened the door and got out. "I'm going to get us a couple of iced caps if you set everything up," he said over his shoulder. Miriam grinned and felt unexpectedly relieved.

"Sure thing. I'll do whatever you want for one of those right now."

Chapter 10

One iced cappuccino and two iced teas each had been devoured before something of interest finally occurred on the security tape.

During some boring hours, they had fast forwarded the tape from Monday morning to Tuesday morning and seen a lot of people coming and going, including Professor Bruchheimer. He came to work at 7:48 a.m. on Monday and didn't leave until 6:30 that evening. Mr. Swanson had been released by the night guard, Annette Meille, a cute redhead in her mid-twenties. She, in turn, had a very uneventful night, which she spent taking notes while looking through a couple of thick books: most likely university studies. She was released by Mr. Swanson at 7:12 on Tuesday morning and left work yawning. Professor Bruchheimer never showed up that morning, which indicated that he had been murdered during that past night.

"I wonder who takes sick calls," Miriam mused and tapped a pen on the table. "Not that I think that the faction or whatever they are, bothered to call him in sick, but you..." She stopped mid-sentence when the employee door on the tape opened, and the false Mr. Bruchheimer came in. Hastily, Cyrus stopped the tape, rewound it, and put it on normal speed. Both of them leaned forward intently. The time on the tape showed 12:32. Miriam scribbled it down in her notebook.

"About half an hour before we arrived," Cyrus mumbled.

The old man stepped forward to Mr. Swanson and seemed to talk to him a couple of minutes before taking a step back. They could see the blank face of the security guard as the inner door opened and let the false professor in. Concerned they glanced at each other.

"That looked really odd," Miriam said. "Do you think..." She fell silent. "I don't know."

Cyrus stopped the tape and rewound it once more. "Let's watch it again."

They watched it in silence. The door opened, the old man in his worn corduroy jacket came in, went to the security cube, stood with his back towards the camera exactly two minutes before stepping back, showing Mr. Swanson's totally blank face. Cyrus halted the tape just there. They both leaned forward and watched his face intensely.

"He looks like he's sleeping, don't you think?"

With a slow nod, Cyrus squinted and drummed his fingers on the table. "It's hard to make any conclusions of course, but..." He hesitated.

"He's been manipulated with. I'm almost one hundred percent certain. Cy, I don't think Mr. Swanson will have one bit of memory of this guy."

"Yeah, I think you're right. Does it mean that the old man's part of the faction too? No," he corrected himself, "but he has been. That's why he knows about their skills, that's why he recognized the eels, and that's why he's at the museum before our other friends arrive. He's trying to escape the faction." Cyrus frowned. "I don't think he'll succeed."

"And he told us as much as he dared to in the hope that we'd be able to catch them?"

"Probably."

"Do you think he's infected too? He was so afraid of the eels."

"Bet he was!" Cyrus' cheeks turned pale. "But I couldn't tell. It's possible." He looked thoughtfully at the back of the false professor on the screen. "I don't think it's his area, though. He's probably specialized in something else, hence, the encrypted papers you saw."

Miriam gave up a triumphant cheer. "He must have gotten away with them! That means that the other us didn't get what they wanted, why is why they brought me there! They thought we took them! They don't know about this guy yet!"

Cyrus smiled at her enthusiasm. "Not to discourage you, Claire, but it depends on what questions they asked you and you don't remember, do you?"

"Damn! You're right." She felt disappointed.

With a slight frown, Cyrus continued to look at the still image on the screen again, seemingly thinking over the situation on the screen. Then he tapped on the table with his fingers again.

"But I do think your conclusion is correct, though. If we hadn't arrived just then, they probably wouldn't have bothered about us. It was the old man's luck that we removed any suspicions that might have come his way, giving him a chance to get away from them."

Miriam nodded, slightly rosy-cheeked and lighthearted at the acknowledgment.

"Which means that for his sake, it doesn't really matter what kind of questions they asked me. Before that night was over, they must have known about his existence." The lightheartedness disappeared, and there was a lump in her throat when she thought of what may have happened to him. Cyrus glanced at her.

"Don't feel sorry for him, Claire. He's probably the one who infected that family in Finland he was talking about. I don't think he knew what it was back then, but that doesn't change the consequences of his doing."

"If he was part of the faction."

"If he was," Cyrus admitted calmly. "But at this point, it seems that our conclusions are correct. Let's keep an open mind until we know more, but work on this track for now."

"Okay," Miriam said, acknowledging his right to decide their course.

He turned on the film, and they saw how the false professor went through the inner security door. Mr. Swanson sat still with his blank face about two minutes after the door closed before coming back to life, reading his paper as if he had done nothing else for the last hour.

The tape fast-forwarded again, and they were the next to arrive at around 1.00 p.m., Cyrus with the white box containing the eels in his hands. Miriam saw herself half turn around, searching for the security camera and looking straight into it for a second, while Cyrus talked with the guard. There was nothing new to be seen, and they sped up the film. The meeting with the false professor went quickly, and they were out of the museum in less than half an hour.

At 1:56 p.m., the old man opened the security door, and Cyrus put the tape on normal speed again.

"That must be the things they were looking for," Miriam remarked and pointed at a big bag he carried over his shoulder.

Mr. Swanson didn't even peek up from the paper he read when the so-called professor went past the security cube and exited out of the door.

"Hm." Cyrus sounded just a bit admiring. "Whatever it is they do, it seems to be very effective."

Miriam looked at him from the side. "Yeah? I guess you'd like to learn it, right?"

"Why not? Think about how handy it would be, never being remembered and never have to answer difficult questions from authorities ever again. Oh, I'd like that." He got a thoughtful expression in his face. "If that guy at the hospital ever wakes up from his coma, I might try to... convince... him about this really splendid idea."

"Cyrus!" Miriam protested.

"What?"

"They're the enemies!"

"So? And I would be just a little careful calling them that, especially around C. They do horrible things, true, but 'enemies'? We're not at war."

"You're just twirling my arguments around," she protested.

He grinned at her. "Yep and I'm good at it too." She scoffed angrily. "And what would be better," he continued

115

without taking any notice of her anger, "than to use their own weapons against them?"

"Just turn on the damn tape, will you? Caesar will probably be here in just a couple of hours, and I'd like to have gone through as much as possible by then."

He laughed kindly at her, but turned on the tape without saying anything else.

The tape showed 2:05 when Cyrus entered the museum the second time, spoke to Mr. Swanson, and got in.

"I missed him with nine minutes! Can you believe that?" Cyrus burst out. "Nine minutes!"

"Wait! Stop the tape, Cy!"

The door had opened again at 2.51 and three persons came in. Cyrus groaned as he put the film on normal speed.

"This must have been my lucky day. Totally awesome."

Neither the two men nor the woman looked at the security camera, but Miriam recognized them anyway; the chubby brown-haired teenager, the older man who now lay silently in the morgue, and a slender woman with a black veil covering her face. They all stood as close to the window in the security cube as they could get, blocking the sight of Mr. Swanson. It only took a minute before the inner door opened and the three of them went through. The security guard lay with his head resting on his arms, seemingly asleep.

"Someone else had a rough day too," Miriam remarked uneasily. "It must have been his luck that no one of the staff actually seems to have caught him sleeping. That could've ended his career just like that."

"Yeah..."

"You know what I find intriguing, Cy?"

"No, what's that?"

"She doesn't seem to have any trouble walking. It's as if she can see, even though she obviously can't." Cyrus stared at her, wide-eyed, and then he shivered violently. "What?" she asked uncertainly, hadn't really expected that reaction.

"Can she see? Is it possible that she can see?"

116

This time, it was her turn to shiver as she thought of the possibility. She exhaled and shook her head.

"I don't know..." she said hoarsely, and they fell silent, shying away from the thought.

The film went on and the minutes went by; five, ten, fifteen. Finally, the inner door opened again, and Cyrus came running out, throwing a glance at the sleeping Mr. Swanson before running out of the exit door. Not even a minute later, the teenager followed him out. Cyrus sighed deeply beside her and threw a hand through his hair.

"I don't remember this. He probably got me right outside. Weird, eh? One would've thought that I could've taken a youngling like that down."

"He might've used some other spell on you," Miriam said, and Cyrus nodded hesitantly. "Well, at least we know more or less what happened."

"That we do." He seemed to be saying something else, but closed his mouth tightly and fast-forwarded the tape again.

Mr. Swanson came back to life at 3:31 p.m. and apparently did not notice the veiled woman and the older man when they exited one hour later. Miriam shook her head.

"I don't like this one bit. I mean, how many times have they had the opportunity of questioning us without us knowing? The times we're aware of – are they the only ones?" she asked. Cyrus just shrugged and grimaced at the thought. "The other two must have questioned you during those hours when we investigated Professor Bruchheimer's house. I wonder what they got from you." With a frown, he grimaced again, and Miriam turned silent.

The tape and the minutes rolled on. Closing hour at the museum came and went together with the staff, and at 7 p.m., Annette Meille once again released Mr. Swanson.

Suddenly, the door behind them opened, and Caesar came in, smiling at them, with a tray of three hot steaming coffees in his hand.

"Hi there. Any progress? Anyone up for some caffeine?" Miriam snickered wearily, and Cyrus frowned. Caesar raised an eyebrow. "What?"

"Well, take a seat, C, and look for yourself. It shouldn't be more than a couple of tape hours before Claire comes in with the false me and, while we wait, we can brief each other."

Caesar sat down beside Miriam with a heavy sigh and handed over the cups to them. Then he looked inquiringly at them. Miriam breathed in the lovely smell and took a small sip of the hot, black coffee.

"So, C, we've seen a lot of interesting things here… Can you hand over the notes, please, Claire, and let him check them out. Roughly speaking it seems as if… but this is of course just my hypothesis…" He paused a second and Caesar nodded.

"They're usually right, though. Go on."

"Yeah… I believe that the false professor is a defector from the faction since he seems to share their knowledge about mind control. We saw him carrying a big bag out from the museum, and we take it that he gathered some papers and maybe books that the other us wanted to get their hands on." He frowned thoughtfully. "We should ask the Faculty about his research area. Anyway, that's probably how we managed to get their attention; they saw me at the museum, most likely when I got out of Professor Bruchheimer's office, but I don't remember that. What we do know is that they followed me. What happened after that I can only guess, but I have no doubts I got caught and got my memories erased. Well… that's the short story."

"Well done," Caesar acknowledged him.

"And we've seen them using the mind control, or whatever it is, several times on the poor guard," Miriam interposed.

"That's alarming." Caesar frowned. "We have to let the Faculty know so they can take measures."

"Right! I should've thought about that!" Cyrus said, but Caesar just waved that away.

"I've done my research too." He brought out his old, well-used notebook and turned over the pages until he found what he was looking for. "First of all, the lab results you got me don't show a thing we didn't suspect already. At least we have it confirmed that the murder victim is indeed Professor Bruchheimer. Secondly, it is as Claire thought." Caesar cleared his throat and started to read out loud. "According to the Faculty, a religious group called the Skoptsy was founded in Russia sometime before seventeen seventy-one. This was the year when the Russian authorities came to know about them and created a file on them. The Skoptsy believed that when Adam and Eve were ostracized from the Garden of Eden, the forbidden fruit was cut in half and embedded onto their bodies in the form of female breasts and female and male genitals.

"That's one way to read the Bible, I guess," Cyrus said dryly.

"The word *skoptsy* is plural," Caesar continued, "and come from a Russian archaic word, *skopets*, which means *the castrated one*. The men and women who followed the Skoptsy believed that when they removed their breasts and genitals, they fulfilled Christ's counsel of perfection and were restored to the pristine state before the original sin."

"Oh, my God!" Miriam said and shook her head.

"Yeah, the things done in the name of religion…" Cyrus muttered.

Caesar didn't take any notice. "The Skoptsy also believed that all things sexual, including beauty, was the root of all evil and prevented the human race to communicate with God. This was called *lepost*." He looked up at the two researchers. "Apparently there were two ways to castrate males: the 'lesser seal' takes away the testicles and the 'greater seal' takes away the penis as well. The male used a cow horn to help him urinate after that. Also, they used simple shaving knives and no anesthetics."

119

Miriam just shook her head and couldn't find something to say. The mere thought of the pain these people went through for their belief made her shudder, and she got a lump in her throat of empathy.

"And the women?" asked Cyrus. "Did they also go through the lesser and greater seal?"

"The history is vague on that point," Caesar said.

"As always," Miriam muttered under her breath.

"Yeah, it's as if people at all times want to silence women with the history of men," Cyrus surprisingly agreed with a frown. She gave him an astonished look, which he met sternly.

"There are some notes, though," Caesar continued with a frown of his own, and they turned their attention to him again. "The first record of a female castration dates back to eighteen fifteen and that woman removed her breasts. The removal of the labia is more rumor than anything else."

"Well, we have some concrete evidence lying in the morgue, right C?"

"I should think so, yes."

"Was there anything more?" asked Miriam. "Did they say something about ritualistic murder? Is that something that's included in their beliefs? That they have to make an example of people who don't follow them?"

"In one way, I wish that would be the case. It would make our job so much easier, but sadly, no, there's nothing about murder or offerings, ritualistic or otherwise. On the contrary, the Skoptsy were allowed to have families and one to two children. They celebrated purity and life, not purity and death. They used to dance ecstatic dances like the dervishes, and they dressed in white, calling themselves *The White Doves*."

Miriam let out a frustrated huff. "So now what?" she asked. "Is this a small, more distorted branch of the Skoptsy, are they just imitating the castrating part of the Skoptsy, or are they something else entirely? Does the Skoptsy still exist anymore in the way you've described them, Caesar?"

Caesar sighed. "Those are excellent questions, Claire," he said, and she lit up by the unexpected praise. "As far as the Faculty knows, they might still exist, but it's more likely that they died out after being repressed by the communist regime in its early stages."

"All right," Cyrus remarked, "let's keep an open mind. Until we know more, we work along the lines that this is Skoptsy that we're dealing with, but if new evidence points us in other directions, we shouldn't dismiss them."

"Yes, I agree with you, Cyrus. Hopefully, we can get the young man at the South Side Hospital to talk once he wakes up from his coma."

"Do they mention the Virgin Mary at all? Skoptsy, I mean?" Miriam asked.

"Virgin Mary?" Cyrus asked inquiring.

"Well… I'm thinking about the writing on the wall: *Mother, Accept Our Offering…* It could be Virgin Mary who is referenced, right?" Miriam frowned. "Or does that even make sense?"

Cyrus nodded. "It could make sense. There's a kind of logic to it.

"Anyway," Caesar continued dismissively, "let's move on. The other things I've found out is that there are no records of the Stevenson's at all in the FBI files and that the girl isn't mentioned anywhere. No hospital records of Stella Stevenson giving birth, no school records of any Emilia Sabrina Stevenson, nothing."

"I saw that too, in the ordinary records," Miriam said, "but I forgot to mention it when we got so busy at the professor's house. Sorry."

Caesar gave her a disappointed look from the side. "Well, you should start using your notebook, Claire. It really helps. Next time the lack of information might lead to our deaths."

For a moment, she stared at him with burning cheeks, before she shied away with her gaze.

"Yes… sorry…" she mumbled. An awkward silence fell in the room. Miriam felt so embarrassed that she could die, and she had to force back a lump of tears forming in her throat. The tape whirled on its fast-forwarded speed, making a humming noise.

"It's weird, though," Cyrus said eventually. "I mean, could they have kidnapped the girl?" He drummed his fingers on his leg and shook his head at the idea. "It sounds unlikely. I never got any impression from either of them that they were hiding anything. Usually, I do if that's the case."

"We'll see if we can find anything that can throw some light on this tomorrow, and, speaking of the girl, she has finally begun decomposing, even if it's not much. The blood has not yet really coagulated. My guess is that the two cases are connected. It'll be very interesting to follow this. I've never seen anything like it before."

Caesar's eyes gleamed with excitement and goosebumps appeared on Miriam's arms. This was the part that she never managed to understand: Caesar's fascination with death.

Silence fell in the room again, all watching the fast rolling security tape where Annette Meille studied her books. Finally, at 9:16 p.m., the door to the museum opened and Cyrus and Miriam came in. Cyrus put the tape on normal speed, and all three of them leaned forward.

"It certainly looks like you," Caesar remarked.

"I know," Cyrus said, frowning.

Annette Meille put her books aside and looked inquisitorially out of the cube window when the two researchers approached her. Suddenly, Miriam staggered, and Cyrus caught her by the arm. The security guard frowned and said something. Cyrus gestured and laughed, pointing at Miriam, who stood half-turned towards the security camera, looking dazed and a little confused. Then he grabbed Miriam's badge and flashed it, still talking. The guard nodded and gave him a pen and paper fastened to a clipboard. He signed. The inner door opened and let them in, Cyrus still with a hard grip around Miriam's arm.

Caesar leaned back with a heavy sigh and shook his head. "No, Cyrus. That is clearly not you. What unprofessional behavior. I'm ashamed."

Cyrus' pale cheeks had turned red during the intermezzo, and he threw his hand through his hair, but Miriam couldn't tell if he was angry or upset.

"It's really... unnerving... seeing yourself like that without remembering a thing of it..." she said slowly and shuddered. No one answered her, and the tape whirled on. One tape hour later, Annette Meille started to get a concerned expression in her face as she checked the time. She grabbed the visitor list, reached for the phone, and dialed a number. They saw her wait for a minute before she started talking, and then wait some more. Finally, she apparently got a hold of someone in a position to help, because she talked for some time while continuing to check the list. She then fell silent, nodded, talked some more, and hung up with a satisfactory expression on her face.

"Huh..." Cyrus said admiringly. "She got suspicious. Good girl, checking us out. Too bad it didn't lead anywhere."

"Or maybe it was a good thing for her," Miriam added quietly. Cyrus gave her an appreciative look from the side, but Caesar just frowned as he watched them. The tape showed 10:33 p.m. when the inner door opened again, and the woman with the veil came out.

"When did she arrive?" Miriam said alarmed. "I never saw her enter again."

Cyrus frowned. "Not me either."

The veiled woman went forward to the cube where the guard put away her books. She put her back towards the camera, lifted up her veil and placed her face inside the cube. The clock on the screen ticked on. Exactly two minutes of absolute stillness went by before the woman covered her face with the veil again and leaned forward, into the cube, stretched her arm at something, and the inner door opened,

123

showing an empty corridor. When she got up, they saw the security guard sitting unmoving with her eyes opened and a blank facial expression as if she were a statue. Then the veiled woman switched off the light, and the place was hidden in darkness. Cyrus groaned.

"Put it on still, Cy," said Miriam. She stood up, heading for the room's light switch, and then folded the blinds. "Okay, you can put it back on now."

"Good thinking, Claire," Caesar said in acknowledgment and Miriam couldn't help blushing. Cyrus turned on the tape again. Helped by their own darkness, they were able to discern two individuals carrying a third, faintly lit up by some light in a corridor further away, before disappearing into the darker security area. The exit door opened, and the two persons with their burden got out, indistinctively lit up by the gloomy green exit sign. The light turned on, the inner security door closed; the veiled woman exited the museum without a glance back at the security guard, who still sat with her blank face looking out in empty space.

Chapter 11

The morning sun had already heated up the pavement. Miriam saw the shimmering heat dance around the car. Her car. She smiled affectionately and petted the steering wheel. The AC cooled the air inside, and she felt comfortably refreshed. It was when she got home from the spa yesterday evening that she heard the message from the workshop that the car finally was ready for pick up, and she went there as soon as they opened this morning.

She was so happy that she could sing, which she had also done all the way from the workshop. Now the soft music of *Peer Gynt* wrapped itself around her like a blanket. With a satisfied sigh, she leaned back in the car seat with her eyes closed, relaxing. Clean clothes, a clean, well-scented and relaxed body, her own car, an AC that tempered the summer heat, beautiful music... what more could she ask for? *A vacation?* a low inner voice asked her, and she frowned.

"Yeah, thanks," she muttered and glanced involuntarily up at the gray, worn out apartment complex where the Stevenson family had lived until about a week ago. She closed her eyes demonstratively, let the music carry her away from duty a little while longer, and let her thoughts wander.

Yesterday evening, she had finally called her sister, and they had shared a long, nice talk. Just as she'd predicted, Bethany was overjoyed to take care of Luce, and she was coming over this very evening. It felt sad. Miriam had gotten more attached to the little bird and his happy chirping during the past days than she had expected, but she couldn't think of any better place for him. Ten-year-old Markus loved animals and had already decided that he wanted to become a veterinarian like his mom when he grew up.

"You're asking at the totally perfect moment," Beth had said with a laugh. *"Ted has finally given into Markus' nagging and*

promised him a pet. He'll just be relieved it'll be a canary, not a Rottweiler... Don't you worry one bit, li'l sis. We'll take care of him."

After that, they had talked about everything else: the latest happy-go-lucky-movie that they both wanted to see; the next time U2 would have a concert in the nearby area; Bono's pros and cons as a singer and songwriter compared to those of James Hetfield (who Miriam had a secret crush on); Markus and his need of loneliness – something that always worried Beth and Ted; the vacation trip to their old summer house in Massachusetts in late August; Mom's and Dad's upcoming fifty-year-anniversary next April; Ted's work as a practitioner; Bethany's as a veterinarian; memories of the golden retriever Petronilla; and the cats Dreams and Stars.

"And speaking of Dreams and Stars," Bethany finally said, *"it's time for bed. I'll see you tomorrow, and I'm bringing you the biggest carrot cake I can find with so much icing that you'll drown in it, in exchange for Luce. Lovely name, by the way. You've always been good with those."*

Miriam opened her eyes and glanced at the digitalized car clock. It showed 08:46. Caesar and Cyrus should arrive any minute. They had decided to go with the schedule as planned, in spite of the new information from the day before. Even though no one had said it out loud, Miriam had a strong feeling that none of them really knew what to do with all the new evidence. The puzzle was certainly clearer, but there were still lots of pieces missing. They needed some kind of a real breakthrough soon or else the trail would grow cold. *No wonder these people manage to stay secret, whether they belong to Skoptsy or not*; she thought. *Everyone who's unlucky enough to run into them ends up either dead or with their memories erased...*

Caesar's car pulled up behind hers, and he met her eyes in the rear-view mirror with a broad grin.

"You've got your car back! Good for you!" he greeted her when he opened the passenger door and got in. "And *Peer Gynt*. Good choice," he continued approvingly.

The tone was remarkably brisker than it had been these past days and he had more color in his face. The spa

126

session had apparently been good for both of them, even though he had refused to get his toenails painted. Cyrus, on the other hand, had surprised her by choosing a hot pink color that he smilingly flashed at her dark violet ones, and she had laughed helplessly at him. If there ever were a next time, she would suggest ocean-blue or moss-green that would go better with his skin tone.

"You're feeling better." She smiled affectionately and touched Henry's hand gently.

"Well, I got a full night's sleep. That does wonders to an old man like me."

When Miriam snorted, he laughed at her and gave her knuckles a light kiss.

"I spoke to Beth yesterday, and they've set the date for Massachusetts to August twenty-third."

"Really good news. If we've solved the RP by then, then nothing can stop me, Mimi. I love that old house and the quiet lake and the woods."

"And Ted's cooking?" Miriam teased.

"And Ted's cooking," he admitted with a gentle smile, caressing her hand. "And evening strolls with you in the sunset, and bathing in the lake, preferably with you naked..." His smile deepened as he leaned in to kiss her. Miriam blushed heavily. Then a car drove past them and parked in front of them. With nothing more than his breath touching her lips, Henry straightened up, and his voice got all professional again. "Ah, here's Cyrus. Good. Good." He let her hand go and got out of the car. Miriam sighed quietly to herself and followed him a bit slower.

"Look who's got her car back," Cyrus greeted her with a big smile. "Looks as new as a newborn kitten. A big, green kitten, that is." The disappointment of not getting that kiss disappeared and she laughed as gave him a friendly nudge on his shoulder. "What?" he protested. "I like kittens."

Caesar cleared his throat, and his face had a stern expression when his eyes met Cyrus'. Miriam looked at him with surprise. *What's wrong?*

127

"I've got the keys, so shall we?"

Cyrus' open smile vanished at the stare and, seemingly involuntarily, he took a step back towards his car. "Yeah..." He looked away. "I just... um... I..."

Miriam gave him a surprised glance too. *What's going on? It's not like him to hesitate like that.*

"What?" she asked and heard the alarmed tone in her voice. "What happened?"

"I... went to HQ before coming here..."

"Yes?" Caesar folded his arms over his chest. Cyrus met his gaze again, while his face got covered by that old unreadable expression of his that Miriam hadn't missed one bit. She frowned and looked back and forth between the two men, trying to grasp what was going on between them.

"The guy at South Side committed suicide this morning."

"What?" Miriam burst out.

Caesar's stern expression gave way to a concerned look, and he released his crossed arms.

"When did he wake up from his coma? I never got a notice about that."

Cyrus shook his head. "No one seems to know. He was still out when they checked on him at ten p.m. last night, but this morning they found him crushed on the pavement. He jumped from the roof." They both stared at him, and he shrugged. "Yeah, someone's going to pay for that, that's as sure as sugar. The door to the roof wasn't locked."

Caesar sighed. Miriam thought that he looked old again.

"Nothing we can do about it right now anyway. He's arrived at the morgue?" Cyrus nodded. "I guess I'll have to take a look at him later." Caesar frowned and put his hands into his pockets, looking like a grumpy child as he stared at the pavement and kicked some loose gravel. "They're a lot of trouble, this bunch. He could at least have had the courtesy to wait until we've questioned him. Quite annoying."

128

They all stood in uncomfortable silence a couple of minutes, Cyrus looking at Caesar with something that Miriam thought might resemble defensiveness had it not been so unlikely and Caesar still glaring at the ground. Finally, he sighed, straightened his back and shot them both a weary glance.

"Whatever. Let's get this apartment done and see if we find anything."

As they entered the building and went up the stairs, the corridor on the third floor was almost entirely dark. There were a couple of flickering lights at the end of it, which made Miriam feel dizzy as if the whole corridor swayed back and forth. The weight of her gun in its holster calmed her nerves, making it easier for her to maintain the sense of being if not safe, at least relatively protected. Caesar stood at the white door to the Stevenson's apartment, searching for the keys in his pocket.

"I could've sworn I put them back..." she heard him mumble.

Cyrus' face was expressionless as usual, but his stance was tense and, just like her, he didn't have his hand far away from the gun. Caesar searched the other pocket. Eventually, he looked up at them without meeting their eye. His cheeks blushed.

"I must've put them in my jacket," he said sheepishly. "I'll be right back."

He turned around and went away toward the staircase. Cyrus' cold gaze followed him as he took the stairs down. As Miriam saw him leave, a worry in her stomach arose that she didn't want to voice. Still staring at the now empty staircase, Cyrus did it for her.

"He's getting too old."

"No!" Miriam turned violently towards him. He glanced at her and his expression softened.

"Claire..."

"No, I don't... I don't want to hear it..."

129

"Claire." His eyes showed the sympathy he felt. "His mother's death took him harder than he wants to admit. He's getting unfocused."

She turned half away. "No."

"You know it too. I've seen it in your eyes. We need to be more alert from now on, especially if we get into danger." She couldn't answer. There was a lump in her throat and her eyes burned from tears she refused to spill. "Claire?"

"Yeah... I hear you." Her voice was a tad hoarse, and she took a deep breath, turned away from him, and faced the door. She hated it. It had shown both of them Caesar's weakness and she couldn't deny it now that Cyrus had voiced it. Frustrated, she wrenched the doorknob and the door opened. "Wha..."

Cyrus reacted immediately, drew his gun and pulled himself to the wall. Miriam managed to get a quick glimpse of the hallway before he grabbed her arm and pulled her aside. She stumbled towards him, but got back up on her feet immediately and drew her gun, pressing her back towards the wall. Daylight lit up the opposite wall. All got quiet.

Cyrus and Miriam exchanged a glance.

"Shall we go in?" she breathed in his ear. "The hallway was empty."

He shook his head. "We don't want to shoot C by mistake when he comes back. Let's wait." She could just barely hear him, but she nodded her approval, and they waited. The minutes went by, eerily quiet. Her own breaths seemed to resonate in her head.

"I don't think anyone's there," she whispered after a while, unable to stand the anxiety any longer, but Cyrus just shrugged, still tense and alert, facing the open doorway. The sudden steps echoing from the stairway sounded abnormally loud. Cyrus didn't move an inch from his watch, so Miriam turned to face whoever was approaching, much relieved to see Caesar climbing the last stairs. He stopped for second, immediately taking in the situation while releasing his gun and quickly making his way towards them.

130

"Clear," Miriam breathed to Cyrus. He nodded. Caesar was with them within the next moment, raising his eyebrows in a question towards the open door. Miriam leaned in towards his ear, inhaling the faint scent of his eau de cologne.

"It was open," she whispered.

Caesar rolled his eyes in disgust seemingly intended towards himself. Then he tapped her on her shoulder and pointed towards the other side of the doorway. She nodded, crouched, and rapidly went to the other side, while quickly looking into the hall. A short figure disappeared around the corner. She gasped, startled, and froze for half a second. Cyrus inquiringly caught her eye, and she nodded affirmatively towards him and Caesar while pointing towards the hallway and raising her index finger in the air to show that she only saw one person. They all raised their guns, and Caesar took a step forward.

"FBI. Please come out with your hands above your head." The sudden sound of naked feet on laminated floor running in the apartment reached them. They looked at each other, and Caesar inhaled deeply. "We're coming in," he called out.

Cyrus went in with Miriam close behind. A door slammed shut somewhere in the apartment. As Cyrus had remarked on Monday, the apartment was empty as a mousetrap, but Miriam did not get the feeling that it was totally abandoned. It didn't feel empty. Could the Stevenson's have moved back? Or was it some very short homeless guy who accidentally found it and made himself a home there?

The door to the left was open. She saw the dirty white walls of the bathroom behind it. A toilet paper roll lay on the floor, and there were wet spots everywhere. Water from the faucet dripped slowly into the sink. It sounded awkwardly loud. There was an arch leading to the kitchen on their right. A loaf of bread lay on the counter and placed beside it was a butter box with the knife still in it. At the end of the hall, they entered the empty living room, where a piece of yellow police tape lay abandoned on the beige carpet covering the floor. To the right were the now closed doors that led to the master and the guest bedrooms.

Caesar and Cyrus placed themselves at each side of one of the doors, while Miriam backed them up. Caesar busted it open, took a quick look around, and went in. She could hear him open a closet before he came out again. They all gathered around the last door. Miriam felt her heart race as the adrenaline hit her even harder. She held her breath and pointed the gun at the door when Caesar busted it open. After another quick look around, he went in. Empty. She saw him open the closet and close it again with a confused frown. He came back to them as she lowered her gun.

"All right, team. What have we missed? We all heard someone running and a door shut, right?"

"Yeah," Cyrus said. "Is there a balcony here?" he asked as he turned around looking at the living room wall. They all checked the rest of the apartment again, but there was no balcony to be seen anywhere.

"Weird... really weird..." Miriam said with a half-whisper. The two men looked clearly confused and worried. Cyrus went through the whole apartment once more with the same result. Miriam went into the two bedrooms for a new inspection. There was something... something odd with them. With a deep frown, she scrutinized them closer. "Wait a minute..."

She went into the minor bedroom and started to twirl around slowly, intensely examining the walls. The two men stared at her, but she ignored them. Then she went out to the living room, carefully checking the walls and then into the master bedroom, twirling around in there as well. An excited blush started to show on her cheeks, and she met the other two's gaze with a broad smile.

"What?" Cyrus asked.

She came closer and leaned in towards them.

"Take a look at the dimensions," she whispered in their ears. "The rooms are smaller than they should be."

Caesar and Cyrus both started to scrutinize the walls.

"Damn... You're right..." Cyrus said admiringly, his eyes shining. "Do you think...?"

Without completing the sentence, he went towards the left wall and opened the closet. Caesar and Miriam were just behind him. Without being able to contain herself, Miriam dived down on her knees in front of Cyrus, wanted to be the first who found the secret. Almost feverishly she examined the floor and the back wall of the closet. A faint, practically undetectable light shone through where they met. She drew her fingers lightly over the wall. To the far left was a small edge. She quickly secured her gun and put it in her holster before grabbing around the edge with her fingers. As she started to push it to the side, she couldn't stop grinning like a madman, feeling both excited and proud as the edge of light became bigger.

Suddenly, the faint light went out, and a sense of danger hit her a quarter of a second before something attacked her.

Chapter 12

A muffled scream was all she managed to produce as furious blows landed on her face in a rapid stream. Her eye got a well-placed smash from a fist, and the flashing pain made it water. A high-pitched scream of rage came from her attacker when the assailant was removed from her. She could hear Cyrus grunting and high-pitched continuous screams along with the sounds of a fight.

Groaningly she sat up and tried to take in the scene around her, but her eye was still blind and watery. Caesar's big hand touched her face gently. It hurt, and she twitched with a grimace.

"That was a surprise." His voice was colored by some kind of amusement, which he apparently tried to hide. Miriam made an attempt to look at him. Amusement? She shook her head lightly. When had he ever been amused in a hostile situation? She must have gotten the wrong signals again. Irritated, she wiped her eye and tried to open it once more. This time, she could discern Cyrus as he struggled with holding someone firmly in his grasp.

"I'm fine," she said with an annoyed tone. "Go help Cyrus. I don't need you right now."

"Well... I think he can handle a small child on his own, but who knows, you might both need a course in babysitting."

With a light chuckle, he left her and took a couple of quick steps towards Cyrus and her attacker. Dumbstruck she sat still on the floor, blinking away water from her runny eye until she finally was able to see relatively clear.

Cyrus stood panting, holding a scrawny little girl, maybe eight years old, in a tight grasp. Her long, dark-brown hair hung greasy and lank over her face and covered her eyes. Caesar kneeled in front of her, hands resting on his kneecaps.

"Hi there. You took us quite by surprise, didn't you?" The girl didn't move or make a sound, just continued to stare down at the floor. Caesar tried again. "So what are you doing here all by yourself? Where are your mom and dad?" Still not a word. "You know," Caesar said in a friendly tone, "we can help you."

Slowly the girl raised her head and looked at him, her eyes as black holes in her face, too old for a child.

"No one can help us."

Small trickles of tears started to run silently over her cheeks. Cyrus caught Caesar's eye.

"Can you take Claire to the car, C. She needs something to drink."

Caesar got up immediately with an expression of mutual understanding and reached out for Miriam. She took his hand and got up on her feet. Neither Cyrus nor the girl moved. The girl just stared blankly out into empty space, completely void of all feelings.

When they got out, Miriam studied her face in the side mirror of the car and was pleased that it wasn't that bad. The only damage was the light pain in her eye and a couple of small red spots on her left cheek.

"When Cyrus gets here with the girl," Caesar said, "I'll take them to HQ, but you need to stay here and search that closet room. The quick look I got off it didn't give much, but you never know. There might be fingerprints, other secret storage places, or something. Maybe a whole binder with detailed information about a certain secretive faction... Who knows?"

She managed to laugh at him. "I wish. Don't set your hopes too high, though. I'd be surprised if they were a part of it." Then she frowned. "So who's this girl? Another unregistered child of the Stevenson's?"

A tired sigh heaved Caesar's chest. "That would be my guess, but she could be a relative, or maybe a playmate that turned up at the wrong place at the wrong time." He fell silent a moment before he continued. "If she's an unregistered child, we might have a problem." Miriam gave him an inquiring glance, and he looked back with a weary expression. "I mean, how many children do they have in that case? Thirteen?"

Miriam snorted. "Don't be ridiculous. They couldn't have had more than three; otherwise, Cyrus would've gotten to know about it when he questioned the neighbors."

He shook his head slowly. "I wouldn't be too sure about that. In a neighborhood like this, you know, people tend to be more blind and deaf than at other places. You noticed how many people that didn't open their doors to check us out? As long as the children behave and don't make a lot of ruckuses, no one cares. Not that I actually think that they had thirteen children."

An irritated frown showed on Miriam's forehead. "Hopefully, she'll talk with Cy and, if we're lucky, we might even get some answers. If she doesn't... At this point, I'd gladly hold her at gunpoint to make her talk." Caesar raised his eyebrows at her, but kept his silence. She looked away, embarrassed, and changed the subject. "Okay, so what about the guy at South Side and his so-called suicide?"

"I like the way you think, Claire," smiled Caesar.

"Well, you're the medical expert here. What would be most likely: him waking up and committing suicide because of unknown reasons, him still in a coma getting tossed off the roof, or him waking up with some kind of mental order to commit suicide?"

"Any of the first two. To be able to discern if the last option is possible, I need to get more information about what sort of mind control these people are able to work and how strong it is. For now, I'll just pass on that one and concentrate on the other two. I would say that it depends more on what form of injury he was suffering from, and we don't have that report yet. I need to get the records from his doctor before I can come to any conclusion on it." Caesar paused before continuing with an almost regretful tone: "I don't think that's the priority, though. We need to concentrate on the living now, not the dead." His voice trailed away and his gaze rested on the gray building before them with a faraway expression. The windows reflected the sunlight and looked down at them like watchful eyes. Goosebumps appeared on her arms, and Miriam folded them across her chest while leaning on her car. The metal burned through her clothes with unbearable heat, but she didn't move. The street lay practically empty. A teenage boy with a thick black leather jacket walking a German Shepherd on a leash was the only person in sight. He and his dog disappeared around the far corner of the building complex. She gave up an inaudible sigh, turning half away from the watchful windows and glanced towards Caesar. He still fixed the building with a stern, unforgiving expression in his face and Miriam sighed. It was no use talking to him while he looked like that.

Twenty minutes later, Cyrus and the girl came out of the building. It always surprised her how good Cyrus was at getting children's confidence, even though she knew that interviewing child witnesses was what he did when he wasn't assigned to a research project. This girl clung to his hand almost desperately. Her greasy hair framed her thin face like curtains and, even at a distance, Miriam could see those enormous eyes as the girl, on the edge of panic, trying to look in every direction at once. She felt ashamed of herself for even thinking that she could hold this terrified girl at gunpoint. As they came closer, Miriam didn't move a finger to avoid any alarm. In the corner of her eye, she could see Caesar leaning casually toward the car as well, exuding calm and safety. When the two reached the car, Caesar nodded in a friendly manner towards the girl, but she didn't seem to notice. Cyrus kneeled in front of her.

"All right, Paulina, I'm going to say a couple of words to my friends here, so you can just jump into the car and then we're off. You're safe with us now, and we'll not let anything happen to you."

She looked him in the eyes with a terrified expression that made Miriam's stomach twist in sympathy and breathed

137

something that she couldn't hear. Cyrus leaned in closer and his red hair tangled with her dark.

"No," she could hear him say in a low voice, "I'm not going to leave you, Paulina."

They remained positioned like that – he on his knees, she clasping his hand so tightly that her knuckles whitened – for about half a minute before he opened the door and she got in, curling her body together like a cat. Cyrus closed the door and leaned protectively towards it. Miriam and Caesar strolled over to him as if they were out in the park on a nice Sunday walk.

"Her name's Paulina. She's the younger daughter of the Stevenson's," he said quietly when they stood together, practically nose to nose. "Adopted, that is, both she and the other girl. They're not related."

"Adopted?" Miriam said in as low a voice as Cyrus'. "That could explain a couple of things, like the non-existing birth records."

"Yeah. Her story's like *Annie*, but I believe her. Abusive foster parents; she and the sister got adopted by the Stevenson's a year and a half ago or something. It was like going from hell to heaven. Heaven didn't last, though. Sometime last fall, the family started to get visits from... people..." Cyrus hesitated.

"People?" Caesar repeated.

"Yeah. She doesn't know who they were, but the Stevenson's got really scared and they packed their things and moved from wherever it was to another place the same day. A couple of weeks later, the same people showed up again. They moved again. This time, it took longer before they were found, but it's the same weary song. Finally, they ended up here. They thought they were safe. The people didn't show up. Daddy Stevenson built the secret room 'just in case,' the girls started homeschooling and later summer school, and life seemed to normalize." He silenced with a grim expression.

"But?" asked Miriam.

"Eventually, they were found. Paulina hid in the secret room, but she heard her parents and the people argue. Emilia got home during the argument and didn't manage to hide. Mommy Stevenson apparently said something like 'Don't shoot'; and daddy got angry for the first time and threw them out."

"'Don't shoot'?" Caesar asked.

"She didn't hear any shots and mommy got mad at her when she asked, but... one week later Emilia died from the eels."

"No!" Miriam burst out, and Cyrus hushed at her with a concerned nod at the girl in the car.

"You asked her what the people looked like, I take it," Caesar broke in calmly.

"Yeah. Two men and a woman with a veil. They don't match the description of our two men from how she described them, but I have no doubt whatsoever that it was them."

Caesar nodded, and silence fell for a couple of seconds.

"Then what?" Miriam asked. "What happened to the parents? Why did they leave her on her own? Where did they go?"

Cyrus drew a hand through his hair. "They were apparently going to move again. The Stevenson's went away with the furniture the same evening I questioned them, but they were going to come back for her. They never did."

Miriam's stomach turned again, and she got cold and sweaty. She swallowed hard.

"They're dead, right? They must be."

Cyrus gave her a sympathetic look. "I don't know. I don't know how long time it takes for the eels to get to that ferocious stage."

Miriam rubbed her cold arms. "The other Professor Bruchheimer said that it differs depending on the human and her diet."

"Yeah."

139

Caesar watched them with a frown. "Does she have an address?" he asked Cyrus, who glanced at him and his face showed that incredibly unlikely expression of insecurity again.

"Um... maybe..." He cleared his throat. "She said she has a note in the secret room that daddy left her, but I didn't want to touch it in case there are fingerprints on it... Anyway... that's the sad story..."

Caesar waved the remark away and continued without looking at them: "Let's take her to HQ and call a social worker. Claire, go up and work on the room. Call us when you're finished." Then he crossed his arms and stared down at the street, looking vexed.

"Um... okay...?" she said and felt like a berated child who doesn't understand what she's done wrong. Cyrus made a tiny awkward movement.

"What?" Caesar demanded and shot him a glare that Miriam interpreted as angry, even though she couldn't figure out why he would be. Cyrus hadn't done anything wrong; on the contrary.

"Do we really need to take her to HQ? It's nicer at my place."

Caesar stared at the younger man, the angry flare slowly disappearing. "You want to take her home to you?" he asked unbelievingly.

Cyrus didn't meet his eye. "Well... yes."

"That's breach of protocol, Cyrus."

When Cyrus shrugged and looked down, Caesar just sighed. "Fine. You lead the way." He turned his back to them and walked away towards his car. Miriam frowned confused after him before glancing at Cyrus. He shrugged awkwardly and gave her a crooked smile, hands in his pockets, like a shy schoolboy.

"Don't take too long, Claire. If they're still alive, they need to get to Bernard a.s.a.p."

"Yes, I hear you. I'll be as quick as possible."

He nodded, stepped into the car and closed the door. She saw him turn to Paulina and say something. The girl

140

looked up and reached for the seatbelt. Cyrus started the car, gave Miriam another smile, and drove away. Caesar's car drove past her, following Cyrus'. She waved, but Caesar didn't acknowledge her.

With a concerned frown, she watched them as they turned right and disappeared around the corner. As she slowly started to walk towards the building's entrance again, she pondered Caesar's odd behavior. If she hadn't seen the other Caesar at the morgue and if this Caesar hadn't been so... so... him... this morning, she would have come to the conclusion that he was a shape-shifter. As it was now, she had to trust that she eventually would get to know what was bugging him, because clearly there was something. With an awkward mental shrug, she tried to let go of him and concentrate on the task that lay at hand.

The silence in the empty apartment hit her as soon as she entered. It felt thick, waiting, aware. A slow, cold shiver ran down her spine, and she hurried to lock the front door behind her. *Just to be on the safe side*, she thought nervously, *just to be on the safe side*. Without thinking she patted her gun in its holster before hesitantly heading towards the secret room, peeping into every other room she passed on the way, heart thumping heavily in her chest. She was still alone.

Her breaths became less shallow as she deliberately relaxed her shoulders and turned her focus to the secret room. It was really cleverly built. Mr. Stevenson must be an extremely skilled carpenter. Miriam had a hard time believing that anyone without her eye for form, space and details would have found it.

There was a light switch on the inside of the left wall, she found, and she turned it on. A faint light bulb lit up the dark wooden walls and the smoothly polished floor. The room was very small, technically just an empty space between the two bedrooms. She doubted that the whole Stevenson family would have been able to do anything in there but stand tightly packed together.

Still with her feet on the outside of the room, she let her trained eye scrutinize the walls. Cyrus had said that there should be a note in there, but since it wasn't visible, she had to presume that there was another hidden space somewhere. So far, she couldn't see anything. It was, of course, a little bit suspicious that the floor was wooden when no other floor in the apartment was. On the other hand, she had no idea how to build anything, so as far as she knew; the floor might have to be there to support the walls. She looked up. The inner ceiling was wooden as well. She knelt down, opened her toolbox and brought forward a flashlight. Still on her knees, she let the light sweep over the edge where the walls and the floor met. There was no joint that could reveal another secret space.

She poked around a little in her box until her fingers found the well-known shape of the container with fingerprint dust and the belonging brush. Then, leaning in, she methodically started to dust the joint all around the room. No fingerprints showed up. She tilted back on her heels with her hands thoughtfully wrapped around her knees and took another meticulous look around the walls. There were no irregularities at all, nothing that gave away any concealed area, not even where the wooden panels met. It was even hard to discern the space between the panels...

"That must be why the light is so dim!" she suddenly exclaimed to herself. "I need better light!"

Thrilled, she got up to her feet and went speedily into the bathroom where four adorned light bulbs decoratively were placed over the mirror. After checking that they were bright enough for her purpose, she brought one of them with her and replaced the faint light bulb. Suddenly, the secret room bathed in light. Miriam blinked a couple of times to get used to it.

This time, when she investigated the walls, she found a place far down to the left on the back wall that looked just slightly different than the other walls, with a panel that had just about an undetectable joint. She took her dust and brush again and dusted the area. Large fingerprints appeared, and she gave up a triumphant laugh. Still smiling she put on latex gloves, captured the fingerprints and placed them securely in her box. She brought out her camera and took some pictures.

Lightly, she touched the dark wood where the fingerprints still showed. It didn't feel any different from other panels. Cautiously she tried to push the panel inwards. Without a sound, it opened, and a hidden space came into light. Miriam's heart pounded so hard with excitement that she couldn't hear anything else. A broad grin played on her lips, and she had a hard time not giving into the mad impulse of dancing around the empty bedroom. Instead, she fell back on her rear and took some deep breaths to calm herself.

A couple of minutes later, her rushing pulse began to slow down, and she was able to look into the compartment. What the light revealed was a part of a relatively broad shelf, empty as far as she could see, but it continued behind the wall. She grabbed her flashlight again and let the light play over the shelf while she peeked into the concealed area. A white sheet of paper was nailed to the outer wall just at the edge. She removed it carefully and put it in an evidence bag. A new smile showed when she saw an address written on it with blue ink.

Once again, the light lit up the hidden shelf. There was something laying on it at the far end. Miriam put down her flashlight and reached into the opening. She had to stretch so much that the edge of the outer wall cut into the flesh in her armpit before her fingers reached the object and managed to bring it forward into the light. It was a regular white box about 11x8 inches big. With trembling fingers she took it out into the room and sat down crisscross with the box in her lap. Somehow, she knew that this was what she had been looking for all the time; this was the answer. Her heart pounded as she opened the lid. Inside laid three objects; all draped in old and faded black velvet. Miriam swallowed hard, vividly remembering the sacrificial tools found in Henry's closet. She took a couple of pictures of the box with

143

its content before choosing the object to the far left and started to unwrap it with slightly unsteady hands. When it unfolded, the sunlight shone on it from over her shoulder, making it glisten.

"It's beautiful…" she whispered in awe, turning the Fabergé egg around in her hands. Its outside depicted a forest in relief on a background of dark-green enamel. The trees were delicately made out of gold for the trunks and branches, and tiny green jewels, maybe emeralds, for the leaves. She had never seen a Fabergé egg other than as photographs in books. To actually hold one in her hands was… humbling. Its beauty created a longing in her heart for something she couldn't even put a name on, but it was the same longing she felt when she heard a beautiful poem or viewed an enchanting landscape. She examined it closer. If it were like the other eggs she had read about, it should be able to open. There was no hatch, but the ground that the trees stood on seemed to be a line that followed the egg around. Miriam put just a light pressure on it and, without a sound, it opened.

The scene depicted inside almost made her drop the egg in terror. A crude altar made out of a gray rock was the centerpiece. Red enamel colored parts of the altar blood-red. A faceless human lay sacrificed on it with all the intestines placed around the body connected with the entrails. The details were frightening, and the whole scene glittered in the sunlight from the gems that had been used.

"*Mother, accept our offering...*" Her voice sounded muffled and hoarse. It made her shrink inside and, without any warning, Miriam felt trapped. The sunlit room suddenly seemed suffocating and narrow. That was the moment she knew that she wasn't alone, and a dark shadow blocked out the sun behind her and fell over the egg.

In an instant, she had swirled around with her right hand already on her gun and a scream trapped in her throat. There was no one there, no shadow, no person, no living being at all. Her heart raced panicked in her chest, and the sound of it made it impossible for her to hear anything. With

144

a shaking hand, she drew her gun while pushing the white box down on the floor. Then she forced herself up on legs that felt as solid as running water. Without being able to stop her body from trembling violently, she closed in on the closet and the secret room, prepared to shoot. The little room was empty. Quickly she went to the door. From her position, she could see the living room, the hallway leading to the front door, and the open door leading to the bathroom. Still not another sound, except the extremely loud pounding from her heart. Logically, she knew that whatever it was that had cast that shadow, he or she could not have escaped the room without her seeing it, but logic was not part of her being right now.

She drew a trembling breath and stepped out, trying to look at all directions at the same time. No one ambushed her. With her back to the wall, she moved towards the other bedroom, trying to keep an eye on the hallway meanwhile, and peeked in. It was empty. Only the kitchen and the bathroom left. Once more she moved with her back to the wall, this time towards the hallway. The two doors faced each other, and she kept her focus on the bathroom as she closed in. She stopped with her shoulder touching the kitchen doorway, trying to look into the bathroom without being seen from the kitchen, realizing it to be impossible.

Her breaths became even shallower as she prepared herself to be attacked. A quick peek into the kitchen and not even a second later a peek into the bathroom. Both were empty.

Cautiously she went to the front door to try the handle. That was when she realized that she still held on tightly to the egg. She shook her head and put it cautiously down on the floor, careful not to damage it. The door handle was cold to her touch, but the door was still locked. Miriam's eyes narrowed. Something was wrong, terribly so. She knew it. Someone had been there, might still possibly be there with her somewhere.

With continuous fast-beating heart, she picked up the egg again and, tremendously on guard, went back to the secret room. It was still empty, but the air felt stale and hard to breathe. With an eye on the door opening, she put the egg back in the box with its wrapping and put the whole box in an evidence bag, grabbed her flashlight again and took another look in the hidden compartment. The light fell on something that looked like a photo. Miriam reached for it. It was a Polaroid photo picturing green meadows with pink flowers, trees, and snow-capped mountains in the background, a glint of water, and some houses. On the back, the word *Bettles* had been written with what for Miriam's untrained eyes looked like the same handwriting as the address she had found.

She flashed the light once more just to make sure that she hadn't missed anything, but the shelf was empty. The Polaroid got placed into an evidence bag, the panel got put back into place, and the latex gloves got thrown into the toolbox. With the toolbox in her left hand and the gun, not quite steady yet, in her right, Miriam hurried out of the apartment and closed the door behind her. With a concerned frown, she glared at the lock and realized that Caesar had forgotten to give her the keys. She had to call him. He had to get here so no one else could enter the apartment.

She was just about to reach for the cell phone when that sinking sense of terror came over her again, and her whole body felt like water once more. The daylight that leaked out from the thin space between the door and the threshold suddenly disappeared as if someone had stepped in front of the door on the other side and for a terrifying moment, it looked as if the handle moved slightly downwards.

Miriam drew a stuttering breath, almost like a sob, and was unable to move. She could reach out for the door handle, open the door, and stand face to face with whoever had hidden in there together with her. She didn't move. The feeling of danger snuck up behind her, enclosed her, and she

146

forced herself to take one step back, away from the door, then another one and another one. She didn't stop staring at the door until she got to the stairway. With all her willpower, she managed to turn her back at the door and rush down the stairs, out into the heat and the afternoon sun, and into her car, which was as hot as a sauna. Her hands shivered so badly so she nearly didn't get the keys out of her pocket, but finally, she got the car running and, with a jumpy takeoff, she drove away.

Chapter 13

Warm light shone through the crack between the door and the threshold when Miriam rang the bell and when Cyrus opened the door with a friendly smile, soft music met her as well, making her feel doubly welcome, and made her still trembling body begin to relax. Some of the stress just melted away, and she smiled in return as she walked into the tiny hall. It was weird that she felt so at ease in his presence suddenly, but he was a friendly human being, which was something she needed badly right now.

"I like the music," she said, trying to sound casual. "So soft. What is it?"

"*Morcheeba: Who Can You Trust?*" A mischievous glint showed in his eyes as he winked at her and took her bag. Miriam raised her eyebrows.

"Fitting," was all she said and he chuckled.

Henry rose from the sofa when she walked into the incense-smelling living room. He took the few short steps towards her and embraced her fondly. Miriam stiffened slightly. He had never shown her any warm feelings in front of Cyrus before, except during that situation with his mother, and she felt terribly awkward. On top of all the other feelings and all the stress, this was almost more than she could handle. He held her tightly a little longer than necessary, and she blushed wildly when he finally let her go.

"Tea? Coffee?" Cyrus asked from the kitchen.

"Tequila," she answered half-jokingly. Henry stared at her, and there were a couple of quiet moments. "Just kidding," she muttered. "What kind of tea do you have?" Just to get away from Henry, she went over to Cyrus in the kitchen where he was putting about a dozen different tin jars on the counter. She opened one of them, a metallic blue with golden stars all over, and sniffed at the contents. It smelled richly of something she recognized, but couldn't place.

"Loose tea," she remarked. "Why Cy, I didn't know you're such a gourmet."

He just gave her a friendly shrug. "There's a lot people don't know about me. That one's chocolate and champagne. Very rich flavor."

She glanced at him.

"Chocolate tea?"

"Mhm."

"Okay. You recommend it?"

"Absolutely."

"Okay."

He filled a tea holder and waved her out of the kitchen. She went back to the living room and sat down beside Henry, who immediately took her hand and squeezed it. She couldn't help giving him a surprised look, but he just smiled back at her without a word, still with her hand in a tight grip.

Miriam drew a mental sigh of relief when Cyrus, a few minutes later, came in with her steaming tea and she could loosen her hand from Henry's and grab the mug. Steamed milk topped it, and she drew in the rich smell with a content sigh. A small sip made her smile at Cyrus.

"Lovely. Exactly what I needed right now. "

"Good." After a short pause, he continued: "Then maybe you could tell us why you looked as if you'd seen a ghost when you came."

Miriam jerked and spilled some of the tea on the table. With trembling hands she dried it up with her napkin, while the tension crept back into her shoulders. She gave up a nervous laugh, but avoided his scrutinizing glance. "No, no, no. You first. Where's the girl?"

"A social worker picked her up."

Henry opened his mouth for the first time since she arrived. "Cyrus is going to take her to Dr. Bernard tomorrow."

"Okay… Nothing else? Nothing new?"

Cyrus shook his head. "Not really. She was too afraid and upset today to give us anything else. I'm picking her up at eight in the morning. Hopefully, she's feeling better then."

"Okay…"

There was nothing more to add and the two men looked urgently at her, Cyrus with some concern written on his face, Henry with a slight frown. Miriam squirmed.

"Well?" Henry sounded impatient and had clearly switched back to being Caesar.

"Did you find anything?" Cyrus asked with a kindness in his voice that she was totally unaccustomed to. Usually, he was the impatient one. Eventually, she nodded unwillingly, deciding to approach the situation professionally, but couldn't really meet their gaze.

"You were right, Caesar. There was another hidden area in there." She looked for her bag on the floor. Cyrus got up immediately and brought it in from the hall. "Thanks, Cy." She opened it and took out one of the evidence bags. "Here's the address."

Caesar took it from her. "Hm. North side of the city. Probably around Belvedere."

"That's one rugged area," Cyrus remarked.

Caesar nodded. "We need to go there all three of us, just in case. How long time do you think it will take with the girl?"

"An hour maybe. Probably not more than that." He rotated his own tea mug between his hands and looked into it as if he could find some answers in the leaves. His hair fell down in his face, and the soft light made it shine like golden copper. "You don't think we need to go today then, C?"

"Today?" He checked his watch. "I guess we could. It'll be late, though, and we need to eat before. I do, at least. I don't know about you two youngsters."

"I wouldn't mind a bit of Chinese," Miriam said and tried to sound casual, and Cyrus nodded approvingly.

"Chinese it is then," Caesar confirmed. "Did you find anything else, Claire?"

150

"I... um... Yes, I... In fact I did."

She brought forward the Polaroid and gave it to him. He read it out loud.

"*Bettles*. Is that a name of a place?"

Both he and Cyrus frowned, and the younger man reached for the photo.

"Well, it has to mean something," Cyrus said. "It wouldn't be logical to hide it otherwise. Let me look it up on the laptop later." He placed the evidence bag with the photo in it on the table and scrutinized her face, still with that weird kindness shining through. "This can't be why you looked so upset. What happened?"

"There... there was one more thing ..."

She reached into her bag once more and brought out the box. Caesar leaned towards her, took it from her hands and opened the lid.

"What's this? These look like they could belong to those ritualistic objects we found in my closet. Give me some gloves."

After a little rummaging, she finally found a couple of unused latex gloves big enough for the men and handed them to him and Cyrus.

"Thanks," Cyrus said.

Caesar was already digging into the box and took out one of the velvety wrapped objects. The egg with its beautiful jeweled forest looked quite small in his hands when he brought it out. Cyrus gave up an impressed whistle. Without taking his eyes from it, while slowly turning it around in his hands, Caesar said: "Another evidence bag."

Miriam brought one forward and held it up for him. He let the soft, black velvet fall into the bag and turned the egg right side up. Without a word, he studied it. Just a couple of raised eyebrows showed any kind of emotion. Miriam wriggled nervously on the sofa.

"Um... you can open it..."

Caesar gave it back to her, and she found the line. When the lid opened, she gasped. It was another scene than the one she saw earlier.

"What?" he demanded, but she couldn't take her eyes away from the scene. The inside was covered with what looked like pitch-black forest spirits with their trunks on tiny hoofs and the branches made into a horrifying mass of tangling tentacles, all ending in puckered jaws, spilling green, jeweled drool onto the ground. The worst thing was that the tentacles actually moved. *There must be some kind of mechanism underneath the ground plate that makes them move.* Miriam swallowed hard and finally managed to tear her gaze away from the scene and hand the egg over to Caesar.

"It's... it's a different one than the one I opened at the apartment..." she said feebly.

"There are more?" Cyrus asked. "Could you hand me the box, please, C?"

Caesar just grunted and gave it to him. Cyrus unwrapped the last two eggs and put the velvet into evidence bags. All the eggs looked the same on the outside. He studied them thoroughly.

"How do you open them, Claire?" he asked, and she came over to his side of the table and pointed to the line where the trees stood.

"It's this line here. Just press it gently and it should open."

He followed her instructions and the lid opened up soundlessly to the scene with the sacrifice.

"Oh... damn..." he mumbled as he tried to take in the scene. Caesar came over with his egg in a thorough grasp.

"Hm." was the only thing he said when he saw what was depicted and handed the moving tentacle egg over to Cyrus whose cheeks started to turn pale. Crouching on each side of Cyrus' armchair, they watched him put down the two open eggs and take up the last one. Miriam suddenly found it hard to breathe. The silence in the room felt thick and syrupy when his slender fingers found the line and clicked the egg open.

An enormous, voluptuous woman without a face dominated the scene. She was naked, and her gigantic breasts reached down to the colossal open vagina between her spread legs. In front of the vagina, a small naked man stood on his knees with his hands stretched up in the air, seemingly worshipping the woman. On each side, two of the black wood spirits flanked her with their jaws open, still drooling.

The seconds ticked by while they all silently took in the scene. After what seemed like ages, Cyrus finally moved and cleared his throat.

"I think we all can agree that the Skoptsy's purity ideal and this scene here do not coincide," he said hoarsely, looking shaken and pale.

Caesar made an agreeing noise and reached for the box. "Let's put them away, shall we?"

"Yeah. Hand me the velvet, please, C. If you don't think otherwise, I'd say these should go to the Faculty rather than into the evidence bin at HQ." Caesar didn't even hesitate, just handed the evidence bags over to Cyrus, who took out the fabric, closed the worshipping egg, and started to wrap it up. Just as he was about to put it down into the box again, he stopped and examined the box. "Hey, look! There's something else in here."

As Miriam and Caesar leaned in to look, Cyrus lifted up the bottom and revealed three golden stands for the eggs.

"Huh, how did I miss that...?" Miriam said, feeling ill at ease and truly annoyed with herself. Cyrus gave her a quick scrutinizing glance before putting back the false bottom and the wrapped eggs. Caesar heaved himself up.

"All right, folks, I'm starving. Claire, you take them in your bag for now, and we'll talk more about our theories and the action plan during dinner."

She nodded and put the box back in her bag while Caesar went out the door and didn't even wait for the slow-moving elevator. Cyrus lingered to lock the door's security locks behind her.

"You can't fool me, Claire," he whispered to her as she took a step towards the stairs to follow Caesar down. She stopped dead and turned towards him with beating heart and flushed face. "I know something else happened. Is it me or C or both of us you don't want to tell?" Miriam didn't know what to say, but she was not in the least surprised that he had seen through her again. "Hey, Claire, I'm talking to you."

She exhaled, trying to calm down, but couldn't stop her hands from trembling again. "So I noticed."

"And?"

She made an irritated gesture with her hand, as to shove him away. "Yes, something else happened, but I don't want to talk about it."

"You don't want to talk about it? Seriously?" He made an astounded pause before continuing with something that resembled irritation in his voice: "You can't reason like that. It might be important." She didn't answer, and he took a deep breath as to calm himself down before continuing: "I remember you saying not too long ago: 'You can't make such a decision on your own.'"

She glared at him. He glared back.

"That was a different kind of situation."

"Oh, really? In what way?"

She exhaled angrily, and the words just tumbled out of her. "If you need to know so desperately, someone was in there with me, someone who hid so cleverly that I couldn't find him, but he was there. I don't know what he saw. I don't even know if it was a 'he' or a 'she.' It might even have been an 'it'!"

Cyrus stared baffled back at her. "An it?" When she grabbed her bag and with a scowl turned her back at him, starting to walk down the stairs, he put a hand on her shoulder to stop her. "Wait. What do you mean by 'an it'?"

Surprised she turned around and saw his concerned face. She drew a deep breath and started to speak so quietly so he had to lean in towards her to hear. He smelled discretely of eau de cologne. For some reason, that calmed her down, and she was able to talk without being angry.

"Something came up behind me when I first looked at the sacrifice egg. A shadow fell over me and blocked the light from the window. Whatever it was, it wasn't there when I turned around, and I looked through the whole apartment without finding anything. When I left something... someone... stepped in front of the door inside the apartment and blocked the light again, and... and tried the handle."

Cyrus frowned tentatively. "Did you go in again?" Miriam's cheeks burned with shame, and she avoided his gaze. "Don't worry, Claire. It was probably a good thing that you didn't." When he fell silent a couple of seconds, she was relieved that he didn't berate her. Then he surprised her by saying: "Maybe we can go there together after Belvedere? At least we can see if we can find something, some trace or something."

The heat disappeared slowly from her face, and she managed to look at him again. He gave her a sincere look back.

"Thanks for believing me, Cy."

He shrugged with a tired grin. "What's not to believe? Besides, we're in it together, right?"

She embraced his arm for a second, just because it felt good, it felt true. They were in it together, and they were going to come out of it together, and – most importantly – they had somehow managed to become friends.

Part Three

nightmares

Chapter 14

It was another ghastly scene. There was no blood, no hideous murders, just the frightening expression of unbearable pain on their dead faces. Their bodies lay twisted on the floor as if they've been writhing in agony. Tears trickled silently down Miriam's cheeks. With some of his old kindness, Caesar lent her his newly washed checkered handkerchief. Cyrus watched the scene with an expressionless face, arms folded. Caesar sighed.

"Not much we can do for them now. Let's get them to the morgue and I'll perform an autopsy on them later." He brought out his cell phone and dialed a number. "Andy? Henry Wittinger here. We have a code yellow at a hundred and seventy-second Brisbane Road, level nine, apartment nine-four." He listened for a moment. "No, I'll deal with it when I get back." He hung up. "All right, team, let's get started. Cyrus, you work your usual magic on the neighbors. Claire, you check the apartment. I'll do a quick examination of the bodies and start filing the report."

They both nodded. Cyrus brought out his notebook and a pen and vanished through the door. Caesar put on his gloves and knelt beside the female, all professional looking and unreachable. Miriam turned her back on him, wiped away her tears, and blew her nose before putting on hand sanitizer. She reached for her camera and a pair of latex gloves of her own.

The apartment was just about as abandoned as the other one. It seemed as if Robert and Stella Stevenson had barely managed to get their bed frame and kitchen utensils to their new place before dying. It took her just fifteen minutes to go through the whole apartment thoroughly. There was nothing to be found: no diaries, no letters, not a single trace of personal things except for the basics, and definitely no hidden areas.

"They didn't even have a toothbrush," she remarked to Caesar when she wrapped up her notes. "All their things must be in a warehouse or something."

A thoughtful frown showed on his forehead as he looked up at her from the body on the floor.

"Do you really think so?"

"Why not? This is hardly all their belongings."

Caesar sat himself down beside the body's mid part and rubbed his chin.

"True, true, but just look at them. There's no bread to speak of here. A warehouse isn't cheap. And you can track it down. They would've needed to give their information, you know, driving license or such, maybe a cheque for pre-deposit. I would be surprised if they dared do anything like that."

"So where do you think they've put it?"

"What about if our friends the sect members have taken it?"

A faint smile turned up at the corners of her mouth.

"'The sect members'?" she asked, teasing him mildly, but Caesar just shrugged and scowled. Feeling rejected again she forced herself to continue, the smile fading away as if it had never been there: "Well, you do have a point. My guess, if that's the case, is that they were looking for the eggs, but didn't have the time to search through the inventories here and thus brought everything with them, even the furniture, to search the seams and things like that. Which means..." she added thoughtfully after a short pause, "... that we might need to put someone on guard here. Who knows if that part was someone else's job? We still have no idea how many are involved in this... this sect. And if it was someone else who was supposed to examine the objects, how long would it take them to go through everything? And when they don't find what they're looking for, they'll most likely be back, even with all the chaos we've caused them. I'm quite sure it's the eggs they've been after the whole time. It won't surprise me if these eggs are the solution to everything."

158

"Hm." was Caesar's skeptical answer and Miriam glanced uncertainly at him as the doubt of her own theories built up. "Better to put up some surveillance cameras," he remarked without acknowledging her ideas, and continued: "Another erased memory is of no use to us. We can put some up in the other apartment too, just to be sure that we don't miss anything."

As she thought about the trip she and Cyrus had planned to do anyway, but of which Henry knew nothing, she blushed faintly with guilt. Despite that, she heard herself blurt out: "Cyrus and I can get that done tonight. I need to lock the door. You didn't give me the keys."

With surprise Caesar looked up at her, his hand reaching for his pocket. Then he paused for a second as he seemed to analyze her face, and whatever he saw made him scowl. Her face heated even more and confused she shied away.

"Nothing to waste your energy on. We'll put Andy and his angels on that." Henry's voice was final.

Miriam hesitated slightly, but decided to try to coax him. She needed to know what was wrong with him. If he suspected that they were keeping secrets from him, it was better that they cleared that now. Nervously she sat down on the floor beside him.

"Henry... What's wrong?"

The scowl on his face deepened. He looked down at the body beside him and idly started to play with the hem of the dead woman's linen. Miriam felt close to tears. They burned in her throat as she tried to choke them back.

"Please, Henry, can't you tell me? I know something's wrong." He didn't answer, and she inhaled, trembling. "Have... have I done something? Are you... are you mad at me? Did I... fail something?" When he didn't answer she was close to giving up, but then a thought struck her. As ridiculous as it did seem, she needed an answer. "Do you still think that Cy's someone else? I've spent a lot of time with him lately, and I can assure you..."

159

"It's nothing, Claire."

The use of her FR-name together with Henry's cold tone and angry eyes made her stiffen, feeling both rejected and humiliated at the same time. He turned his back towards her and started to fiddle with his notebook instead. As tears trickled down her cheeks despite her attempts to stop them, she dried them away hurriedly, glad that he didn't see them. Desperately she tried to breathe normally so he didn't hear that she was crying. If he did, he didn't act on it. After a while, she managed to compose herself, and she watched him, feeling confused, lost and betrayed. As if that wasn't enough, a slight guilt hit her for feeling betrayed when it was her and Cyrus who deceived him.

The tears began to flow again without her being able to stop them this time either. With an angry gesture, she wiped them away with the back of her hand and got up on her feet. If he didn't want to speak, then there was nothing she could do about it. At least she had tried.

She had reached the doorway to the kitchen when she felt his hand on her shoulder. It was surprisingly gentle and warm, begging her to stay.

"I'm just a silly old man, Mimi, failing miserably at being professional," he mumbled. She frowned confused, but stood still. "I'm... I... can't really... I'm... just silly... and old... and... and not on top... but I'm not giving up on you, Mimi."

Slowly she turned towards him and watched him confused.

"Not giving up on me? What are you talking about?" When his whole face reddened she squinted as another, even more ridiculous, thought was born in her head. It felt weird to even express it, and she couldn't hinder the skeptical tone in her voice. "You're not... You're not... jealous... are you?" He didn't answer, but he shied away with his gaze and looked slumped, beaten. Miriam couldn't believe it. With her hands on her hips, she stared at him. "You... are jealous. You're jealous of... of Cyrus?" Henry grimaced and half-turned his back towards her. With a perplexed look at him, she

160

continued: "Why? It can't be because I've spent time working with him. I do that on every RP. It's how we work, how you want us to work."

"Can we... just... not talk about it?"

"What do you mean, 'not talk about it'? Of course, we need to talk about it. How can we otherwise solve this situation?"

"No. I... I can't do that right now..."

She watched him blush heavily, looking everywhere else but at her. The seconds ticked by and she still felt too baffled to believe him. Then the realization dawned on her; she had never been friends with any other man in the team before, and Henry didn't like that she and Cyrus finally got along. With a deep frown on her forehead, she felt anger rise inside her. It suddenly felt as if he wanted to cheat her on some positive emotions in her everyday work situation and she couldn't understand why.

"Why would you want me to work with someone who doesn't like me when I can work so much better with someone who does?" Seeing his expression turn from embarrassed to annoyed made her anger vanish and be replaced by self-doubt. "Please, Henry, don't... don't cheat me on this. Please? It's... it's nice not feeling loathed all the time. I... I'd like to continue feeling appreciated at work. It's... it's just Cy..."

With a new flash of anger crossing his face, Henry glared at her and turned his back on her. She stared silently at him as he went back to Stella Stevenson and started to file the report again, ignoring her very presence. Without being able to stop the tears, she went into the kitchen. The rest of the time in the apartment, they stayed away from each other.

When Miriam finally got home that evening, tired and miserable, she could smell the amazing aroma of her sister's home cooked dinner even from outside the door. A smile appeared on her lips as she opened and got in. Beth emerged from the kitchen looking absolutely stunning and as radiant as usual. Her hair was as raven-black and elegantly coiffured

161

as always, and she looked intelligent enough to be the president of the science department at MIT, even when dressed in Miriam's blue-checkered apron. Miriam put down her FBI bag on the floor and gave Beth a big, warm hug.

"How do you manage that, Beth?" she asked with a smile, feeling better just being in the arms of her beloved sister.

"Manage what, sweetheart?"

"Always looking so elegant and so intelligent? I mean, just look at you! You're just pretending to be out in the kitchen cooking. How can you be my sister?"

Beth just laughed. "I'm a natural," she winked and gave her a big wet kiss on the forehead.

"Blech," Miriam said and wrinkled her nose, vigorously wiping away the kiss.

Beth laughed even more and hollered over her shoulder as she returned to the cooking: "Join me in the kitchen and help out with the salad and then you can tell me everything about why you're so ridiculously late."

Miriam smiled and, as usual when her big sis was around, everything felt as if it was going to be well and good in the end. She took off her FBI jacket and hung it in the closet. If she could avoid seeing it until tomorrow morning, no one would be happier. Beth was singing along with Bono on highest volume when she came out to her as she stood at the counter, crumbling feta cheese in a bowl. Together they massacred *Even Better Than the Real Thing* in a way that probably would make Bono cry if he could hear them.

The salad was done with lots of chickpeas, carrots, and fresh baby spinach with an abundance of homemade dressing, and the deep red wine was poured into the glasses. Miriam was delighted. She rarely drank alcohol, since it had been forbidden for the Star Students and the habit was too strong to break. Therefore, a glass of wine was a nice treat, especially one that had such a rich bouquet as this one. Beth put the steaks with the melted feta cheese on top and the garlic roasted potatoes on the plates, and through the whole apartment, a heavenly aroma spread. They placed everything on the large table outside on the terrace to be able to enjoy the last bit of sunset while they were eating. The air was mild and dry, and the potted flowers and herbs spread an amazing scent.

"It feels like Greece, don't you think?" Beth said dreamingly.

Miriam nodded. "Ah, yes… Greece…" She sighed with pleasure as they both shared ten-year-old memories of radiating colors, of the stunning blue sky and white houses, of the heat during the day, and the everlasting bouzoukis during the nights, accompanied by the loud chirping of large crickets.

"We should try to save up for another trip, but with all of us this time; you and me, Ted and Henry and Markus. It would be unforgettable." Beth watched the darkening sky with a faraway, dreamy gaze and didn't see how Miriam frowned. "I'd love taking Markus to Greece. You two could wander all those ruins together and get lost in history. He'd love that, don't you think?"

Miriam smiled again, her forehead smoothing out, as she thought of her introverted nephew who she loved to the moon and back.

"Yes, he would."

"Where would you like to go, Mimi? The mainland or Rhodes or Crete?"

"What a question." She grinned at her sister. "How could you think I'd like to go anywhere else than Crete? I mean, Minoan, right? You've just got to love their culture, so rich and so much alive still, and of course friendlier than the Mycenaean."

Beth turned her head and laughed at her.

"Minoan, Mycenaean. Who cares? It's the wine, Mimi, and the food, and the beaches, and the elderly people up in the mountain villages, and the beauty."

"There's beauty in Knossos, Beth. You have to admit that."

163

"Just lots of dust and withering pillars…" she answered with a mischievous glint in her eyes.

"Columns," Miriam interrupted.

"Whatever." Still smiling she shook her head. "Truthfully, Mimi, I've never understood that fascination of yours for the ruins."

Miriam swirled the wine around in the glass, watching Beth over the rim. Then she decided to make a new try. She put down the glass, leaning forward, looking her seriously in the eyes.

"It's because you've never asked before, Beth, not really, I mean. It's not the building itself as much as the people, the souls who still inhabit it, how they lived, how they loved and laughed and cried, how they fought for what they believed in, what they won and what they lost, how they felt, and what they thought about when they were alone at night, and how they eventually died. The people who built the palace and the people who inhabited it, they watched the same sky as us, studied the same stars, bathed in the same water as we do today. Don't you think it's fascinating, Beth?"

Beth rested her chin in the palm of her hand and studied her with a genuine interest that gladdened Miriam deep in her heart.

"I've never thought about it like that before," she admitted, "but I like the images you create in my mind. It is beautiful, Mimi. You're right." She raised her glass. "Let's cheer for those long lost people and for our upcoming vacation."

They clinked their glasses together and drank in silence as the last golden streak disappeared from the sky above them and gave way to a velvety darkness.

Beth turned her head towards her again. "And speaking of vacation, what about this new Star Student case of yours? Is it finished soon? Do you think you'll be able to join us at the lake in time?"

Miriam bit her lip and looked down at her plate, shoving a piece of potato around with her fork. She really didn't want to talk about Henry right now. *I don't even want him to come to the lake with me...* a rebellious thought appeared, and she blushed in stunned shame. *God, what am I thinking? Okay... don't worry about it. It's going to feel better tomorrow. It usually does.* To her relief, the blush disappeared as she calmed down, and she took a sip of the wine, while Beth patiently waited for her to answer.

"I actually don't know. I... hope so, but... Right now, we're... well... not really stuck, but not really moving forward either. Just, you know, trampling around in mud, as Carl probably would say."

"Who's that? I can't recall that name. Is he part of the Star Students too?"

To her own surprise, Miriam suddenly blushed wildly. *What the hell...?* Trying hard to appear casual, she rested her chin in her hand and looked out at the city view, feeling that her awkwardness was clearly detectable. *Damn you, Henry, for making me feel guilty! Damn you for not wanting me to have friends at work! Damn you!*

"Mimi?" Beth's voice was suddenly worried. "Are you seeing someone else?"

Miriam turned towards her, almost surprised over the question and very irritated with herself that she wasn't genuinely so.

"No, of course not," she said and felt her cheeks burn even more. Beth gave her a penetrating look that she couldn't meet.

"So what's going on? Why are you blushing and looking like you're having a secret? Who's this Carl?"

Miriam sighed at how transparent she was and turned to watch the view again, while she poured more wine into her glass to save some time.

"You're right," she said eventually. "We work together; as Star Students, Henry and Carl and I, and we're... we're a really good team. Really good. We complement each other."

"Okay?"

165

"Carl's relatively new. We've only been in a couple of cases together, last summer. I haven't talked about him, because... well...honestly, we haven't gotten along very well before. At all, actually, and... yeah... but now... I don't know..." Miriam hesitated.

"You don't know what?" Beth inquired suspiciously.

"I mean... it's just that..." She scowled down into her wine glass.

"What?"

With a deep, irritated exhalation she looked Beth straight in the eyes.

"Oh, God, it's such a mess! I just can't believe Henry!"

"Why?"

Miriam let out all her frustration and waved impatiently with her hands in the air. "Well, how long have we been a couple? It's almost four years now – and he's suddenly jealous?"

"Of Carl?" Beth asked, and Miriam nodded unhappily, but felt that she'd already said too much. She didn't want Beth to know about Henry and his weird reaction, and certainly not that he seemed to want her friendship with Carl to end. That was too... too owning... and she felt ashamed of his reaction. *I shouldn't have said anything. She's going to pry everything out of me and then she'll be worried about our relationship again. Goddamn... I don't need this tonight.*

Beth didn't let it be, of course. "So what happened?"

Miriam sighed and looked down at her plate again. "Nothing, really..." she tried, but Beth just gave her that big-sister-look that showed Miriam just how much she didn't believe her. Miriam made a disarming gesture. "Okay, okay. He said that he's 'a silly old man who can't think properly anymore.'"

"That's it? Come on, you have to tell me," Beth said as she didn't answer. "There's something else. You can't hide it from me, sweetheart."

166

Desperately trying to talk about anything else than what really made her sad and worried, she said: "I don't know. Suddenly he seems concerned about the age difference between us. It's never been a problem before. I mean, I don't care that he's older than me, but now... He keeps on calling us, me and Carl, 'youngsters' and himself 'an old man.'"

"Well," Beth said with her dark, soothing voice and sipped her wine, scrutinizing her intently, "he's never had reason to be jealous before. He probably doesn't know how to handle it."

"As if he has a reason now! Carl's not a threat to him!" Miriam lashed out.

"Apparently he thinks so." Miriam scoffed, and Beth smiled at her, with a hint of teasing. "So tell me about this Carl," she said curiously. "I want to know why Henry reacts so strongly to him."

Miriam cringed, knowing exactly what made Henry go out of his mind with this, even though she couldn't understand it. Then she hesitated a moment, trying to come up with an explanation that wouldn't sound like Henry wanted to lock her in. Apparently Beth misinterpreted her silence and gave her a stubbornly inquiring look, so Miriam gave in to her sister's curiosity, realizing that it would only look worse if she didn't answer.

"Well..." she stalled for time. "I don't know what to tell... What do you want to know?"

"Let's start with how he looks and how he is, how he treats you, what he's interested in, and if he likes animals."

Miriam managed to laugh at her big sister, which felt good. *And I think I've led her around that pit. If I tell her about Cy, she won't ask anything else about Henry.* Then she hesitated again, pushed Henry to the back of her mind and tried to put Cyrus into words instead.

"Well..." she started. "He's a couple of years younger than me. Redhead. Looks good enough, I guess. Maybe a tad like a young Robert Redford. Probably a bit Irish."

"Sounds nice. I've always liked Redford. He's sexy."
Miriam rolled her eyes, had problems combining Cyrus with
'sexy', and Beth snickered. "Go on," she pried. Miriam glared
at her, but gave in.

"Yeah, good-looking enough, if that's all you're after,
but he's so closed up. I've never met someone so... so...
locked up inside himself before. He hides all his emotions,
and you can't even guess what's going on inside if he doesn't
want you to, and that's so damn infuriating. He's a damn
tower!" Miriam let out a puff of frustration before she
continued with another frown. "And then he's hotheaded. At
least sometimes. Just, you know, rushing into things...
situations... without even thinking about the consequences,
and then usually creates lots of trouble on the way. But he's
very intelligent, and I'm starting to like him..." Miriam
paused as the thought struck her. "No, that's not fair," she
said slowly, feeling surprised. "I do like him, which is really
weird. When he lets people in he's both caring and funny and
we're actually enjoying each other's company now, which is
also weird, now when I think about it." She frowned again.
"But there's one thing I really, really hate about him, and
that's that he can read me like a book! It bugs the hell out of
me!"

Beth laughed. "He sounds intriguing and complex
and totally different from the guys you usually fall for."

Miriam shook her head at her and took another sip of
the wine. "The first year I loathed him, couldn't stand the
sight of him, but now..."

"Aha! I knew there was a 'but'!"

"Beth!" Miriam protested and continued to defend
herself. "It's not like that at all. I'm not falling for him. God,
the thought... No, we've started to become friends, and I
think we could become really good friends if we got the
chance, and... and I'm so very happy about it. I... I don't have
to work with someone who... who loathes me anymore..."

Beth reached over the table and took her hand,
caressing it gently.

"Oh, *zissele*," she said with distress in her voice and Miri felt the damn tears lurking, wanting to fall. She cleared her voice.

"At this point, I'd even consider calling him if I needed to talk about something. I haven't had a friend like that since... since... university, since Noreah. You can't even imagine how it is, Beth. Sometimes... sometimes this job is so very lonely... and scary... and you lose people... and you try not to attach yourself too much to someone because... because... you never know when they're going to... to die."

Beth caressed her hand again, looking devastated. "I'm sorry, hon. I was just teasing you, and it was the completely wrong thing to do. I know it's a terribly tough job you have."

Miriam shook her head. Beth would never be able to understand how powerless they all were in the end, how they never were able to control the situation, and how the only thing they could do was to ride the storm at the best of their abilities and hope that the outcome would not be anyone dying or going insane. She just ignored Beth's last remark and concentrated on something her sister would understand, unwillingly stumbling into the pit anyway.

"And you know, the thing is, Henry can't handle us being friends, apparently. Everything was fine between us when Carl and I could barely talk politely to each other, but now... It's like he wants to show Carl some kind of ownership over me. He doesn't own me, Beth! He never has. That I want to please him doesn't mean that I'm a doormat." She exhaled, feeling her cheeks burning in agitation. "I'm my own, Beth. It's my body, my mind, my actions, my feelings, not his."

Beth nodded seriously and held her hand hard. "And it frustrates him that you don't play along with him, right?"

"Yeah... I guess..." Miriam looked down, suddenly ashamed of the whole situation and of how embarrassed it made her feel.

169

"You need to make that clear to him, Mimi. It won't be easy, but you won't be able to let this go if you don't, and he's going to push you away if he continues like this. You need to take control of the situation and show him that he can't play with you."

Miriam nodded and felt a tear slowly run down her cheek. It surprised her that Beth gave her advice on how to make things right with Henry. She had never been particularly fond of him, for some reason, and from time to time she had expressed concerns about their relationship. *Maybe she's right;* a traitorous voice whispered in the back of her head, and she scowled. *So what? I love him. We can work this out. He just needs to understand that he can't boss me around.*

Beth got up and around the table, hugging her gently as more tears found their way from her eyes. Miriam wasn't really crying for Henry being jealous. That thing wouldn't be too hard to solve with time. She cried because she desperately wanted to have a friend again. Until this evening, she hadn't realized how much she longed for that, and she felt so at a loss at Henry's reaction. She also cried because she was so scared of this project right now, so tired, so bone-tiredly exhausted, and she couldn't handle Henry's unexpected outburst. *I won't give in to him. I'm going to stand up for myself. I need that.*

Carl had started to mean something more to her than she ever thought that he would, and she was not going to let Henry destroy that. If he did, she had a feeling that he would also destroy something precious between the two of them, something that would not be easily repaired. She dried her tears and tried to explain that to her sister.

"And this case, Beth… it's just so scary, so weird, and I think it gets to us all. We're all so damn tense! And we need to be able to let go of personal feelings right now. We can't let them take over. We need to be able to focus and work together again, as a team."

Beth hugged her harder.

"You're afraid."

"Damn right I am! Everyone in their right mind would be."

"I wish you could tell me about it, Mimi. I know you can't, but if you need something, anything, just let me know. I'll take a day off, let Tamsin be chief in command at the clinic, and help you out."

Miriam felt her heart overflow with love and hugged her back as if she would never let go.

"I love you, Beth, to heaven and hell and back. You're the best sister in the world!"

Chapter 15

Later that night, the stars had begun to shine. A mild breeze played with Miriam's hair as she sat alone on the terrace, drinking the last glass of wine, surrounded by the scent of late July and the soft music from the stereo. *Morcheeba.* She had stopped by at the store and bought the CD on her way home. It felt a bit silly now, considering the circumstances, but she had honestly fallen in love with the music immediately, and it had nothing to do with Carl or her feelings for him. That she had to reassure herself about that made her a bit touchy. It upset her that a man and a woman could not become friends without the whole world believing there was romance in the air. Thanks to Beth and Henry and their crazy ideas, her cheeks blossomed hot every time she thought of him now, and that distressed her even more. Just thinking about the combination of Carl and romance was… weird and out of place.

To herself, Miriam could admit that she wondered if this was another big mistake. Every time she had gotten emotionally attached to another Field Researcher, that FR had perished in some gruesome way. She was terribly afraid that something would happen to Carl too, and if it did, she wasn't sure that she could handle it had they become close friends. Suddenly she felt ashamed of herself, being so selfish.

"I'm always thinking solely of myself," she muttered and twirled the glass in her hand, watching the deep red liquid splash around. "Maybe he needs a friend too. He seems pretty lonely." If that was the case, she decided, she couldn't let herself shy away from it just because she was afraid of what might happen in the future. "That's just cowardly. And yes, I might be a coward, but I can fight that too." Satisfied with herself, she took another mouthful of wine.

She hadn't told Beth that Carl had invited her home for tea that very evening. She would just have continued her matchmaking game, and Miriam was definitely not in the mood for that.

He had never done something like that before, she mused, inviting her out somewhere after work, which of course was understandable. He was a sane person after all, not someone who liked to surround himself with people he didn't like or who didn't get along with him, but tonight, just as they left the Stevenson's apartment complex, he asked her in that casual, friendly way she now knew was the real Carl. It touched her because she finally understood how rare it was for him to show that side to anyone. She suspected that he, just like her, had stopped having friends years ago.

"Just chilling. Thinking of something else than the project. Maybe talk or watch a movie. Drink tea. It sure would be nice not to be alone for a while."

She had felt bad when she told him that Beth probably was at home waiting for her already. There had also been a tang of disappointment in her heart, which had taken her by surprise. Then she had amazed them both by asking: *"What about tomorrow?"* and he had smiled that rare smile of his and nodded.

As they went to their different cars, they were both relieved that the apartment still had been "as empty as a shoe box" as Carl had expressed it, and that they got the door locked. To go home knowing that the door to a crime scene stood unlocked was something she never thought she would be able to do, but now she could confess without feeling too ashamed that she would never have had the courage to go back there alone.

Her gaze drifted away to where Luce's cage used to be, and she gave up an inaudible sigh. It had been love at first sight between the canary and Beth, not that she had expected anything else, but it wasn't until now that she fully realized how much she would miss him. It didn't matter. As long as she actively worked as a Field Researcher, she wouldn't be able to keep an animal. Miriam sighed. She had always loved animals, all animals, even the rats and snakes and lizards, but

173

she did not have that magical touch with animals as Beth did. It was like Beth could communicate with them telepathically. Miriam had always secretly envied her that gift, and when they were kids that envy had transformed itself into teasing. Countless of times, she had called Beth Snow White in that annoyingly little-sister-way that she herself hated nowadays, and none of them were able to watch that movie anymore. Ah well, it was all in the past now, thank goodness.

Hurriedly, she emptied her glass and heaved herself up from the chair, a little bit tipsy. She locked the terrace door with its three different security locks before going into the kitchen. While she washed the dishes, she leaned her forehead towards the cupboard and hummed to the music, just letting her thoughts drift toward pleasant daydreams of the future.

Half an hour later, she laid tucked in on her bed, dressed in that silky, rosy nightie that Henry liked so much and her old, worn teddy loosely embraced in her arms. Surrounded by gentle light and soft music, she drifted off to sleep.

She wasn't sure how long she had slept when a heavy thump woke her up. Before she even knew that she was awake, she sat up in bed with her teddy in a cramped grasp; her chest tight and hurting from the shallow breathing. With eyes wide-opened in fear she stared out into the softly lit apartment. Nothing seemed to move.

With pounding heart and the painfully shallow breaths, she tried to force limbs that had turned into hot water to move. She couldn't even hear the music play over the heavy beating in her ears. With jerky movements, she managed to let go of the teddy and shove the duvet aside, getting her stiff legs off the bed. With her gaze still fixed on the doorway, she groped for her second gun, which always lay under the mattress. The cool metal against her fingertips started to calm her down, but when she grabbed it with trembling hands and raised it, she could see it wobble.

Even though the naked wooden floor was chilly under her feet, and the air conditioner cooled the night air so much that goosebumps appeared on her arms, big drops of sweat trickled down her forehead and wet her armpits when she forced herself towards the doorway. There was nothing to disturb the calm, yet she knew that something was wrong. She felt it deep down in her bones and in how the soles of her feet hurt.

She saw it immediately when she cautiously looked out in the living room. Her FBI bag lay on the floor, opened, with all her CSI tools and evidence bags scattered all over. When she guardedly went through her apartment, no one was there, and both the front door and the door to the balcony were locked, as were all the windows. *Morcheeba* sang with gentle voices from the stereo, trying to calm her down, but failing miserably. The whole while it took her to gather her things and rearrange them in her bag, she felt the rigid uneasiness in her spine, as if someone was watching her. Every now and again, she caught herself glancing over her shoulder, feeling like a hunted animal. Finally, the bag was re-packed and placed at its usual spot in the hallway, and she went into her bedroom again, sliding into her bed, but this time hugging her gun instead of her teddy. She lay stiff, on guard, not able to close her eyes. The minutes went by; five, ten, fifteen…

Suddenly another thump came from the living room. Miriam gasped and clutched the gun. This time, she flew up from bed with the gun raised in front of her.

No one was there, but just like before, her FBI bag lay on the floor with its content scattered all over the room. A new search of the apartment gave nothing. There was no one around. She returned to the living room and collected her things with trembling hands and put them back orderly for the second time.

This time, she didn't even get into her bedroom before the bag skid over the floor behind her back. As she swirled around, she saw the lock open by itself and the entire content slide out. Without letting her gaze fall away from the bag, she backed into the bedroom, closed the door, and locked all the locks. Then she curled up in her bed with her teddy tightly squeezed to her chest with one hand and the gun in the other, while she heard the things from her bag scatter throughout the floor in the living room. With the teddy still in her arms, she stretched out for the phone and dialed a number with trembling fingers. One signal went through, then another, and another.

"Um... Wittinger..." Henry's deep, comforting voice was sleepy. At the sound of it, the tears broke free, and she started sobbing. "Mimi?" His voice lost the sleepiness and got worried. "Is it you?"

Miriam managed to whimper a "yes."

"What happened? Are you hurt? Where are you?"

"I'm home... I can't get out... Something's throwing my bag around, and it won't stop..."

"I'll be over immediately. Don't go anywhere."

The click from when he hung up on her made her feel more lonely and vulnerable than before. Outside the door, her things continued to rummage around on the floor.

The forty-five minutes that passed before Henry called on her cell were probably the longest minutes she'd ever experienced in her own home. Her belongings in the living room had stopped rummaging around after eight and a half minutes, but she hadn't dared poke her nose out there. She sat on her bed with her gun and her teddy cramped in her arms and the duvet tightly wrapped around her body, almost covering her face. She felt like the worst coward in the world, but she couldn't release her body, couldn't order it to go out there, not on her own, not without the team. It was her home, for crying out loud! She was supposed to be safe here! Nothing bad was supposed to happen here! As the tears ached in her throat, she knew now that she had fooled herself when she repeatedly told herself over the years that she was prepared for anything that could come for her in her home.

"Liar. Damn fricking liar."

176

When her cell finally rang, the gun's handle was wet from sweat as she released it to grab the phone.

"I'm right outside, Mimi, but the door is locked."

"Damn! Damn, damn, damn! Not just a coward, but a stupid coward as well! I'm coming."

She hung up before he could respond. At least the phone call made her body parts feel like they were actually part of her again and she could move. She dried her sweaty hands on the duvet, put down the teddy on the messy bed and grabbed the gun again, moving carefully towards the door. Nothing seemed to stir outside, but then again, it was hard for her to judge since her heart beat like a hammer in her chest, made the blood boil with rage in her ears to the extent that she felt deaf.

She took calming breaths and turned the different keys, then opened the door and peeked out. The contents of the bag lay in a mess on the floor, but it was a non-moving mess. In spite of that, Miriam decided to wait with the deep breath of relief. Instead, she snuck past the chaos on the floor with a suspicious glance at it and at her FBI bag while rapidly moving towards the front door. A quick look through the door viewer showed her Henry outside. A heavy sigh of relief made her calm down and finally start to clear the anxious fog that had replaced her capacity of thinking.

With shaking hands, she unlocked the security locks, but suddenly she froze. The feeling of someone watching her had returned, stronger than before. The hair on her arms stood up, and the soles of her feet hurt. Slowly, she began to turn around. During a split second, she heard a sharp metallic sound, a muffled vibration in the air, and then the fleshy thud when one of her scalpels went straight through her left hand and fastened it to the door. Miriam shrieked in pain. Blood gushed down her hand and arm and the only thought that seemed to occupy her mind was: *I can't let the blood smear the nighty, I just can't, I just can't, it's Henry's fav, I just can't let it smear it!* The door pushed opened, and she screamed again as the throbbing pain gave way to flashing pain.

Henry charged in with his gun raised, taking in the scene in just a moment, and rushed by her, looking for the perpetrator. Two minutes later he came back, gun tucked away and a towel in his hand.

"It's clear," he said.

"It's not clear," she breathed painfully through her teeth. "You just can't see it."

Henry gave her a worried look, but didn't say anything more, just came with the towel for her bleeding hand and examined how it stuck to the door with the scalpel.

"We need to free your hand, Mimi."

"Yeah? Good idea. Really good idea. Appreciate it. Can you do it now, please, for everything good in the world?"

"I don't want to injure anything, a muscle or anything like that. I need to be..."

"Just... take... it... out!"

"All right! Fine!"

He frowned as he watched the scalpel's angle and depth, and then, with a rapid movement and heavy force, he managed to drag it out. Miriam screamed again as the pain flashed sharply when her hand got released and fell down without her being able to stop it. Henry grabbed the towel, wrapped it around her hand, and made her sit down on the floor.

"You need to put pressure here. I'll get some first aid before we leave for Dr. Bernard. You'll need some stitches, I believe."

She couldn't do more than nod faintly. The pain throbbed and spread, making her feeling weak and sick. She lost track of time and didn't know if Henry had been gone for five seconds or five minutes when he came back with the first aid kit, looking at her with a strange expression on his face.

"Why have you put up the eggs on your fireplace, Mimi? It's evidence."

She just stared at him, bewildered and confused.

"The... What? I haven't done that." A cold chill ran down her spine. "No..." she whispered. "It's the thing... It's

178

here. It followed me... Oh, my God, it followed me! *A brock! A brock!*"

Henry's face got concerned.

"What followed you? Mimi, are you all right?"

"No..."

He sat down beside her, took away the blood soaked towel and started to put a tight pressure bandage on the wound. She gasped in pain, but tried to relax and breathe.

"This doesn't look good. We need to leave immediately. You've lost quite some blood."

She nodded eagerly and felt a bit dizzy. "Yes, let's... let's go. We... need to go. We have to lock the door. Where are the keys? I need my keys."

"I'll get them for you. Don't worry." Henry's voice was very calm and reassuring as he stood up and started to rummage through her shoulder bag. "I have them. Can you stand up?"

"Sure I can. It's not that big of a wound, and it's in my hand, not my legs."

He helped her up, and she silently cursed her own weakness when she staggered just ever so slightly. Henry led her out, carrying her bag, and locked the door behind her. Blood already soaked the bandage, and she wrapped the almost drenched towel around it to prevent the blood from dripping.

Henry drove like crazy through the backstreets to Dr. Bernard's house. At least there was no waiting there, as it would have been at the emergency. Only a few minutes after Henry rang the doorbell, Dr. Bernard opened the door dressed in an orange kimono-like nightgown and a pair of pink slippers. *He looks as well-rested as if he's just been on a three months refreshing vacation. No dark smudges under his eyes this time;* Miriam thought sourly as she leaned heavily towards the outer wall. When a cold shiver violently shook her body, she suddenly realized that she wasn't wearing anything else but the nighty, but she was in too much in pain to care.

"Miriam. Henry. Come in. I would offer you tea or coffee, but I think we need to get you into the examination room immediately. What happened?" he asked as he ushered them both in.

"I got a scalpel thrown at me, and it nailed my hand to a door," Miriam muttered annoyed.

"Really!" Dr. Bernard whistled a surprised tone. "That must have been one hell of a talented knife thrower."

"You could say that," Miriam muttered again.

"Was he human?"

She shrugged. "Who knows."

Dr. Bernard gave up a short barking laughter. "Yeah, who knows," he agreed, then glanced at how the blood dripped through the soaked towel. "You've lost some blood. How do you feel?"

"A bit dizzy. Cold. Throbbing pain. It's not that serious. I've been through worse."

"All right."

He opened the door to the examination room and waved a hand towards the bunk. She sat down and Henry threw himself into a chair out of the way. Dr. Bernard wrapped a blanket over her shoulders before he took the swivel chair and wheeled towards her.

"Unwrap it."

She did as he asked and even though she knew that she'd been telling the truth, that she'd been worse wounded before, the wound looked terribly serious, deep, meaty, and still gushing blood. She swallowed hard.

Dr. Bernard put on a pair of latex gloves and reached for a needle, a glass bottle with clear liquid, and a bottle rubbing alcohol. He filled the needle with the liquid and pointed it at her skin beside the wound.

"This'll sting a tiny bit, but it's anesthetics so it will take the pain away somewhat when we clean it."

As they waited for the anesthetics to work, he examined the wound with a deep frown on his forehead, which scared her. Eventually, he started to clean the wound

180

carefully, and even though it was numb, it still hurt like hell. Tears of pain filled her eyes, and she tried to keep back the raw moaning without really succeeding.

"We need to stitch it, Miriam. It goes right through the hand, and one of the larger muscles has been damaged."

"How bad is it?" she asked through gritted teeth.

"I wouldn't say terribly bad, but it's not the clean cut I was hoping for. You won't be able to use your hand for some time, and when it's healed, you'll probably need a few weeks of physiotherapy to get it back in shape."

Miriam sat silent for a couple of seconds, letting it all sink in.

"Damn," she said. "Damn it all." Then she sighed. "At least it's not my right hand. *A brock*, let's get it over with. I need to be able to work tomorrow."

Chapter 16

The early afternoon sun shone through the vanilla-colored, bland curtains and bathed the briefing room in soft, calming light. Miriam's hand throbbed through the Tylenol 3 she had taken a couple of hours earlier, and she had a difficult time keeping it still. For the time being, she was alone in the room. Henry had gone to pick up her FBI bag, the eggs, and the other evidence she found at the Stevenson's' apartment, and Carl hadn't shown up yet.

She and Henry had used the hospitality of Dr. Bernard and slept in one of his patient/guest rooms during the few hours that followed the minor surgery. That way, they managed to get two more hours of sleep than they would have gotten had they gone home to Henry's, since she flatly refused to enter her own apartment again, at least not until those cursed eggs were removed. She didn't even want Henry to drive by to pick up some clothes for her. Instead, she had put on a tunic, a pair of jeans, and a summer jacket, that she had in her locker, so she didn't have to go around in her nighty.

She didn't know if Henry believed her or not, and right now it didn't matter. She just wanted the atrocious things out of there. After that, she could start worrying about people believing her or not. Nervously, she picked on the bandaged hand and grimaced when a slightly stronger flash of pain hit her. At least he hadn't tried to talk about their argument, which was a huge relief. At this point, she wouldn't be able to take it. It would be too much on top of everything else.

When the door opened a couple of minutes later, Henry and Carl stepped in together, seemingly on good terms. Henry had a tray steaming, hot coffee in his hands and Miriam felt the first genuine smile this day appear on her face.

"Aw, look! Coffee! You're definitely my hero today, Caesar!"

He smiled back at her, and his face showed her that kindness she loved. Her eyes filled with tears at the mere sight.

"I thought you needed one, and a large one at that."

Carl threw his bag on the table and sat down on the chair beside her. Without being able to restrain herself, she glanced nervously at Henry, but he seemed occupied with his bag.

"Caesar told me what happened," Carl said with genuine concern that warmed her heart. "How do you feel?"

"Have been better, there's no doubt about it, but it's no big deal. It's not my head or my eyes or my legs. I can function."

"Great. That's what I thought you'd say. I'm glad to hear it."

"I put the eggs in our usual bank deposit box," Henry broke in. "Hopefully, you'll get some peace tonight."

"Yeah," Carl said, "it's annoying if things start to move around over there, but it won't disturb anyone."

"We're going to send them to the Faculty as soon as I get a hold of Anna's new address. I'm quite sure they'll find them intriguing," Henry added.

Miriam was so happy she could sing; they believed her! Spontaneously, she threw her arm around Carl and gave him a big hug and a smashing kiss before getting up and giving Henry another. They laughed at her, Carl with suddenly red cheeks, but both of them friendly. It relieved her so much that Henry didn't seem to mind. Maybe that argument yesterday had made him come to his senses after all.

"So, team," Henry said in a brisk, professional Caesar voice, "let's get to business."

They all settled down around the table, and Caesar took out his notebook and a pen. The gentle light smoothed out their faces, making them all look younger and less stressed out than they were.

"During the night, I thought about what we discussed at the restaurant yesterday, and the more I contemplate it, the more I sense that you're right, Claire. That last egg probably depicts a fertility goddess and her human worshipper, possibly with origin from the Fertile Crescent – also your suggestion, Claire, but since we can't either confirm or deny it as for now, I don't want to make any assumptions. What we most likely can do without assuming too much is, as Cyrus suggested, excluding the Skoptsy. Their belief in purity and their view of sexuality as evil do not coincide with what this last scene seems to suggest, and when I called the Faculty this morning, Anna hadn't found anything that suggests that they were engaged in human sacrifice. My own, most unprofessional hypothesis in this matter, since I'm not an anthropologist, is that the Skoptsy got inspired by some specific traditions from this, at least for us, unknown, most likely ancient, religion, adopted them into their own faith and performed them with another meaning than the original. However, we can't know these things for sure, which of course makes it all quite difficult to pursue. Anyway, do you agree with me or do you have other theories?"

Miriam shook her head. "I think it sounds plausible, and until we can get in contact with a GFS Researcher with expertise in fertility cults, this is what we have, right?"

"Yeah, I agree," Cyrus said and brought out a book from his bag. "I borrowed this from the library today. If I remember my university lessons correctly, Erich Neumann discusses the female figure throughout history from the perspective of the Great Mother, and the different aspects of her as beautiful and terrible. I haven't read it for years, but I remember it as very interesting, and it popped up in my head yesterday when we talked about the fertility cults and how widespread they are."

Miriam reached out for it.

"Can I take a look?"

"Sure, go ahead."

While she skimmed through the pages, Cyrus took out the Polaroid photo from his bag. "I did my homework last night as well, and checked this out, and I think that we finally have a lead here, especially when I put it together with some other info I got this morning. Bettles is a small Alaskan town located on the banks of the Koyukuk River, thirty-five miles north of the Arctic Circle. Well, 'town' might be a tad exaggerated. It's actually more like a village with only twelve in population. That's one family and one household, according to the latest census."

"Go on," Caesar said when he paused.

"The previous census, however, showed Bettles to inhabit forty-three people, sixteen households, and nine families."

"Huh." Miriam frowned. "That's a decline with three-fourth in just ten years. That doesn't seem normal."

"A bit out of the ordinary, I'd say," A dark shadow appeared on Cyrus' face.

"What?" she asked, suddenly concerned. "Did I say something wrong?"

He shook his head. "No, I just think I have some idea of what's going on up there. There wasn't much to go on from the internet, but I got the full story — at least I think it's the full story — out of Paulina this morning before we went to Bernard, and it's bad, really, really bad. But at least she's free of eels. Good for her, poor little thing."

"What do you mean 'bad'? Worse than *Annie*?"

He gave up a humorless chuckle. "Annie would consider herself lucky to just have to deal with an alcoholic housekeeper. Where these children come from, there's no hope of a sun tomorrow."

"Spit it out, Cyrus," Caesar said impatiently, and Miriam glanced wearily at him.

"Yeah... Emilia and Paulina's families knew each other. They were neighbors in Bettles. The parents got murdered, sacrificed, in front of their children's eyes, and the two girls and Paulina's older brother Lucas were brought to

185

something that Paulina describes as a kind of foster home. Records show that the farm is owned by a William Phillips. He's married to a Margery Phillips, and there's also an adult daughter, Roxy, and a teenage son, Warren, who live at the place. Paulina says that there are lots of children there. She named them, and there are twenty-two kids. That was, of course, one and a half year ago, so that may have changed."

Caesar raised his eyebrows.

"Twenty children in a foster home? That's way too many."

Cyrus nodded grimly. "Problem is, they don't have any permit. They're not an official foster home. They're just listed as a regular family and self-supporting farmers."

"That's great news, Cyrus," Caesar said pleased. "That means that we can shut them down without it having to be a big operation."

Cyrus watched him intently. "In any other case I'd agree with you, C, but I'd say that it depends on whether we want to stop them or if we just want them to relocate and continue."

"Stop them? From what?"

Cyrus pulled at his hair and exhaled. "Paulina told me that three males live there too. They're not registered in the census, so I don't have any last names. I don't know the relationship to the family, but Robert, Gregory, and Jesus constantly abuse the children physically, mentally and sexually. Yes, they do rape them," he acknowledged when Miriam let out a low groan. "The women comfort the children, and if they start praying to the Great Goddess, the abuse stops."

"The Great Goddess...?" Miriam repeated slowly.

"Yeah, they call her the Great Mother."

They all glanced at the book in front of Miriam, where the words *The Great Mother* were printed in a large font.

"It must be her, the fertility goddess in the egg, and also whom the writing in professor Bruchheimer's bedroom

186

refers to. It just must. It all makes sense now," Miriam said urgently.

"I wouldn't draw too strong conclusions just yet, Claire," Caesar warned her, "but with what we have it seems possible."

With a nod, she turned to Cyrus again. "So what happens to the children who don't pray to the Goddess?"

Cyrus looked down with a grim expression. "If they don't, they... disappear."

"Lucas disappeared, I take it," Caesar said.

"No, he became one of the new believers and got... privileges. He raped her."

"What?" Miriam burst out unbelievingly. "His own sister?"

"Yeah..."

The silence in the room was stunned and shocked for a moment.

"I feel sick..." Miriam mumbled at long last.

"She doesn't know how the rumor started, but a couple of days after that, whispers about Emilia and Paulina's rebuke started to circulate. They were going to go the same way as the other lost children, into the building where the goddess lives and be punished, also according to the rumors, by Lucas."

"So... does the punishment mean death?"

"I don't know. Possibly. The penalized children disappear. That's the only thing Paulina knows."

"This obviously didn't happen since both children ended up at the Stevenson's," Caesar remarked.

"How did they get there? Did they flee?"

"In a way. Same day the Stevenson's came to visit. They were apparently close friends with Emilia and Paulina's families, but didn't live in Bettles."

Caesar raised his eyebrow. "That sounds like a miscalculation from the Phillips' septuplet."

"Sure does," Cyrus agreed. "Paulina doesn't really know how her new foster parents managed to get them out

187

of there, but it seems that Stella Stevenson upheld the family while Robert Stevenson 'spoke weirdly' to the guards who fell asleep and they could get out."

They all looked at each other.

"Have we seen that before or what?" Miriam said with a grimace. "I was so wrong; they were part of the sect."

"Fleeing," Caesar reminded her.

"Why, yes, but they must've been part of it at one point or another. How would they otherwise know that sleeping thingie kind of spell?"

"'Sleeping thingie kind of spell'?" Cyrus chuckled lightly. "Well, that's one way of describing it, I guess."

Caesar raised his hand impatiently. "Did you get anything else out of the girl, Cyrus?"

"Just personal matters. Nothing that relates to the RP."

"Are you sure?" Miriam couldn't hide the slightly concerned tone in her voice.

"Yeah, quite so."

"Like what? Just tell us, please."

"Sure, but it would surprise me a lot if Paulina's lost teddy Herbert was a big, breaking clue."

She unexpectedly stuck her tongue out towards him, and he laughed at her.

"You mentioned that the girls' parents were sacrificed, Cyrus," Caesar said, with that cold tone in his voice again and Miriam hunched involuntarily at his gaze before she composed herself and sat up again with a straight back. "Did she describe how?"

Cyrus shook his head. "Not really, which isn't very surprising. Margery told the girls and Lucas that they had been naughty in the eyes of the Great Mother and that their parents had to go to her and pray for forgiveness. Then the Great Mother had come and swallowed them."

Silence fell heavily in the room. Miriam stared at Cyrus, fear clutching her stomach.

"Um… what do you mean, 'swallowed them'?" she asked eventually, feeling anxious.

He sighed and drew his hand through his hair several times. "I actually don't know. She's not lying. She believes that this is the truth. The Great Mother swallowed her parents. She is absolutely certain about this."

The silence stretched out in the room, and Miriam felt the trepidation grow around the table. Eventually, Caesar put his notebook down on the table and leaned forward on his elbows, watching them intensely.

"No matter what, we need to stop this cult."

There was another bit of silence before Cyrus sighed and stretched.

"I thought you'd say that. Looks like we're off to Alaska then. When are we leaving?"

"Hold on, hold on, hold on!" Miriam said. "We can't just leave things right now. There are some threads we need to tie down first."

"Like what?"

"Our suicide victim at the South Side for example. And the two professor Bruchheimers. And what about Paulina?"

"You're right, Claire, but so are you, Cyrus. I need to check the other you from the hospital before we leave. When it comes to the two Professor Bruchheimers, our best lead is to investigate these 'foster parents'. The eggs and Paulina's story make his murder very much connected to them. We have no lead of where the false Professor Bruchheimer is, but it's likely that we'll find some information about his whereabouts in Bettles. Cyrus, I want you to tie up the loose ends when it comes to the girl. You need to do it today. Claire, you book flight tickets for us to Alaska for tomorrow and rent a car. Choose the closest city to Bettles that has an airport. After that, you can take the day off. You need it."

Miriam nodded and rose, grabbing her bag.

189

"Thanks," she said and headed out towards her minuscule office to book the tickets. Today she couldn't leave work fast enough.

As soon as she managed to leave HQ, only thirty minutes later, she decided, despite knowing better, being hurt and under the influence of strong painkillers, to drive by the nearby Superfresh to pick up some groceries. Thanks to it being mid-day and low traffic, she managed to get to the store without incidents, even though she was sweating and clenching her teeth at the throbbing pain. The rest of the day, she spent picnicking in Millwood Park downtown together with the rest of the city, as it seemed; sunbathing and reading a lighthearted romance novel which she had also picked up at the store, sternly concentrating on the somewhat silly story just to be able to relax.

At five p.m. that afternoon she knocked on Carl's door with mixed feelings of nervousness and excitement, blended together with a strong sense of guilt that she hadn't told Henry about this 'tea date,' whatever that was. It wouldn't have made anything better, telling him about it. Miriam knew perfectly well that it would just end with him getting more weird ideas into that thick head of his, and she wouldn't be able to relax tonight.

Carl answered the door with a rare genuine smile and invited her in. As he took her tomato-red summer jacket and hung it in the closet, she suddenly felt as shy and awkward as a schoolgirl on her first date. She frowned, ill at ease, with cheeks as burning red as the jacket. *Damn you, Henry!* she cursed to herself. *Damn you, Beth! This is NOT a date, damn it!*

The thought that Carl probably knew exactly how she felt embarrassed her even more, but when she shot him a glance, he just took her confidently under the arm and brought her into the kitchen where he opened his amazing tea cupboard.

"Here, have some fun. Choose something."

The air was filled with a sweet and fresh aroma, and the sun that shone into the apartment turned the wooden

190

luster of the cupboards golden. Casually leaning towards the kitchen island a couple of yards behind her, giving her the space she needed, Carl continued talking: "I thought we could start with tea and order pizza later. Not what I originally had planned, but let's just make it easy and cozy tonight."

As she finally let go of all embarrassing thoughts and feelings, and smilingly digging into the rich treasure of tin jars, opening the lids, smelling the different teas, she found herself relax quicker than she thought she would.

"Easy and cozy sounds great," she agreed wholeheartedly. "I'm all for that." Then she held up a red and golden tin jar that even with its lid closed spread an appealing scent. "What's this? It smells heavenly."

"Chai. Perfect for a soft evening."

She looked over her shoulder. "Good choice then?"

"Oh yes. I make one of the most ultimate chai lattes you've ever tasted in this country. Pinkie promise."

Miriam grinned amusedly. "Since I've never tasted one, I'm sure you're right."

He gave her an astounded look. "You're kidding, eh? How can you not have tasted chai?"

With an easy-going shrug, she turned around and leaned towards the cupboard, facing him, still with the jar clasped loosely in her uninjured hand.

"Honestly, I've never been much of a tea fan. I have my chamomile tea with honey, and my lemon-balm slash peppermint tea, also with honey, and that's about it. This here," she gestured towards the tea treasure, "is just crazy. I mean, how can you drink all of this?"

When he surprised her by giving up a friendly laugh, she felt warm in her whole body.

"That's no problem. Trust me," he said, still smiling, before continuing: "But your choice of tea is great. Chamomile and honey loosen up frazzled nerves, and that's very called for sometimes." He reached for the jar in her hands. When she gave it to him, and he opened the lid, the aroma that filled the air made her think of the Arabian restaurant where they'd lunched the other day. "But since you haven't, you simply must taste this. Chai with hot milk and golden sugar is like something even the Queen of Sheba would've enjoyed."

She gave up a friendly laugh. "The Queen of Sheba? Wow, you really mean business here, Carl."

He laughed with her. "You'll see. I bet you'll never again taste anything as good as this, at least not if you're not traveling to India."

As they changed place in the tiny kitchen, and he began to prepare the tea, she mused that it was something like a soothing ritual over it: the boiling of the water in the kettle, the filling of the tea holder, the exact amount of milk and sugar in the pot, the stirring of the milk as it slowly rose to the perfect temperature. It all made her very curious.

"Why tea, Carl? Why not coffee or wine or something?"

He grinned, clearly amused. "Wine? For a Field Researcher? Why, Miri, you surprise me."

The unexpected version of her pet name that he so easily slipped made her heart suddenly beat faster and colored her cheeks rosy. He didn't seem to notice, but she knew better by now. She cleared her throat and looked away. Carl fiddled with the cups.

"We were three in my Star Student class..." he began.

"Three?" Miriam looked back at him, almost not believing what he said.

"Yeah, it'd never happened before. Crazy. Anyway, it was me and Sonia and Simon – they were twins, believe or not – and they were totally nuts when it came to tea. One of their grandfather's grandfather's father or something like that had opened the first tea store in New York, so they had it in the blood, more or less. They taught me a lot. We used to have tea parties in the middle of the night with home baked treats, sharing secrets, giggling like teenagers. Well, yeah, we were still teenagers at that point, so no surprise there, really." He smiled at the memory, and his face turned soft, while

192

Miriam, fascinated, listened to this unknown part of his life. "It was as if we got high and drunk on it. Weird. I mean, tea, eh? But we had fun. And now I can't live without it."

"And you're a great advocate for it too."

"You shouldn't get me going. I can talk about it for hours, the history and the flavor and the difference between black, green, rooibos, herbal..." He laughed at her mocked terrified expression. "Don't worry. I won't."

"I suddenly understand my sister," Miriam admitted. "You know, I could go on and on and on about the Minoans when we were younger, details about their architecture and art and religion, things like that, and she just yawned and then I realized she'd fallen asleep and I'd been talking to myself for the last twenty minutes."

He chuckled and handed her a large mug of tea that smelled delicious. "Funny you'd say that. It's one of my favorite eras in history too. I actually wrote a paper on it once for history class at Western Shore, about the religion. I never thought the difference would be as big as it was compared to the mainland religion."

She felt herself beam towards him. "You did that? Really? I've never even met someone who cares about it before. Yeah, except Dr. Stewart, of course. Wow, you almost make me teary-eyed here." She smiled and continued: "You know, when I was a kid we spent a whole summer on Crete, and I just fell in love with everything: the people, the art, the nature, the culture... When my sister and I went back as adults, it was like coming home."

"Yeah, I noticed your art on the walls when we checked your apartment. Very beautiful."

She radiated at the compliment and had to laugh at herself and how it made her feel.

"I'm feeling silly here," she admitted, "but it means a lot that you noticed it. No one ever has."

He gave her a glance that she couldn't interpret, and then he said with a nonchalant tone: "Well, none of them might recognize beauty when they see it. Don't care about them, Miri. They're not worth your time."

With a smooth grip around his tea mug, he walked out of the kitchen, leaving her squinting suspiciously at him with rosy cheeks and high pulse. *A brock...* she cursed silently at herself, but then she shrugged. She read in anything in everything now, after Henry's outburst and Beth's teasing. As she followed him slowly, careful to not spill anything as she held it tightly with her uninjured hand, the steam that rose from her cup was alluring, and she couldn't stop herself from taking a sip. The full, warm liquid awoke all her taste buds at once in a minor explosion, and she sighed with content.

"Oh, my... Carl, I'm almost fainting here. I had no idea tea could taste like this." She noticed his expression when he looked over his shoulder at her, and she grinned. "Yeah, you've all the right in the world to gloat. And here's another one for you, now you've just got to tell me the history of chai."

He laughed out loud as they took a seat on the sofa. "Do you have all night?"

"Well, technically, yes, but what about the rough details?"

"All right." He took a sip and leaned back, put up a foot on the seat and placed his hands on his knee. "Chai's not the exact word for what we're drinking. It's *Masala Chai*, which means 'mixed-spice tea' in Hindi. *Masala Chai* was originally used in India as herbal medicine and the earliest mention of this particular kind of tea is from Ayurvedic medical texts."

She looked astounded at him. "Really? Wow, I had no idea. That's actually very fascinating. What kind of illnesses was it used for?"

"Mostly to improve digestion and clear up mucus."

"I would claim to be sick every day if this was the medication."

He grinned. "The Ayurvedic traditions are really interesting. It's a lot of body and mind connection, of course. I mean, it's Ancient India we're talking about after all."

"Okay? I mean, sure, I know some tiny bits and pieces about Ancient India and so, being a Star Student and all, but I've never really dug into it very much."

"Fair enough. I guess that when you need to calm down for some reason, you go and get yourself a cup of chamomile and honey, right? Maybe you read a book, or you take a walk or a hot bath, or you just sit and breathe?" She nodded. "Yeah? Well, I do something else. I make my own *Masala Chai*."

She stared at him. "You... you make your own tea?"

"Mhm."

She held up her mug. "Did you make this?"

"No, not this one, but I could if you'd like, later on tonight."

"Yes, definitely. How do you make it?"

Carl looked absolutely delighted by her genuine interest. "First, I place the different spices in small ceramic jars. It's part of the tradition to make it look pleasing. If it doesn't please you, it won't taste good."

Miriam nodded. "Body and mind. I hear you."

"Then you have to touch the ingredients with your fingers. I usually close my eyes and let my fingertips feel the texture. Is it crunchy or soft or silky or downy? Do they have a sound? Do they crack or squeak?" Miriam couldn't help laughing at the thought of squeaky spices and Carl smiled. "After that, I take up the small containers and smell the spices. What kind of smell is it? Does it arouse any memories? What kind of memories? Then I let myself indulge in the sensations and let them form images in my mind. All this is called *The Five Senses Ritual*."

"That's beautiful, Carl," she said sincerely. "Do you think you could you teach me?"

"Sure. It'd be my pleasure."

She took her mug and curled up on the sofa, half turned towards him. While she sipped her wonderful tea… no, *Masala Chai*, she studied him covertly. She hadn't known what to expect of this 'tea date', but it had definitely not been to sit and actually have an interesting conversation about tea. It struck her that only a week earlier, the idea of sitting in Carl's apartment and being totally relaxed would never have occurred to her. If she'd thought about it at all, it had been as a complete contradiction. She smiled and shook her head slightly.

"What?" he inquired.

With a faint blush from being caught, she gave up a slightly embarrassed laugh. "Well… It's just… We've argued so many times… disliked each other for so long…I never thought that you and I would ever be able to have a decent conversation, but now… just look at us."

"I know. It's weird, eh? I'm actually happy that you're here, Miri, and that's really crazy." They laughed together, and she glanced at him again, feeling amazed at the whole situation. "You know what," he said and tilted his head, "there's one thing I've always been curious about. Why did you choose Western Shore University?"

"Hm… Except for the Star Student opportunity, you mean?" He nodded and she felt excited that someone actually wanted to know. *When did that happen last?* She couldn't even remember. "Well, mostly because of their great rep. I mean, being such a small university – which I believe is on purpose, by the way – makes it relatively easy for them to take good care of their students. For me, Western Shore, well, it always felt like home, even from the first day, and the respect that I experienced there… Of course, I met people, both teachers and students, that I didn't like and who didn't like me…"

"Let me guess," Carl interrupted with a smile, "Dr. Atzmüller, eh?"

She looked astounded at him and then burst out laughing.

"Dr. Atzmüller, yes, absolutely."

"Thought so. Probably the least popular teacher at the whole campus I'd say, but I interrupted you. Sorry. Please, go on." Miriam gave him another astounded look. *Apologizing for interrupting me? Really? Henry never does that.* She cleared her throat and tried to find the lost thread. "Respect," Carl helped her.

"Yes, right. Um... there was always this respect for you, both as a person and for your knowledge, you know. And the people that you did like, they became more like a family than anything else. I had done lots of thorough research before I applied and everyone, and I do mean everyone, said the same thing: that the care and respect for the students and teachers were unmatched, and that the teaching methods were different from everywhere else, and that the teachers actually were passionate about teaching. All that just blew my mind. It was very intriguing to me. And then, of course, the Star Student program. I had put my mind to it that I was to become my grad year's Star Student, and then when Noreah got called up on the stage instead of me... my world just collapsed."

Carl was still paying attention, to her surprise. "So you were two that year, or did you reapply?"

"No, we were two, which I'm very happy about. I loved Noreah like a sister, and I think I'd feel very lonely without her. We promised to keep in contact, but afterward, we got into different teams. Her specialty was archeology and, the last time I heard from her, she was going to Iraq on an excavation. That was years ago. I never knew what happened to her. She... she might not even be alive today."

In his face, Miriam saw empathy and understanding.

"Mm... I know that feeling... It was the same thing with Sonia and Simon. Not that I lost contact with them, but they disappeared somewhere on a boat trip. Their bodies were never found."

A sad silence fell for a moment; both of them in thoughts, but then Carl grimaced and moved restlessly on the sofa, reaching for the phone.

"Easy and cozy, I said, and we're talking about death and disappearances. Let's order pizza instead. What do you want?"

She brightened up and let go of the sad thoughts. "Gourmet veggie pizza with lots of tomatoes, artichokes, and black olives."

"And fresh mushrooms and garlic."

Miriam grinned approvingly. "Let's order a really big one. And lots of Coke and garlic bread. If we order from that Swedish-Italian pizza place down on forty-fourth, we can get some of their special coleslaw to go with it."

Carl raised his eyebrows. "Swedish-Italian? Now that's an intriguing combo for a pizza place."

She rummaged around in her shoulder bag. "Here. This is their card."

"Sure thing, if you recommend them."

He took the card and dialed their number. While he ordered she drank the last of her *Masala Chai* and brought their empty mugs out to the kitchen. The sunset drenched the apartment in golden light, and she realized that she felt genuinely happy for the first time in days. Carl came out to her, putting down his cell phone.

"It'll be here within the hour."

"Great. Can't you show me how to make that tea of yours while we're waiting?"

"Now? You don't want to wait 'til after dinner?"

She smiled openly at him, surprised that she felt she could ask for it, even though he hesitated.

"You're funny. I won't be able to swallow a bit after all that food."

"All right." Carl looked pleased after all. "Let's make a small batch. This is a bit different than what we've already had. It's heavier, fuller, so we don't need a lot."

As he started the tea making ritual, she watched his slender fingers work and listened to his melodic voice. As he stepped away and let her try, she realized that he was right; it was very soothing, very uplifting, and very calming. It opened up her senses in a way she hadn't expected and when they sat down on the sofa again, sipping the heavenly liquid from the small Indian glasses, she felt total bliss.

"Carl," she said sincerely, "this has been the best evening in a very long time. Thank you."

To her surprise, he blushed and looked down at his glass. A knock on the door announced the pizza delivery girl, and he got up and came back with enough food for a small army. The smell hit her already sensitive senses, and she realized how hungry she was. She helped him put out plates, cutlery, and glasses on the coffee table and he lit the candles in the tall floor candleholders on each side of the sofa. Miriam poured some Coca-Cola in their wine glasses and swallowed a Tylenol 3.

"How's your hand?" he asked when he saw that.

"Well…" she half-smiled. "Bad. Hurts like hell, but whatever. It'll pass."

He frowned. "Yeah, sorry to hear that. Such weird shit going on in this project…" He stopped abruptly. "Anyway, no job talk, eh? I like watching a movie while eating pizza. That's all right with you?"

"Sure."

"Have you seen *Cold Comfort Farm*?"

"I've read the book and liked it a lot, but I didn't know there's a film too."

"It's a good adaptation of the book, in my opinion, and good actors too."

"Sounds awesome."

They ate pizza and coleslaw and garlic bread, watched the film and laughed a lot; something that felt strange and liberating at the same time. They drank more tea and then they started to watch another film. She should go home, she thought with a grimace. She didn't really want to admit that she was afraid of that entity that might still be there, waiting for her in the dark. Just the thought of it made her heart beat faster and sweat break out on her body. With a glance at the time she saw that it was getting late. *Yes, I really need to go home.*

It's going to be relatively early tomorrow, getting to the airport and all. Need to pack a few things too. But if she was completely honest, even without the entity, she hesitated to leave. It felt so comfortable sitting on the sofa, casually watching a movie with a friend for the first time in years, without feeling any kind of social pressure. *That has never happened before, not with him;* she thought, covertly glancing at his relaxed face beside her, and without caring about if it was rude or not, she decided that she was going to stay until he asked her to leave.

Somewhere near the middle of the film, Miriam started to yawn and had problems keeping her eyes open. *No wonder;* she thought and tried to focus on the screen, but it was just a blur. *Too little sleep, too much pain and stress, combined with strong painkillers... That'll do the trick...* As she closed her eyes and her head gradually slipped down to rest comfortably on Carl's shoulder, she thought about Henry and made a mental shrug. It felt as if she should care, but right now she didn't. Right now she wanted to indulge in the feeling of being happy in the presence of a friend, to feel completely at ease, and to feel a tiny bit like a teenager: spontaneous and carefree. When he put his arm around her, stabilizing her, her heart skipped a beat, and her body stiffened slightly, but with a deep breath, she relaxed again, realizing that she felt completely safe and satisfied with everything. The warmth and the nearness of his body and the faint smell of his eau de cologne worked like a tranquilizer. Soon sleep overwhelmed her.

Much later she became half aware that the film had ended. Carl eased away from her, only to come back to put a pillow under her head and a duvet on top of her. A smile softened her lips as she took comfort in the fact that she was right; she was safe.

"Thank you..." she mumbled before she curled up under the duvet and gave in to sleep again.

Chapter 17

After an early morning that had been nice and relaxed, and – to her surprise – not at all awkward as she had suspected it would be waking up at Carl's place, she had gone home to pack a bag. The whole time at her apartment she had been on her guard, sweating in fear that something would happen, but nothing had stirred the silence. That silence, on the other hand, had felt deeper and more ominous than it should. With way too much time on her hands she had fled the apartment and taken her refuge at a coffee shop until it was time to leave.

Now, coming off the plane in Alaska, the bustling, energetic atmosphere at Fairbanks International Airport struck Miriam as soothing, and so bursting with everyday life that it appeared that nothing strange could ever happen there. She even found herself smiling at the whole commotion. When she and the two men closed in on the exit after picking up their few luggage bags, she went towards the car rental office and, despite knowing better, having a hand that didn't work properly and filled with painkillers as she was, called out over her shoulder: "I'll drive today."

Ten minutes later, she had the keys to a Ford Fiesta in a vapid blue color and was hauling their baggage into the trunk with her healthy hand. When she sat down in the front seat, it dawned her just how much she really wanted the freedom of the road and the power of the engine in her hands. Carl met her gaze in the mirror and winked at her with a little smile. She smiled back and realized that just a couple of weeks ago, heck, just the other day, the fact that he could read her like a book would have ruined her whole day completely, but now she just felt safe and cared for.

When she got out from the airport area, trying to ignore the throbbing pain in her hand and the awkwardness it made driving, Henry opened the window and let a refreshing breeze into the car. It was strange, she reflected; how they all seemed to share the impression of being on vacation, rather than following a strong lead in a research project. *And I wouldn't even mind a vacation with just the three of us...* she thought to herself, somewhat surprised. *At least not as long as Henry keeps a grip on himself,* she corrected. The flight had been smooth, though, which was a relief. They had been able to keep the small talk going without any catastrophes, and Henry had tried his best to behave reasonably. Neither she nor Carl mentioned her visit and sleep-over to Henry. Not that she thought Carl would be that stupid. He'd probably seen through Henry right from the beginning. It irked her, though, that she had to hide it from him as if she had cheated on him.

She glanced at Carl in the back seat, wind blowing through his red hair as he was watching the scenery with a peaceful expression on his face, and at Henry beside her, who gave her one of his old loving smiles, which made her feel warm in her whole body and soul. She let out a happy sigh and gave herself up to the wind, the green countryside, the warm sun, and the silent, but content friendship between the three of them.

The motel she chose had a porch with a white rocking chair and a tiny yard with green grass and a birch. It had to be a good sign, she decided. Carl booked the rooms. Being the end of summer, but still tourist season, she got a room on the ground floor, while Carl and Henry had rooms at opposite ends at the second, and highest, floor. Her room overlooked a small park with a pond on the other side of the road, and she took that as a second good sign.

Miriam put her small personal bag in the closet and went into the blue-themed bathroom. With the dim light in there, she felt like being in a cave or under water. She peed, undressed, and took a long, soothing shower, still indulging herself in the 'I'm-on-vacation' sensation. The alarm clock showed three thirteen when she came out. That was all right, she decided. It wasn't like they were going to start working until tomorrow anyway.

Half an hour later, Miriam stepped into Henry's room. Carl lay casually sprawled out with his lanky body over the bed, arms folded over the big pillow he had brought to the foot of the bed, reading his library book. Henry sat at the only tiny table in the room, absentmindedly going through his notebook. They both looked up at her, Carl with a friendly grin, Henry with a professional nod. She sighed inaudibly at his expression, but shrugged. It probably was best to start working as soon as possible. *But it had been nice with a day off...* She sat down on the floor under the window, toes playing in the square of basking sunlight on the beige carpet. Caesar folded his notebook with a clasping little sound.

"Everyone's ready? Good. I spoke with Health and Social Services. They're open until five. We can just make it if we go now."

The drive to the Department of Health and Social Services was short, but beautiful with the sun shining abundantly from the amazingly blue sky. The many green parks and trees that dotted the city and riverbank made her heart happy. *Green and blue, that's what this city is all about,* Miriam thought as she sat in the passenger seat, resting her throbbing hand, and then: *I could live here.* She pictured herself as a retired, seventy-something grandma, surrounded by children and grandchildren, working in her garden, playing with her pets, and making homemade preserves. Then she scoffed at the thought. *More likely that I'll end up in one of the locked, padded cells at the psychiatric ward. And the winters here would be terrible.* Still, it lingered in her mind, that picture of her as a happily retired woman, enjoying life without fear or nightmares.

Caesar turned left into the parking lot outside the Alaska Department of Health and Social Services' brick-red building and parked opposite the entrance.

"All right, team. Cyrus is going to be the talker here. Claire and I are only here for show and to put some pressure on the caseworker if needed."

"Yes, sir," Cyrus agreed, and Miriam nodded affirmatively.

They took the stairs up to Children's Services on the third floor. A bell jingled merrily when they opened the glass door and stepped into a nice, almost cozy, reception painted in light pastels. The elderly woman behind the desk looked all but merry, though, when she wearily watched them as they approached. She had dark smudges under her eyes and tired lines at the corners of her mouth. The nametag on her gray blouse simply said "Dana."

"Yes?" she asked as they stopped at her desk. Her voice struck Miriam as lifeless and depressed. Cyrus brought out his badge.

"I'm special agent Carl Hansen from the FBI."

"Oh, dear!" the elderly woman burst out with a sudden glint in her eyes. "She got murdered? We all thought it was suicide."

"I'm sorry?" Cyrus said.

"Oh..." She hesitated. "I thought... You're not here for Mary? Mary O'Shannigan? No? Oh dear, I'm so sorry." Her pale cheeks blushed red, and she tapped a pen nervously. "What are you here for then?"

"We're interested in speaking with the caseworker handling the area of Bettles."

The woman looked silently at him a couple of seconds before her gaze wandered towards Miriam and Caesar. Miriam tried a friendly smile without any success. Cyrus waited patiently. Eventually, she looked back at him.

"Bettles?"

"Yes, Bettles. It is the Fairbanks office that handles Bettles' child service, right?"

"Well, yes, but... I don't know..." She frowned and looked down at her pen. Then she pressed a button on the intercom, and an energetic voice was heard.

"Yes, Dana?"

"Kendra, can you come out here for a moment?"

"Sure, just a sec."

204

Dana turned towards Cyrus again.

"Kendra will be out here soon. You can just sit down for a moment."

Some minutes later a young, sweet-looking brunette came out to the reception area. She got a curious expression in her face when she saw the three of them on the sofa, before turning to Dana.

"What's up?"

Cyrus got up from the sofa and went over to the desk in three smooth steps.

"I'm special agent Carl Hansen from the FBI."

The young woman blinked, clearly taken by surprise. "Um... Kendra Swann. Nice... um... Nice meeting you." She nervously gave him her hand, and he shook it with a warm smile. "So how... how can I help you?"

"We're interested in the Phillips family from Bettles. What can you tell us about them?"

She looked at him, puzzled. "The Phillips family from Bettles?"

Miriam imagined that she could hear Cyrus' mental sigh although his friendly expression didn't change.

"Yes, Margery Phillips. She and her family are running a foster home in Bettles. According to my information, it's the Fairbanks' office that handles the town of Bettles."

"I've never heard of her. Sorry," she added when she saw Cyrus' raised eyebrows, "I haven't worked here more than a month." She turned to the elderly woman. "Lorraine should know. It's her area."

"She's still here? I thought she left an hour ago."

Dana pressed the intercom again. Another voice, tired this time, was heard.

"Yes?"

"Can you come out here a moment, please, Lorraine."

"Okay."

Not a minute later another young woman came out, her long black hair, dull and lifeless, covered her face. Like

Dana, she had wrinkles and dark smudges under her eyes. As soon as she saw Cyrus, she stopped mid-step, and an expression of fear flashed across her face. Then she took a deep breath and composed herself, but stopped a couple of feet behind Dana's desk.

Cyrus flashed his badge for the third time, and Miriam had to admire him for the warmth and trust he managed to put into his voice when he told this new woman his name. She looked a bit confused as if she had expected someone else, but stayed silent.

"Mr. Hansen is here to get some information..." the elderly lady begun when Cyrus interrupted her smoothly with a disarming smile towards them both.

"It's Lorraine, right?" The young woman nodded. "Have you ever heard of the Phillips family in Bettles, Lorraine?"

Lorraine's pale cheeks turned white and for a moment Miriam thought that she was going to faint, but she swallowed visibly and seemed to compose herself again.

"Can I see your badge again, please?" she said with a weak voice.

"Of course."

Cyrus brought it out once more. Without touching it, Lorraine scrutinized it thoroughly and then seemed to compare the photo with the man.

"If you want, you can come into my office, and we can talk," she said without any enthusiasm and showed him into the corridor. Caesar and Miriam stood up and followed. Lorraine halted immediately and blinked nervously while biting her already sore lip.

"This is special agent Miriam Goldblum and special agent-in-charge Henry Wittinger, my co-workers."

They both brought out their badges and let her take a look at them. A couple of silent moments later, after she'd studied their likeness with the person on the photos; she nodded and showed them all into an office at the end of the corridor. It was bright with cream-colored walls, a matching vinyl floor, and big green potted plants standing at the window. Miriam and Caesar took the chairs at the wall and let Cyrus sit at the desk opposite Lorraine. She busied herself with organizing some already organized paper piles. Cyrus gave her a minute.

"Lorraine, what do you know about the Phillips'?"

"I... can't say... I don't really... I don't know anything."

"You don't know anything?"

"No... well, yes, in a way... I mean, I know about them. I've heard the name, but..."

She turned silent and rubbed her hands nervously on her threadbare jeans, as she refused to meet Cyrus' steady gaze.

"Do you have any files on them?"

"No." Her voice became more confident, and she managed to meet Cyrus' scrutinizing eyes this time.

"Have you ever handled a child from that foster family?"

Lorraine's cheeks suddenly blushed red, and she looked down again. "No..."

Cyrus observed her for a moment with that well-known emotionless face of his before speaking up again. "Have you ever visited their place?"

"No, I... can't say I... No, I... really can't remember visiting that foster home..."

A sudden tenseness vibrated in the room, and Miriam could see it in Cyrus' shoulders too. "You haven't visited the foster parents, or you don't remember visiting the foster parents?"

She looked up, strung like a bow, her eyes big and frightened as she fixed them at Cyrus. "I... I don't understand..."

"Yes, you do, Lorraine."

Tears suddenly filled her eyes and trickled down her cheeks. "I... don't remember..."

Cyrus' emotionless countenance vanished as he took a box with Kleenex from the table and handed it to her. She helped herself to one and wiped her eyes and nose.

"Thanks," she said barely audibly and clutched the now wet paper tissue to a ball in her hands.

"Tell me about it," he suggested.

Miriam could see how she shied away from his approach even though she still looked him intensely in the eyes.

"How do you know?"

"The same thing happened to me."

"It did?"

"Yes. It was scary."

Lorraine burst into tears again and hid her face in her hands. Miriam could hear her muffled voice: "Oh, my God! I'm not crazy! I'm – not – crazy!" She cried for a couple of minutes before she managed to compose herself. When she looked up, her tired eyes seemed to shine with relief. She watched Cyrus as trustfully as a well-cared child.

"What's going on?" she asked. "Why can't I remember?"

"We're not really sure," he answered her with his warm voice, "but they seem to use some sort of narcoleptic substance that influences the brain's memory center." His steady gaze and confident tone seemed to make Lorraine accept the half-lie as the truth. "Lorraine," he continued, "how did you realize your memory loss?"

She sighed, a deep, shaky sigh. "I had nightmares," she started, looking out of the window, "about children who chased me with enormous knives, screamed at me, accusing me of leaving them to suffer... Sometimes they got me and killed me and... and I was relieved... like I got what I deserved..." She sighed again. "I thought it was the stress. I mean; we cannot help all the children out there. We try to, but sometimes... most times... it's impossible. They're too traumatized. We just have to... try and live with it... one way or the other... Most foster families are good, really good; they

208

really care about the children, but some…" She shook her head. "Some are just after the money and some… just don't … they just don't care about anything. They just want people to harass. We really try to catch up on those families, but once you've gotten the permit, well…" She grimaced, and Miriam wondered if she was aware of the deep bitterness in her voice. If she was, she didn't seem to care that they noticed it. "I mean, I'm not the only one stressed out here. Stress… does take its toll."

"Like Mary O'Shannigan?" Cyrus asked to Miriam's surprise, seemingly out of the blue. Lorraine nodded.

"Yes, she jumped from Wendell Street Bridge six weeks ago. She'd been under a lot of stress lately, and she said that she had started to see Sandra. The psychologist," she added before Cyrus could ask. "Apparently it didn't help. I liked Mary." Her eyes filled with tears again. Absentmindedly, she wiped them off with her hand. "I've been depressed for quite some time, and when Mary died… well… it didn't really… her death didn't really… help me overcome that, so I started to go through some boxes that have been standing in my bedroom closet for some time. Um… organizing things usually helps me calm down…" Nervously, she started to tear the damp Kleenex to pieces. Cyrus waited patiently for her to continue. "Well… in the last box… there were things there… drawings… notes… that I don't remember that I've made, but it's my handwriting and my drawing style, so clearly they're mine."

"What was it?"

Lorraine fell silent and seemed to shy away from the question, but after a moment she inhaled and continued talking with a low voice: "Bunches and bunches of sketches of different children, screaming, crying, holding their hands out to me… People abusing the children… Living trees trying to catch the children… Ramblings that don't make sense… Names… Children's names, some with a cross after… A couple of drawings of a farm and the name 'Bettles' or 'the Phillips family' on them… Even though I don't remember them I... I thought that I might have had something to do with a family with that name, that something had happened there that I forced myself to forget, so I looked it up, and there is a Phillips family living in Bettles, but according to birth certificates and other records it's only an older couple living there with two adult children, no foster children. They don't have any permission to run a foster home, and they've never applied for one." She paused and swallowed hard. "One of the drawings was clearer than the others. I mean, there were no ramblings, just plain information, and some questions. It pictures three children with the text 'Paulina and Lucas Netro and Emilia James, May twenty-fourth, handed over to Margery and William Phillips. Why are there so many children already? Re-evaluation needs to be done'." Lorraine sighed and looked down on the table and the small ripped pieces of the Kleenex. "I looked through older case files here to find them, but there was nothing, not a single line about either the children or the Phillips'. I have no idea where they came from, or why I placed them there, especially... especially since I shouldn't even consider placing them at a family who is not approved. I don't know what year this was, nothing about their family history, nothing at all." After a short silence, she added quietly: "I thought I was going crazy. I even thought that I had visited them a couple of weeks ago to check them out, but I seem to have changed my mind... The gas tank showed that I'd been driving somewhere that day, but I can't remember where..." She looked up at Cyrus again. "I've been thinking about going to the psychologist, but I haven't dared to. I've been too afraid that I actually am crazy, and I...could never bear being locked up. I'd rather commit suicide. No one here would care about it anyway."

"Why?" Cyrus asked. "Are suicides that common?"

"I don't know what you mean by 'common,' but during my time here, which is four years now, there have been two. And then it was Maisie. She just disappeared. Just walked out of her family and never came back. That was last year."

"What did the police say about that?"

"The police?" Lorraine scoffed. "Um... sorry..." Two red spots appeared clearly on her sallow cheeks, but Cyrus just smiled warmly and waved the remark away. She looked down at the desk for a moment, before shaking her head a bit. "Yes, well, the police... They didn't seem to care too much. They thought that she might have taken a hike to New York. She'd talked about it with a friend apparently. I never heard her say anything about New York, but then again, we weren't very close."

"So two suicides in four years? And one disappearance?" Cyrus said thoughtfully. "Were they all depressed before?"

"Yes, very much so, but Fairbanks has one of the highest crime rates in the US, so depression isn't uncommon."

"That might be the case, but I'm still curious about this department. Do you know if your co-workers went to therapy?"

"We all get the offer to meet a psychologist to get our stress levels down. There's one connected to the office that we go to. Not everyone goes, but I know a few who do. They certainly had."

"But you haven't."

"No, not yet. As I said, I was thinking about it, but now, thanks to you..." Her eyes filled with tears again as she smiled towards him. "I don't think I have to."

Cyrus smiled back. Then he leaned in towards her. "Just a suggestion, Lorraine, don't mention anything about what we've been talking about. The Phillips' are dangerous people, and we don't know what they're up to."

The smile disappeared from Lorraine's face, and she looked frightened again, her eyes black in the pale face. "What do you mean? Am I in danger?"

"You might be."

"What... what kind of danger? Are... are they going to kill me?" Cyrus got a concerned look on his face, and he waited one second too long. Lorraine got a stiff, terrified expression on her face for a moment, and then her eyes seemed to bulge out. "You think that they might kill me. No! No, I won't let that happen! There must be some way for you to protect me!"

Caesar opened his mouth for the first time. "Don't worry, Lorraine. We have a good witness protection system. We will contact the people there as soon as we leave your office."

"Witness protection?" Lorraine's laugh had a hysterical tone to it. "You're kidding me! I told you, I don't remember anything!"

"That's true," Cyrus interposed, "but your drawings and notes do."

"Oh..." With a deep breath, she seemed to compose herself. "Will they suffice? Do you want them? You can have them if you do."

"Gladly."

"Do you have a friend, a boyfriend or a family member that you can stay with tonight?" Caesar asked.

"Yes... yes... I can go home to mama and da."

"Do so. We will get you into the protection program a.s.a.p. Maybe as soon as tomorrow, depending on how close the nearest unit is, but I can't promise anything. If we aren't able to get you into the program that soon, stay at your parents' until we can, and call in sick." Lorraine nodded with the look of a frightened child. "We'd like to get that box this evening. Would you mind following us to your apartment and give it to us? We'll see to it that you get safely to your parents afterward."

"Sure. I can do that. Actually," she glanced at her watch, "I was off three hours ago, so we can leave immediately."

"Good," Caesar said and stood up, "let's go."

"Just one more question," Cyrus held up his hand, "what's the name of that psychologist you all get access to here?"

"Sandra Davies. Why? Do you think that... Oh, my God! They all went to her! Mary went to her! She's been asking me a lot how I feel, if I need to talk!" The ghastly mask of fear that suddenly had covered her face started to crack and give way for relief. "I haven't talked to her. She doesn't know about my box."

Cyrus looked stern. "Let's see to it that it continues that way."

Chapter 18

The drive to Lorraine's apartment was silent and tense with everyone in their own thoughts. When they stepped out of the car at the three-story brutalist-style building, Cyrus and Lorraine started to walk towards the entrance, but Caesar lingered behind and grabbed Miriam's arm. Startled, she turned towards him.

"I'll stay here. I need to make a couple of phone calls. See if you can find anything in her apartment, if she's been bugged or such."

Miriam stared at him. "Bugged? We never checked her office."

Two red spots appeared on Caesar's cheeks, and he looked away with a frown. "I know. Stupid mistake. Just like a beginner."

"Then they might know everything!"

He turned back at her at that faint trace of panic in her voice. "Not everything, Mimi, not everything."

"But enough to be well prepared for us!"

He sighed. "Yes. We got careless. We might have underestimated them."

"But..."

"Claire," Caesar's voice was firm. "There might not be a lot of time."

She nodded. "Yes. I'm sorry." She grabbed her CSI bag and hurried after the other two who were still waiting for her at the entrance. Cyrus gave her an inquisitorial glance when she came over to them with her bag in hand, but she avoided his gaze, not wanting to say anything in front of Lorraine. It was enough to have been careless once. She wouldn't make that mistake twice.

Lorraine led them up to the highest level and took the keys out of her left pocket. Before she could use it, Miriam held up her hand.

"I'm going to look around your apartment a bit, if you don't mind, Lorraine." The young woman nodded. "To do so, I need to have complete silence around me. Please do not talk when we enter so I can work as efficiently as possible."

Lorraine stared confused at her. "Um... Okay... Sure..."

She put the key in the lock with a questioning glance at Miriam, who nodded approvingly. When the door opened and they entered, Miriam caught the amused expression on Cyrus' face. He knew very well that she had lied through her teeth.

The first thing that struck her was the smell of garbage, dirty dishes and stationary, dull air. It was hard not to grimace. The evening sun shone hard and mercilessly into the filthy apartment. Used clothes lay everywhere together with empty pizza cartons and hamburger bags, as well as numerous open cans of soft drinks. Hoverflies clouded around old fruit and houseflies buzzed lazily around the rest of the garbage. The TV was on, showing one or another of the gazillions of soap operas that drenched the American TV stations. Miriam released an inward sigh. How was she ever going to find anything important here?

Lorraine made a gesture of turning the TV off, apparently wanting to accommodate the agent's need for silence, but Miriam waved her away from the control. She could see how the other woman stared at her as if she was crazy, but Miriam just frowned irritated and ignored her, not giving the damn about the inconsistency in her behavior. Cyrus still had that amused expression on his face, clearly enjoying the show. For once it didn't bother her. It felt like he was smiling with her rather than at her, and that made the whole difference.

The table lamps were clean. No bugs there. She was going to need a chair to check out the ceiling lamp, so she concentrated on the landline first. Not a minute later, the phone showed her what she was looking for. Miriam scowled at it and reassembled the phone. There was no need to search for anything else. If there was one, there were probably more around, both here and at Lorraine's office. With a glance and a small gesture at Cyrus, who now frowned concerned, she put down the phone and went through the small apartment, looking for something that might catch her eye, but there was nothing in particular. To be able to do a thorough investigation of the place, Miriam would need at least three days to dig through all the dirt. There was no time for that.

When she was done, she went over to Cyrus, who stood at the door with the big box in gloved hands and Lorraine who stood lifeless beside him. Miriam ushered both of them out and didn't even wait until the younger woman had locked the door. She was out with Caesar way ahead of the other two.

"Yes?"

"Yes."

"Curses!" He looked behind her. "Lorraine. I got a hold of the witness protection group. We are extremely lucky. There is a unit in town already. We're going to meet up with them in thirty minutes. As soon as you go with them, you are safe."

Relief made tears flow from Lorraine's eyes. She hid her face in the palms of her hands and sobbed quietly. Cyrus put a gentle hand on her shoulder and moved her towards the car.

Once more, they drove in silence. Caesar navigated the car to a bustling parking lot at the mall downtown where another car waited for them. The two office-clad men who met them shook Caesar's hand and turned towards the young woman.

"Lorraine Ernest?"

"Yes."

"My name is Peter Mulroney. This is Stephan Babic. Nice meeting you." They showed her their badges. "Don't worry. We're going to take care of you from now on, and we're going to do anything we can to protect you from the perpetrators."

Her face was blank from the overload of stress and anxiety.

"Thank you, sir." She turned toward Caesar and Cyrus. "And thank you. I... I... don't know what to say. I probably owe you..."

Cyrus waved the remark away with a friendly smile. "Your being safe is the only thing we want from you, Lorraine. You take care now, and we'll meet again soon."

He shook her hand, and the two agents ushered her into their car. Miriam could see her pale face looking back at them when they drove away.

They ate their dinner sitting in the car. The false feeling of being on vacation was definitely gone by now, and they gobbled down their burgers and fries in a grim silence. Miriam thought of the social worker and how she must have felt when she found that box of hers and no records at the office, how nothing would have made sense to her, and that nagging fear that she was going insane. *What a terrible thing to do to someone.* Miriam shuddered involuntarily and felt her heart fill with sympathy for the young woman.

Finally, Caesar looked up from his food and gave them that emotionless and professional stare that they hadn't seen since the beginning of the case.

"So, team. I made a huge mistake and because of that, our chances to succeed are... minimal... I take full responsibility, and I'm sorry that I've put us in more danger than was necessary."

Cyrus glared back at him. "Hey, C! You do realize that we're three in this team, eh? That means three brains – or no-brains in this case."

"True," Caesar admitted, "but the responsibility is still mine. As the principal investigator of our FRT and after being a field researcher for thirty-five years, I should know better."

"Caesar..." Miriam began, but he held up his hand to stop her.

"Let me finish," he said and then he turned silent. Miriam moved restlessly on the seat, having a bad feeling about whatever it was he was going to say. Then he spoke again, looking them firmly in the eyes. "When you were up in Lorraine's apartment, I contacted Anna of the Faculty. However this will end, it will be my last project."

"What?" Miriam gasped, not believing her ears.

Cyrus sat silent, while watching Caesar intently.

"I'm losing my grip. It's been obvious for some time now, and you know it. I've seen it in your eyes. I need to step down before I put us or anyone else in more danger."

"No!" Miriam almost yelled. "You can't be serious! You don't mean that!"

"Claire." His voice was sympathetic, but firm, leaving no space for questioning. "Cyrus, you will take over as P.I. for the rest of this research project. I will assist you, of course, and give advice if you ask for it, but the decision making is yours. We will get help too. FRT O6 will join up with us tomorrow. Together, we should be able to even out the odds." Silence fell in the car. Miriam was close to tears. Caesar scrutinized Cyrus. "Any objections to your new role, Cyrus?"

"No, sir."

"Good." He sighed and leaned back in the car seat as if a heavy burden had been lifted from his shoulders.

"Um... Hm..." Cyrus cleared his throat. "All right... My suggestion is that we go back to the motel and check our rooms thoroughly. If we find them bugged we need to check out and find ourselves someplace else to spend the night. If not, then I think that we just need the evening and night off. We can't make any plans until O6 turns up tomorrow anyway."

Caesar nodded. "Sounds good. We're supposed to meet them at the downtown library at ten, at the mystery section."

Cyrus smirked. "Suitable enough, I guess."

"Claire?"

She just shrugged, looking down at her hands, lying limp in her lap. "Whatever."

"All right, let's go then," Caesar said and started the car.

The rooms weren't bugged and, according to the receptionist, no one had been asking for them or entered their rooms. That seemed to make both Caesar and Cyrus in a lot better mood, but Miriam knew that if she didn't get to be alone soon, she would start bawling right in front of the men. She just mumbled something to them that could only be translated as "Good night" in the most generous of terms, locked the door behind her, and crept down into bed, crying her eyes out.

She felt so betrayed and lost. Henry had always been there: her kind, safe hero. Six years! He'd been there for her for six years! He could not have done this to her! Who would she lean on after this? Carl? In the midst of all her tears, a very unfair chuckle broke through. She knew how unfair it was. He had really been there a lot for her lately, and she had always trusted his loyalty, and now she suddenly didn't trust him to take the lead? The chuckle died away as she thought of his caring personality that he hid so well, and then she cried for being so mean towards someone who meant so much to her. It suddenly dawned on her that he had started to help her in a completely different way than what Henry did; he made her believe in herself and her own abilities. He made her feel respected. In the midst of all her self-pity, she had a moment of grim honesty. Carl as principal investigator might be exactly what she needed. He would expect her to stand on her own two feet beside him, rather than holding her hand and pet her on her head when things got rough, and he would expect her to carry her own load. Tears started to fall again, this time out of shame of herself and her behavior. Had she been a burden during all these years? Had Caesar protected her too much? Why had she let him do that? No

219

wonder that no one of the previous FRs in C2 really liked her. The image of Conrad's condescending face came to mind, as did Cecilia's pitiful and Cindy's doubting expression. Burning waves of shame flashed continuously over her face, and she didn't know how long she tortured herself by going through incident after incident in which she'd made a fool of herself during the past six years. *If I hadn't been labeled 'Caesar's girl', they'd reported me long ago. I'm not a real FR. I'm a star struck groupie trying to play in the same league as the big boys.* It felt as if she cried for hours before she fell asleep out of sheer exhaustion.

Dawn broke with a heavy rain hammering on the window. Miriam woke up slowly, feeling dazed, after a night of nearly torpid sleep. In the back of her head, a dull pain tried to work itself through. She looked at the alarm clock. Ten to six. No use in going back to sleep. In spite of that thought, she turned on her side and buried herself under the thick duvet.

The alarm clock sounded one hour later. Her headache had blossomed during that time, drenching the dull ache from her injured hand, and every movement made her grimace in pain. She dragged herself out of bed and into the bathroom where she dug out her loyal Tylenol 3:s and swallowed one with the cold water from the bathroom tap. The shower was hot and made muscles she didn't even know were tense relax. Today, she just wanted to snuggle up under a blanket with a cup of hot tea, and not meet anyone, not look anyone in the face. Instead, she put on the only pair of jeans she had brought with her, old, comfortable and almost velvety in texture, a soft black linen shirt and her likewise black trench coat, before heading to the European café across the street for some hearty breakfast. Her hair was still damp and tousled under the new umbrella she had just bought at the reception desk. *I can't redo these years;* she thought regretfully, *but I can start anew today, behaving as a real FR should, on my own two feet. I will never again hold anyone's hand because it's the easy way out.*

Carl and Henry were already waiting for her. As they enjoyed fresh pressed orange juice, sweet ripe peaches, large sandwiches with cheese, ham and vegetables, thick and smooth Greek yogurt with locally produced honey, cereal and strawberries, and hot black coffee, they watched the rain coming down like there was no end to it.

"It feels surreal," Carl said after a while, "after this whole summer without even a drop of rain and suddenly you can't even see the opposite pavement because of it."

Henry smiled. "I bet the sun is shining back home, though."

"Probably," Carl agreed. "I don't know if this rain is to our advantage or disadvantage, though. I mean, no one will notice us driving to the library, that's for sure, but we'll never be able to blend in once there, especially if we're going to be the only ones around."

"Hm, I think you're right," Henry frowned thoughtfully.

"If someone's trying to track us, they'll definitely see who we're meeting with too," Miriam added. "What do you say, Cy? Shall we split up? I can go meet the O's." She looked down at her jeans. "I'm probably the one of us who'd blend in the best."

Disapproval was clearly shown all over Caesar's face, but she didn't care, and Cyrus didn't seem to notice. *Which is probably what he wants*, Miriam thought. It was a good mask to have; she had to give him that. He tapped his fingers thoughtfully on the table's edge.

"I don't know," he said after a second. "It's probably not safe, and safe is what we absolutely want to be now. I have a distinct feeling that we're closing in on something big, and that we might be in more danger than before. On the other hand, I don't like the idea of the Phillips' knowing that we're getting reinforcements."

"It's possible that they already are aware of that," Caesar said, still frowning. "They might have been bugging our phones or our clothes."

221

Miriam shook her head. "I don't think so. The bug I found yesterday was crude. Lorraine could've found it herself had she just been looking for it. I don't think they know what they're doing when it comes to that kind of technology."

Cyrus checked his watch. "We need to decide now what we're up to, if we're indeed up to something. We'll meet the others in twenty minutes."

"Just let me off a block from the library," Miriam said hastily. "That way you'll be able to see if someone's following me. I'll give you a call as soon as I've entered the place, and then I can probably get a ride with the O's to... say... what about the parking lot at the mall, where we were yesterday?"

Cyrus nodded. "All right, seems like a sound enough plan. Hasty, but sound. Let's go."

As she smiled brightly at him and Caesar glared displeased at them, Cyrus swallowed the rest of his coffee, pulled out the car keys from his pockets and jingled with them all the way to the car. Caesar chose the back seat this time, still with a sullen look, leaving the front to the other two.

The drive downtown took them eight minutes, and theirs was the only car out on the streets, at least as far as she could see. She frowned uncertainly. Shouldn't there be at least a couple of other cars out here together with theirs? *It's still a town, there are still people running errands, even at this time, right?* As Cyrus' had said, it felt surreal, like a dream or a horror movie. Miriam suddenly shuddered.

When she was let off, she pulled out her umbrella and hurried briskly towards a light-yellow sandstone building at the end of the street that gave way to the beautiful, lush park that surrounded the library. The rain pattered at the black nylon above her head and, together with the empty park, it gave her an ominous feeling. Usually, she liked this kind of weather, but now, it only made her feel anxious. Even as she told herself not to check her surroundings, she did just that. There was nothing to be seen, nothing at all, which she perceived as an ill omen in itself.

Finally, she reached the library and speeded up until she jogged over the insignificant-looking bridge that led to the front doors. As she turned and folded the umbrella, she quickly glanced around the park once more. There was still no one to be seen. She pulled up one of the big doors and went inside. The young receptionist behind the desk looked up and smiled at her as she approached.

"Wet outside today, right?" she said with a friendly nod.

"Yes, very." Miriam returned her smile as she covertly studied her, not really trusting anyone at this point. The girl looked innocent enough with her discreet make-up and her long, black hair neatly braided. A tiny silver moon-crescent hung around her neck in a beautifully crafted silver chain that seemed to be an heirloom, and the blue sweater revealed her curves without drawing attention from her pretty face. The deep blue went well together with her own colors. Obviously, she was great at choosing clothes that enhanced her appearance and beautiful almond-shaped eyes. *A bit young, maybe. Do they graduate teenagers at the university nowadays? And no name badge. Shouldn't she wear one if she really worked here?*

"Anything I can help you find, ma'am? Any particular book you're looking for?"

"Not really, I'm just going to look around for a bit, if you're just kind enough to point me towards the mystery section."

"Absolutely. It's a great day for mysteries, that's for sure. Just over at the back wall, not far from the washrooms. You'll see three other cheechako's around there too."

She pointed in the direction. Miriam thanked her and headed towards the large section. *What's a cheechako? Outsider? Tourist? Woman?* She hadn't gotten far before she saw three women sitting around a table reading books. Before she reached them, she stopped and picked up her phone and dialed Caesar's number out of sheer habit, without as much as looking at the sign with a crossed-out cell phone. As soon as he answered, she remembered.

223

"Ah, damn!" she whispered. "I forgot to call Cy. Anyway, I'm in."

Then she hung up before he could reply and put the phone down. One of the women at the table looked up at her in an analyzing way before going back to her book, seemingly dismissing her, which meant that her casual clothes worked. That raised her spirits somewhat. Miriam contemplated the books on the shelf without actually seeing them, while she was covertly watching the three women who were ignoring her. As she slowly let her finger run over the books, she took in all the details. From this distance, she couldn't discern any rings, but she was sure that this was Team O6. They were all three physically fit and dressed in business clothes, and the air of FBI lingered all over them. *Cheechakos;* she thought. *Doesn't matter what it means. They are clearly cheechakos. Can't blend in if their lives depended on it.* As she got closer, she could study their faces too. For some reason she couldn't explain, she thought that the woman with the warm, hazelnut-brown hair, softly made into a bun, was the P.I. She was probably around her mid-thirties, Miriam pondered, with a heart-shaped face that struck her as pretty and unusual. The dark eyes were large and added to the somewhat doll-like appearance. She seemed to be engrossed in her novel, unlike the woman opposite her, who apparently had a hard time concentrating on her novel. Time and again she put it down on the table before her and let her gaze wander around. Every time Miriam happened to meet it, she felt as if she was staring into the eyes of a hawk and she quickly looked away. The air around her was aggressive, Miriam thought, after meeting that restless gaze for the third time, and it had a diminishing impact on her even at this distance. Her thick and shiny black hair hung loose and framed her somewhat long face. Miriam couldn't help admiring her warm olive-colored skin and dark eyes, with a pang of envy. Throughout her youth, she had always wished for a skin color like that herself.

The third woman was African-American and definitely the youngest of them. She had a naïve and innocent

224

air around her, and she seemed to be flanked by the two other women's more dominating personalities. As Miriam covertly studied her, it struck her that the choice of keeping her long, black hair neatly braided in a cornrow hairstyle with orange glass beads at the ends, probably made her look younger than she actually was. *She doesn't look to be more than nineteen, and that can't be the case.*

At this point, Miriam had reached the end of the bookcase. Without looking, she chose one book, and, trying to look casual, she stepped up to the table where a couple of chairs were unoccupied. The women ignored her. She cleared her throat, and three pairs of eyes stared coldly at her. With a friendly nod at each of them, she asked: "Is this chair available?"

The brown-haired woman gave the nearest empty table a meaningful look. When Miriam didn't react on the cue, she shrugged and continued to read her book, but couldn't hide an annoyed frown on her forehead. As Miriam glanced at her, hoping that she hadn't irritated the woman too much, she noticed how her eyes were surrounded by a tiny web of wrinkles, definitely placing her in her mid-to-late thirties. Before sitting down, Miriam quickly eyed their hands to make sure that they wore the rings. Immediately she discerned the tiny band of stars that discreetly adorned the left little finger on each of the Field Researchers, and felt happy that she'd been right.

"I'm Claire," she said as she placed herself on the nearest empty chair. Once again, she was the center of their emotionless, scrutinizing gaze, and she saw them looking for her own Star Student ring. The black-haired lady with the warm olive-colored skin snorted, and her dark eyes squinted in disgust for some reason that eluded Miriam, but the condescending expression instantly made her feel too young and ignorant and insecure again.

"Really?" she said with a contemptuous tone that made Miriam cringe inside.

The brown-haired woman scowled at her team-mate before turning to Miriam again. "I'm P.I. Olwen," she said somewhat brusquely, and once again a happy, proud feeling that she'd been right, rose inside her.

The very young woman opposite her nodded at her with a sweet, friendly smile and put her book down. "I'm Omega. Nice meeting you."

It felt like a relief that not everyone around the table was hostile towards her, and she gave the young Field Researcher a warm smile of her own. As they looked at each other, Miriam had a feeling that the two of them would work very well together.

The black-haired woman inspected her once more, and Miriam shifted focus towards her.

"Oona," she said eventually with a gruff voice. "Why are you alone?"

"Caesar and Cyrus are waiting at the mall parking lot," Miriam explained and hated how her voice became feeble and mouse-like at the other woman's dominant antagonism. "We might be followed and didn't want to raise any attention."

Oona snorted again. "Stupid."

Olwen scowled at Oona once more and got a provocative glare back. Omega got up from the chair with a nearly inaudible sigh as she wearily glanced at the other two.

"It's no use sitting around here, then. Claire probably knows better than we do about the situation and..." Before she could finish her sentence, Oona interrupted her.

"I certainly hope so."

Miriam couldn't help raising her eyebrows in something that felt like a perfect imitation of Caesar. Olwen gave Oona another stern stare and turned towards Miriam.

"Our car's at the back door. Take this library card and borrow that book, then you'll just meet us outside. It's a white Chevrolet."

"Okay."

With a deep feeling of relief for getting away from Oona and Olwen, and at the same time feeling ashamed for feeling relieved, Miriam took the card and glanced at it as she hurriedly walked away. It was subscribed for a certain Ann Wheeler. When she got to the desk, the librarian looked up from her own book with another brilliant smile. As Miriam handed the book over to her, she viewed it with an approving nod.

"*The Further Side of Fear.* Helen McCloy. Great choice. You'll enjoy it for sure, Ann."

She registered it, put it in a plastic bag for her, and gave it back.

"Thank you," Miriam said and took the bag.

"Have a nice and cozy day," the librarian said as Miriam went for the doors. "Don't forget to brew yourself a nice cup of tea."

Chapter 19

After a short ride in awkward silence, the Chevrolet parked beside FRT C2's rented car at the partly underground mall parking lot. Miriam got out as quickly as she possibly could and despite all promises she made during the night of standing on her own two feet, she sought silent refuge with Caesar and Cyrus, who just stepped out of their car. Cyrus gave her a probing glance before turning towards the other agents, apparently looking them over. Olwen and Omega calmly returned his gaze, but Oona crossed her arms over her chest.

"Principal Investigator Cyrus," he said and turned towards Olwen. She nodded with a friendly smile.

"I'm P.I. Olwen. This is my team: FR Oona and FR Omega. We're pleased to be able to help you out with this project. Claire wanted to wait until we were all gathered before she filled us in on the details."

"As if she knew any," Oona muttered under her breath.

Olwen turned on her heel as she angrily stared at the black-haired researcher, lips sternly set, but before she could say anything, Cyrus stepped in.

"Excuse me?" he said, overly polite. "Did you just imply that my Field Researcher does not know her job?"

Omega stared Cyrus defiantly in the eyes. "She doesn't seem to have a lot of routine, that's all."

"'That's all'?" Miriam felt her anger fume, but the words hit her hard and shame flashed over her again. "I've been an FR for six years and don't you dare talk about me as if I'm not here!"

"Oona, it's actually none of your business," Olwen said wearily.

"Yes, it is," Oona answered. "If she lacks routine she can get us all killed."

Cyrus watched the other Field Researcher coldly. "FR Claire does not lack routine, and your superior is right, it is none of your business. You, on the other hand, can be dangerous if you are going to question everything we do. I, along with my team, am in charge of this research project. You will act on my orders or not act at all. At this point, you still have the opportunity to back out if that does not suit you. I do not want you on this team if you are going to cause any trouble. Is that clear, Field Researcher Oona?"

Silence fell, as all of them were watching Oona. Rain came pouring down outside the parking lot, dampening the sounds and hiding them from the outside world.

"It is, Principal Investigator Cyrus," she said, at last, then turned and looked at Miriam with unsympathetic eyes. "If it matters to you, I'm sorry that I questioned your competence."

Miriam, still angry, just shrugged. Then she saw Cyrus frown at her.

"Apology accepted," she muttered.

Olwen let out her breath. "Matter settled," she said. "Let's get this project rolling. Please, Cyrus, fill us in on the details. The only thing we know so far is that we're dealing with some kind of faction that uses unorthodox methods to deal with people."

"That's right. I'll let Caesar do the filling-in for you. He's the real academic head amongst us," Cyrus said and turned towards the older man.

"Yes," Caesar said and brought forward his notebook, turned some pages and cleared his throat. "This is believed to be a faction that seems to have a religious foundation. Evidence speaks of 'The Great Mother,' for example, and one of their customs seems to be to either remove or burn their genitals. There is a religious group of Russian origin which uses the same tradition, but for totally different reasons. Therefore, we believe this to be something else completely. The one place we have found that seems to be a base of operations is a family of child collectors; the Phillips family.

229

Their house is located in the small community of Bettles, situated two hundred and forty miles northwest of Fairbanks. Margery and William Phillips and their adult children Warren and Roxy Phillips seem to brainwash the unregistered children living at their home into becoming sect members, using all kind of torture: physical, mental, and sexual. The children that refuse to worship 'The Great Mother' disappear. Three additional males live at the farm, and they take part in the abuse. We know that the members of the sect have unusual skills, at least all that we have encountered. They can use mind control to make people forget about them and their whereabouts, as well as taking on the appearance of another human being. They don't hesitate to commit murder. The two different *modus operandi* we have encountered are ritualistic murder and the planting of carnivorous eels inside the victims' stomachs. When these eels mature, they eat the victim from the inside." He looked up at the three stone-faced FRs of team O6. "Any questions?"

Once again, the silence was only interrupted by the steady raining. Then Oona took an involuntary step to the side and shook her head.

"There are a lot of 'seems to be' in your briefing, FR Caesar. I take it that you don't have enough proof to go with your statement."

Caesar gave her a steady gaze. "That is correct, and it is also the usual way for us Field Researchers to work, without enough proof, which is why we follow different rules than FBI agents, police officers, and military personnel. As an experienced Field Researcher of GFS, you should be well aware of this."

A fierce blush showed on Oona's face, and she looked angrily down at the pavement. Omega glanced at Oona without any expression at all on her face before turning towards Caesar and raised her dark, velvety voice: "You say that the sect members use mind control. Do I understand it correctly when I say that they make people forget that they've met the sect members?" Caesar nodded. "How do you know?"

"We have firsthand experience of it, as well as witnessing and questioning other people who are victims of it."

Olwen broke in. "If you have firsthand experience, how do you know that you've been exposed?"

Caesar smiled. "A very good question, P.I. Olwen. It doesn't seem to be one hundred percent reliable. Memories slip through, for example."

Olwen nodded thoughtfully. "I see. But I'd think it to be a good enough tool to use in a situation where you want to avoid attention for a difficult project."

"Yes, that's how they've been using it, one on one on security guards and social workers. Very efficient for a short time, but once again – sorry about that, Oona – it seems that a strong enough mind fights against it."

"Interesting," Olwen remarked and frowned. "And dangerous."

"And our specific task is to take down this family, right?" Omega asked.

"Yes," Cyrus said, "and hopefully be able to arrest the adults and rescue the children. If, however, it's not possible to make any arrests, we have clearance to kill them. Any other collateral damage or victims amongst the children are sad and discouraged, but if impossible to avoid, there will be no consequences for us."

"I see..." Olwen said and looked down. "Well, hopefully, we'll manage to save those children. It's most likely that they ended up at that place by mere chance without any connection to its deranged cult, but if they've been brainwashed, we must be prepared that they might fight back. Do we know the age range amongst them?"

"As far as I know," Cyrus said, "there are around twenty children from around three and up to around sixteen."

"Do you know how many of them are teenagers?" Oona asked.

"Not really. The numbers I have come from an escaped witness and are one and a half year old."

"So, what's the plan, Cyrus?" she asked, her previous antagonism gone and she looked resolute instead.

"The Faculty has arranged so we have access to surveillance equipment at the local PD. The plan is to use it to get a grasp of the routine of the family, but we'll have to see how much time we've got for surveillance. They might suspect that we're around." Oona raised her eyebrows with a new condescending look on her face, but Cyrus ignored her, and the expression disappeared quickly. "The one thing I really would like to know is the schedule of their religious ceremonies, if they have any. Are they mainly during daytime, or during nighttime? If they're daytime based, we'll break in during the night when – hopefully – everyone's asleep. That would make things much easier."

"Things are never easy in this job," Oona muttered.

Cyrus nodded to acknowledge her. "True, but one can always hope, eh?" he said with a wry smile. "Another question is," he continued, "if they keep dogs or armed guards, and also how difficult it will be to get in. I think our best bet is to try some manual surveillance for about... say three days and nights before we plan our move. That should give us plenty of time to figure out their schedule."

Olwen nodded approvingly. "I think you're right. What about getting our gear together and then take a nice lunch somewhere warmer than here before we start the journey?"

Everyone smiled, and the atmosphere lightened.

"I think that's a great idea," Caesar said. "There's an Italian restaurant we've been driving past a couple of times that looks inviting. Anyone against that?" When everyone looked eager enough, he chuckled and said: "Well then, let's get into our cars and get moving."

Within the next few hours they had picked up all the surveillance gear and extra weapons at the local police station; bought heavy rain clothes, boots, backpacks, sleeping bags,

232

tents and a kerosene stove at a survival store; and groceries at Superfresh. Team C2 checked out from the motel, and they took turns driving the almost nine hours from Fairbanks to the rural and mostly uninhabited area where the Phillips family farm was located, the whole time covered by the pouring rain. Miriam had started to bless the downfall, since it would be almost impossible for anyone to follow them without being discovered, judging by the complete lack of other cars on the road. On the other hand, it felt downright spooky sitting in one of two lonely cars on an empty road while the rain hammered in wrath on the roof. It was as if the rest of humanity had died.

The landscape was covered with dark-green pine trees, only visible as a darker, almost solid wall through the rain. In the early morning hours, they drove past the insignificant sign that pointed towards the entrance of the farm. From her seat in the back, Miriam could see the white painted houses behind split-railed fences. At some distance from the main house, an enclosed pasture sat where white-and-brown spotted cattle grazed. It looked lonely, but even so, it was impossible to imagine such cruelties taking place here as those Paulina had told Cyrus about. A couple of miles later, Cyrus drove into a clearing and parked to the side, letting team O6's car catch up.

"All right," he said when they all gathered around him, "Let's try to find a couple of good spots for surveillance and a good one for camp. I guess that we have at least the rest of the day hidden, so to say, thanks to the rain. Let's make as good use of it as possible. If we split up, we might have a better chance of finding our spots. My suggestion is that Olwen and Caesar go together, Omega and Claire, and Oona and I make pairs."

When no one objected, Cyrus reached into his bag and brought out six walkie-talkies and three local maps companioned by compasses that he handed out to everyone.

"Where are we going to hide the cars?" Olwen asked.

"I guess that 'hide them' might be an overstatement in this landscape, but hopefully, we'll find one of the desolated farms that are supposed to be around here according to the map, or, even better, a clearing that's more obscured by trees than this one."

"So just let them stand here for now, then?" Cyrus inspected the cars and the landscape with a frown. "You and I can drive our car to this ruined house here," Oona suggested, pointing with her finger at a spot on the map. "It's only some hundreds of yards further down the road and might not be as conspicuous as leaving both cars here."

"Good thinking. Let's do that." He nodded towards the others as he and Oona turned and got into O6's car, Oona in the driver's seat. Olwen faced the rest of them.

"Omega and Claire, if you track in the east-southeast direction, Caesar and I will take the east-northeast direction. Let's keep in touch every thirty minutes."

They all grabbed their backpacks and started walking. The trees of the thick pine forest grew so close that Miriam had to duck all the time to not get too many low-hanging branches in her face and then squeeze between the trunks. The resistance soon made her pant for breath, even though she considered herself fit. Omega gave her a friendly smile over her shoulder.

"Not used to being out of the city, are you?" Her voice sounded a bit muffled coming from inside the thick rain gear.

Miriam smiled back. "Not really. I mean, yes, I'm out at a lake once every year, but I guess sitting by the lakeshore with a drink at sunset doesn't really count."

Omega laughed. "It depends on what you're counting, love."

Miriam laughed too, feeling more at ease with this young woman than with any of the other two in team O6. "So what about you?" she asked with a bit of curiosity. "What's your background? I take it that you're not one to sit behind a desk the whole day."

234

"That's correct," Omega said with her warm smile. "Both Oona and I are Rangers, but even though Oona started as Star Student in her green and innocent youth, I got the chance to take a year-long training course at Western Shore after an op that went fubar three years ago, so I guess I'm not a 'real' FR, according to some." She shrugged indifferently. Apparently she couldn't care less, which made Miriam feel a slight touch of envy. *I'll get there too, one fine day;* she promised herself. "Every now and again we get called in on these kinds of ops. In a way, they're not very different from what I'm used to. We're still out in the field, and we're still shooting the enemies. It's just what you're considering 'the enemies' that changes."

"Huh... Yeah, I guess..." Miriam frowned. "Well, I'm from the FBI, as are Cyrus and Caesar. We usually get the weird cases no one else can handle."

"Like this one?"

"Yes, like this one. I don't know how it works within the Rangers, but it's pretty much standard procedure at the FBI to hand over odd stuff like this to us. Everyone there knows that the former Star Students that work for the FBI are specialized for these kinds of cases."

"Huh..." Omega frowned thoughtfully. "That's... I don't know... trusting?"

Miriam shrugged with a half-smile. "It works," she said. "Every time someone gets a case that seems out of the ordinary in some way, they call Caesar, who takes a look at it and then decides if it's up our alley or not. It doesn't happen that often – maybe once a year or so – and in between, we work as regular agents. Well, except for last year. Last year we had two projects. I've never had that happening before." Miriam frowned at the thought of the two failed projects, but shrugged. There was no need to think of them here and now.

"Very interesting way of procedure, I have to admit. Can't say if it'd work for us, but hey, every organization's different, right?"

They walked in friendly silence for a while. The backpack started to weigh down on Miriam's shoulder, and her damaged hand hurt. She had put a large plastic Ziploc bag secured with several elastic bands on it to protect the bandage from the rain, but even though it was kept dry, it ached nonetheless. Being hit by unfriendly branches twenty times per minute didn't really help either.

They had reported back to the other teams every thirtieth minute for two hours when they literally stumbled upon a perfect spot for a camp, at least that's what Omega told her. It was a small glade flanked by relatively high hills. As Omega said: "It'll be hellish with all the mosquitoes, especially after this rain, but on the other hand, no one will see us light a fire. We can use that area there for a kitchen hut, and I'll dig a latrine on the other side. Good thing we're the ones with the tent, but you can't do anything with that hand of yours, right?"

"Not much," she admitted, "but I can hold lines and such with my other hand if that would help."

"As long as you can function as a counterweight, I can do the rest. Let me just contact Cyrus and Olwen and give them the coordinates. We need to get that kerosene kitchen and the food over here. I don't know about you, but I'm hungry, and I'm craving something hot."

They managed to raise the tent and prepare what Omega called a kitchen in just thirty minutes thanks to the ranger's long field experience. Omega had just started working on a latrine while Miriam with her feet tried to tie down the high grass when Oona came into the little glade.

"Here's the food!" she called out to Miriam with the first genuine smile she'd ever seen on Oona's face. She stopped in the middle of the camp and looked around. "Nice place you gals have found."

"Thank you," Miriam said with an almost genuine smile of her own, determined to stand on her own feet. "It was mostly Omega's work. She's over there, digging the latrine."

"We've found a good spot for surveillance, as well. Cyrus is setting it up right now."

"Good. Let's just hope that Caesar and Olwen are that lucky too."

"Oh, I've no doubts about it. That's the food preparation area?" She pointed towards a small sheltered area with a temporary kitchen bench made out of an old log, and a bowl for dishwater. Miriam nodded. "Good thing you've got it up already. I'm hungry as a wolf."

On Oona's orders, Miriam started to chop carrots, potatoes, and celery while the other Field Researcher got the kerosene kitchen to work. The chunks she managed to cut were uneven and thick, and her hand ached like hell, but she was more than happy to not be a burden. Oona laughed and shook her head when she saw the result, but it was friendly enough.

"I'll do the cooking. That's usually my task during ops and projects, and I'm quite good at it. I hope you like spicy food. Gets you warm inside."

Miriam couldn't help smiling again, completely genuine this time. "I guess we need that. It sure is chilly. And all of us for our part like spicy food, so just do your thing."

An hour later the heavenly aroma of the veggie stew that lay over the campsite made Miriam's mouth water and her stomach growl loud enough for the others to hear. They just laughed at her.

"But you know," Omega said with a grin, "I've taught mine to growl politely. You can't hear it."

"It's actually ready to eat now," Oona said and scooped up a generous portion to her. "Hopefully, the others turn up soon. We can't work attentively if we're hungry, and we can't manage on survival bars only."

As if he had heard her, Caesar walked into the glade with tired steps. "Olwen chased me away," he said. "I was a little bit grumpy about it, but not anymore. I hope you have some of that deliciously smelling food left for a hungry man."

237

Oona scooped up another plate, and Caesar sat down with a heavy sigh beside Miriam. Without another word, he started to gobble the hot stew down. The others followed his example. Fifteen minutes later, Cyrus showed up. As he sat down with a plate of his own, he looked over the camp.

"Very nice work, team. Very nice, indeed. And this food is fabulous. Wow. Just wow." Miriam saw both Omega and Oona smiling happily at the praise, and she felt rather pleased too. *Not a burden this time,* she thought. *Won't be ever again.*

Cyrus continued to talk as he wolfed down his food. "We need to man those surveillance sites. I've already talked this over with Olwen, and we've decided on a guard schedule. During the night, we'll have three-hour shifts, but throughout the day the shifts will be six hours each. That gives us plenty of time to rest and also to get a good grasp of the family's routines, as we've already discussed." Everyone nodded. "There's some bad news, of course. At the back of the main house, there's a dog kennel. You can't see it from the road, but we have a good view of it from our surveillance spots."

"How many dogs?" Omega asked.

"Five. Big German Shepherds, of course. I mean, why would any suspicious group settle for Pomeranians?"

Laughter rose from the small group and the smile on Cyrus' face was wry. "Anyway, as soon as I'm finished here, I'm going to take the first shift at what we now call Site A. If you hand your maps over, I'll mark the spots for you." As they did that, he continued talking: "The first shift will end at midnight. Oona will take the shift from midnight to three a.m., and Claire takes the shift from three a.m. to six a.m. Those are the night shifts at Site A. Meanwhile at Site B, Olwen will take the first shift, Omega the second, and Caesar the last. Day shift at Site A will last a little longer. I think I already mentioned that, right?" They nodded. "All right. So, first shift will be me again from six a.m. to noon, Oona will take noon to six p.m., and Claire will take six to midnight. Then I'm on again until three. We're doing the same shifts

238

and same order at Site B." He looked them all over, but no one raised any counterarguments. "A rifle with a silencer will also be present at each spot at all times. Don't use it for any reason if you're not attacked. We don't want to reveal ourselves." They all nodded again. "All right, I suggest that everyone clean their plates and then get some sleep." Then he followed his own example and went to the kitchen area, where he poured some water in the dishwasher bowl and cleaned his plate and fork, before heading out again. As Miriam watched him leave, she felt immensely proud of his natural leadership style. *It's like he's born to do this. Never thought he had it in him;* she thought, and it struck her that it was true, seeing how team O6 accepted him as the leader without any questions.

Standing up with a grunt, Caesar said: "I'll wash that pot. It's not fair that people who cook also should clean," He was immediately rewarded by a brilliant smile from Oona.

Just then Miriam realized how tired she was. While she was waiting for her turn at the washing bowl, she went in and put her sleeping bag in order. Omega and Oona joined her shortly afterward. Half an hour later the camp was silent, and everyone left was asleep.

Chapter 20

When Miriam had been released the next morning after an uneventful watch, it had stopped raining, and the dawn promised sunshine. It was still damp in the air, and the pines wore dresses of glistening dewdrops. She walked with a smile on her face at the serene beauty. When she got to the camp, she put water to boil on the kerosene stove for tea and helped herself to some sandwiches and Fruitsations, a huge difference from what they ate the other day, but the serene beauty of nature made up for the meager meal. She sat alone on one of the hills and watched the landscape bathe in the rising sun while she drank her simple peppermint bag-tea and ate her breakfast. Birds chirped everywhere and her heart and soul filled with plain happiness at the beauty around her.

The day proceeded slowly. She had time to actually rest for what felt like the first time since this project had begun. She brought out her sleeping bag in the sun and started to read the book she'd borrowed from the library. In the afternoon, she yawningly put away the book and took a long nap in the basking sunshine. When she woke up, she ate dinner, and when it was her turn to take the evening shift, she was refreshed. No one had seen any strange things that day, just children taking care of the farm. They looked well fed enough; Oona said when Miriam released her, with no signs of abuse.

"No adults?" Miriam asked concerned.

Oona shook her head with a thoughtful expression on her face. "None whatsoever. It's weird, now that I think about it. Ah well, maybe they're like Dracula, popping out and showing their ugly faces only when it's dark." Miriam laughed with her and Oona waved and went back to the camp.

She had been watching the empty farm for approximately two boring hours, and she was desperately trying to stay awake while yawning so hard that her eyes watered, when the children, about twenty of them, suddenly came running out from the farmhouse, screaming and laughing. Miriam grimaced. She had never been particularly fond of children, and less so screaming children in groups. They were playing some kind of game, she assumed, some intricate form of tag from what it looked like. She let her eyes wander away for a minute. When she looked back at the farm again, she realized that this form of tag involved not pats on a shoulder, but punches wherever they managed to reach. It seemed to be especially popular to hit someone in the face. When a little boy got a fist right on his nose so hard that it started to bleed, and he began to cry, all the other children whooped and laughed and applauded. Then they physically kicked him out of the game. He disappeared into the house, still crying and bleeding. Miriam moved uncomfortably on the grass, wondering where the adults were. The game went on with more punches leading to bloodshed until there were only three older children, probably young teenagers, left. They put their arms around each other and sang something that even from this distance had the distinct sound of a victory song. Then they too disappeared into the house, and everything went quiet.

At midnight, Carl released her. She told him about the game and he frowned.

"And no adult around during the whole day? Not that I'm actually surprised after what Paulina told me, but it's one thing to hear it and a totally different one to see things that indicate she was right." He sighed wearily and threw a hand through his hair. "Last night was uneventful, just that older lady spending some hours at the barn. If this one follows the same pattern, it would at least indicate that they're all asleep during night time."

"Mm, that would be great. We could use some advantage."

"Yeah. After tomorrow night, we should have a good enough understanding of their procedures to be able to plan our next step." Miriam couldn't stop herself from a long yawn and Carl laughed at her. "Look at you. Well rested enough to swim across the Atlantic and then climb Kilimanjaro."

"Right..." She yawned again.

"Hm, if you didn't notice it yourself, you'll probably need some sleep before your next shift."

She nodded and couldn't stop yet another yawn. "Don't talk about sleep," she said. "I've been relaxing the whole day, but I could go to sleep standing up, right now."

"So stop talking and get to bed," he smiled and off she went.

At dawn, she was up at the surveillance spot once more. Nothing special had occurred during this night either, Oona told her.

"Just that woman being in the barn again. Weird, right? I mean, what do they keep in there? For some reason I truly doubt she's having long, philosophical discussions with her favorite cow."

Miriam laughed with her. "Well, you never know. It might be politics, though, not philosophy..."

With another laugh and a friendly wave, Oona walked away, leaving Miriam to eat her breakfast with only the big binoculars as a company. Nothing stirred the silence until around nine when a tall twenty-something woman with short blond hair came out from the main house with two live hens in her arms. The five German Shepherds that had been loose during the night immediately rushed towards her, barking and jumping. With a loud: "Sit!" she pointed towards the ground and all the dogs sat down. She took a couple of steps away from the dogs and then threw the hens up in the air. They flapped desperately to gain some balance. The woman shouted: "Capture!" and all the dogs were suddenly leaping up, striking at the hens. Miriam threw a hand over her mouth, staring unbelievingly. In the commotion, she couldn't really see what was happening, but feathers were flying around, and the dogs were turning away, one after one, chewing on something, jaws full of feathers and down. The woman stood with her arms at her side and laughed heartily. Suddenly, the windows at the main house opened, and several children leaned out, clapping their hands and whistling. Miriam could hear shouts like, "Bravo, Satan!" and she put her arms around her to stop herself from shaking.

After the woman had ordered the dogs into the dog yard, the children came running out, but all of them avoided coming near her. She seemed to scowl at them. Then a small child, not more than a toddler walked towards the dogs. The dogs growled at her and showed their bright white teeth. The girl stopped uncertainly and just looked at the dogs. One of them threw himself at the fence, attacking the wire, as if to get to her. At that, the blond woman resolutely went forward, grabbed the girl by one arm, slapped her face and then started to drag her away by her hair. The toddler screamed in pain and tears flowed down her cheeks. Miriam hid her face in her hands. Tears of compassion and powerlessness flowed from her eyes.

Later that day, other reports of abuse came in. Apparently, three men had joined the blond woman in abusing some of the children, mostly physically, but Omega reported that there seemed to be some psychological abuse as well. There were children who did not get abused, though, but they were apparently encouraged by the adults to mistreat the other children. Miriam wondered over that, why Paulina had said that the women were comforting the children when that was obvious not the case. The only answers she could come up with was that things had changed during the one and a half year Paulina had been away or that she, being so young, had repressed some memories. She could have asked Carl about his opinion, but for some reason, she didn't want to. Over the camp lay a feeling of disbelief and anger. No one joked or even talked. Everyone seemed to walk around in their own dark thoughts without sharing them with the others. Miriam saw both Omega and Carl wipe away tears from their eyes. She tried to get some sleep before her night shift, but she couldn't relax. The thought that ran through her mind over and over again was: "We need to do something!" and then she had to remind herself that they were, in fact, doing something, and that they couldn't just rush in without a plan. They needed to get the schedule figured out before they moved in. The only good thing with this, she tried to tell herself, was that the people at the farm could not possibly be aware of being watched, which meant that they had not listened to the conversation with Lorraine at her office.

At midnight, it was her turn at the surveillance spot again and this time, she had to drag herself to her shift. She was relieved, though, that it was the night shift and that everyone was going to be asleep. This time, when she met Oona, the other field researcher's face was closed and dark, and she just nodded to Miriam before heading down towards camp. Miriam sat down next to the binoculars and looked towards the farm, thankful for their night vision. Everything was quiet and calm in the, for her, unusual brightness. Only the loose dogs were sniffing around the farmyard. She got up to her feet and moved around a bit to warm up. The night was cold, and the sky was full of clouds. She suspected another rain coming. Once she felt a little warmer, she brought out a survival bar and ate it slowly, trying not to think at all. She longed for this project to be over and solved, for her and Henry, and Beth and her family, to be at the summerhouse with lazy, happy days in front of them. It was her hope that she and Henry would find the time to rekindle their love after this whole silly intermezzo with Carl. She was daydreaming about that when she suddenly heard a door open and... singing voices? No, she corrected herself, chanting voices. She looked through the night vision binoculars and saw the children with an adult, obviously a woman, walking from the main house all dressed in dark, flowing dresses, while chanting. The walkie-talkie crackled.

"Do you see that?" Caesar's low voice was barely audible.

"Yes," she breathed back. "They're heading towards the barn."

"I guess it's time for their Great Mother ceremony."

"You're probably right. It looks scary, though."

The procession halted at the gigantic barn doors and the woman opened them for the children, who raised their voices to a scream before they all went in. The woman followed and closed the doors behind them.

Miriam was just about to take another short walk when she once more heard a door open. She pointed the binoculars towards the main building. A young girl, maybe eight or ten years old, came running out, this one dressed in a white, flowing dress. She was just to turn around the corner of the house when a man came rushing out of the same door, heading after her. The girl looked over her shoulder and Miriam could see the terrified expression on her face through the binoculars. She tried to run faster, but the man was winning on her. He caught her at the fence just below Miriam's surveillance spot with one hand around her long, blond braid. Her head was violently pulled back, and she cried out in pain. Miriam's hands around the binoculars whitened. The dog pack came running. Barking and growling, they surrounded the pair as the man threw the girl towards the fence and started to rip off her dress.

Miriam's heart began to beat faster, and she swallowed hard, feeling sweaty and on the brink of nauseous. He couldn't be doing what it looked like he was doing. Just then she saw another figure in a dark dress closing in, and Miriam started to breathe normally again. Faintly, she could hear the woman let up her voice. Apparently sound traveled in her direction tonight. Miriam recognized the voice as belonging to the blond woman.

"Jesus!"

The man turned his head towards her. "Get those damned dogs away, Roxy," he shouted back to her. "She tried to run away. I'm going to teach her a fucking lesson."

The girl hanged sloped over the fence, face down, trying desperately to kick him, but he just pressed her harder down, hitting her over the back of her head with his closed

245

fist. She turned limp in his grasp, her hands hanging flopped down. Miriam put a hand over her mouth. She couldn't believe that she was sitting here, witnessing this horrendous abuse without doing a damn thing. Roxy crossed her arms and glared at him.

"Take them fucking away!" he shouted again.

"All right, all right, just make it quick. Mom's gotten the other misfits into the barn. Time's short."

"Yeah, yeah. It's not like the fucking monsters will leave until they've got their share anyway."

Roxy threw her arms up in the air and seemed to roll her eyes. Then she whistled sharply three times, and the dogs came rushing towards her. Miriam could hear her talking faintly to the dogs as she turned her back to Jesus and the girl and started to walk away: "Bad dogs. Stupid dogs. You're not getting anything tonight except chicken duty."

The dogs whimpered and tried to brush themselves towards her, but she pushed up the door to the dog yard and locked them in. They all started to bark and throw themselves towards the fence, but Roxy didn't seem to care. Instead, she went over to the barn and got in.

When Miriam turned her gaze towards the girl, she could see that she had started to come back to life again, weakly trying to defend herself from the burly man behind her, who had just ripped off her underpants. His own pants were already hanging around his ankles.

"This can't be..." she murmured to herself in terrified disbelief, closing her fists so hard that they hurt. She could see the white panties landing on the grass as Jesus violently parted the girl's legs and thrust himself in. The girl gave up a high-pitched shriek in agony. She shrieked again and again as Jesus forced himself in and out of her.

Miriam felt something wet on her cheeks and her sight blurred, but the painful shrieks still cut through the violent barking of the dogs. Her hands trembled when they seemingly on their own grabbed the rifle beside her. She wiped her eyes as black hatred towards the man at the fence

246

filled her. The girl seemed to have fainted. She was once again hanging limply over the railing. Miriam looked through the riflescope. Jesus's face came unpleasantly close just as he got a look on his face of utter satisfaction. His body got stiff and his eyes shut. Miriam's finger pressed the trigger. The shot was almost soundless. She doubted that anyone heard it over the dogs' barks. She got a short glimpse of what had once been Jesus's face before he went down on the grass. The girl glided slowly down as well, without anyone holding her.

Miriam threw the rifle on the grass and without her even reflecting over it, she was up on her feet, rushing down the slope. Behind her, the walkie-talkie crackled to life and Caesar's upset voice came through. "Claire! What the hell just happened? Claire? Damn it! Did you just shoot him?"

She didn't stop to listen. In what felt like seconds she was down at the site, grabbed the unconscious girl by her feet and dragged her out under the fence. There was blood everywhere, and the girl's face was white as a sheet. Her breaths were ragged and thin. Miriam watched her in something that resembled shock. Gently, she stroked her cheek. The face was clammy and cold to the touch. She could hear herself mumbling: "Don't die on me now, sweetheart. Don't die."

From somewhere, a dark shadow suddenly loomed over her. With a shriek of her own that fastened in her throat, she looked up. Cyrus' fuming face was virtually touching her, filling up her whole eyesight.

"What the hell have you done, Claire?" His voice was on the brink of dangerous and for the first time ever she was seriously afraid of him. In spite of that, she tried to explain, tried to make him understand.

"I couldn't let him do this to her, Cy, I just couldn't!"

"I don't care! You just destroyed our advantage. You just made everyone aware that we're here."

Once again she felt those treacherous tears running down her cheeks without being able to stop them. "She's dying, Carl."

247

He stared at her for another moment, his face sculpted in anger, before looking down at the girl and his expression changed, softened. A wave of relief washed over her, and she could hear him mutter: "Oh, God... What a damn, fucking monster." Gently he grabbed the girl around her waist and back and lifted her up as if she didn't weigh anything. Her head rolled to the side. "Here, you need to get her to the camp."

"Me? What about you?"

"I need to get rid of that fucking pig-head before anyone finds him." Cyrus put the lifeless girl over Miriam's shoulder. "Go! Now!"

Miriam stumbled under the weight, but managed to find her balance. Slowly, she started to walk. The long grass seemed to try and hold her back, but she just concentrated on putting one foot in front of the other, breathing heavily as she progressed yard after yard. Her hand screamed in pain as she desperately tried to hold on to the girl, but that didn't matter. The only thing that mattered was that this girl should not die.

Finally, when she thought that she wouldn't make it all the way, Cyrus caught up with her. Even in the relative dark she could see spots of blood on his hands. It struck her that she, for the first time in her life, had killed a person, and that she didn't care.

"Here, give her to me. You can barely walk." To her extreme relief, his voice was normal again, and he didn't seem angry anymore. He took the girl carefully in his arms and started to run up the last hill. Already panting for breath, Miriam managed to gather enough strength from somewhere to run after him. She could see the camp below her, everyone being up and awake. When Olwen saw them, she rushed towards Cyrus. Miriam could hear her usual friendly voice lingering on the edge of anger.

"What the hell is going on, Cyrus?" Then she gave the still lifeless girl a look. "Oh, my God!"

"I don't know if she's dead or just unconscious. She's lost a lot of blood."

Olwen turned hurriedly towards the other field researchers. "Give me my bag, a sleeping bag, and whatever warm things you can find: blankets, clothes, whatever!"

Oona and Omega were off immediately, and Miriam had barely managed to reach the camp before they were back. Cyrus put the girl down on the sleeping bag, and Olwen kneeled at her, pressing her wrist and folding up her eyelid.

"She's alive, but in deep shock." She looked down at the girl's lower abdomen, and a grimace flew over her face as she shook her head. "I need to stop that bleeding."

"I'm going to leave her to you. I need to get down there again. Someone will come looking for them sooner or later."

"Them?" Omega asked with alarm in her voice.

"Yeah, her and the guy who did this to her. Claire shot him."

"Good." Omega glanced appreciatively at Miriam and somewhere she managed to find a faint smile in return. Oona stood looking down at the girl with a dark expression on her face.

"I'll come with you," she said to Cyrus. "I know how to deal with people like this one."

Cyrus nodded. "Good," he said.

She grabbed her own rifle and pistol, before turning to Olwen, who frantically worked with the girl. "I'll take a couple of those tranquilizers."

"Just leave me two, will you?" Olwen answered without even looking up.

Cyrus grabbed his walkie-talkie. "Get down here immediately, C. We need to go in, and we need all of us."

"Affirmative," Caesar's voice came through with a crackle.

Olwen glanced up at Cyrus. "If I leave her unattended, she'll die. She's in too deep a shock and that bastard nearly destroyed her. We need an ambulance helicopter."

Cyrus tugged at his hair. "Yeah..." Once again he let his hand run through the hair all the way back to his neck and rubbed it vigorously. A couple of moments later he seemed to come to a decision. Without any grudge towards her he said: "Claire, you heard her. Call for an ambulance helicopter. Give them all the directions and coordinates they need. Go grab your rifle, as well. We'll soon need it." Then he gave Oona a questioning look, and she nodded. They both started to climb up the hill and, a minute later, they were out of sight.

Chapter 21

When she came back down with the rifle, Caesar had already joined the camp. He was sitting really close to Olwen, their heads together, and they were talking with low voices and serious expressions in their faces. Miriam felt a pang in her chest and a chill in her stomach, something that it took her some moments to recognize as jealousy. Then a wave of heat flashed over her face. How could she be jealous at a time like this? She had just witnessed a ten-year-old girl being brutally raped and now fighting desperately for her life and, thanks to her own actions, they had to make a move when they weren't prepared for it. Regardless of that, she couldn't make herself feeling sorry for shooting the man. *I don't care! I just wish I'd acted sooner... And what the hell is this? I mean, jealous? What the hell?* Her personal life definitely had to be locked in somewhere. In spite of that thought, she sat down next to Caesar, closer than necessary, trying hard to not give Olwen a sour glare. They both looked up at her in greeting.

"She'll probably live," Olwen said to the unaired question. "If we can get her to a hospital in reasonable time, that is." She sighed and glanced briefly at the watch. "I hope that Oona and Cyrus don't take too long. We need to get moving if we're to keep anything that can still be called an advantage."

Caesar nodded and turned to Miriam. "How long did they say it would take for the helicopter?"

She sighed anxiously. "A couple of hours."

"That's expected," Omega said as she sat down with them and joined the conversation. "If worse comes to worst, we probably have to leave her here."

Olwen nodded reluctantly. "I don't want to, but there's really no other choice."

"From what we've seen so far," Caesar said with that deep, comforting voice of his, "there doesn't seem to be more than five adults, three young teenagers, eleven children between the age of five and twelve, and the rest – that's four – are under the age of five. Most of them are in that barn. I would say that all the younger children are in the house, hopefully sleeping. I counted nine children in the procession. One of the others is here with us. That gives us eight children most likely still in the house. One of the men is dead. The other two are probably in the house, looking after the younglings. The older woman – I think it would be safe to say that she's Margery Phillips – is in the barn together with the other children. As for now, the younger woman, who most likely is the daughter Roxy we've had witness reports about, is in the barn as well, but she seems to be going back and forth between the barn and all the other places of the farm. She's also the only one we've seen who has control over the dogs. That leaves us four adults. We should be able to outnumber them."

"But," Omega said, "shall we count on those nine children being brain-washed enough to fight us as well if we make a raid into the barn?"

Caesar just shook his head to show his ignorance.

"I think," Olwen said grimly, "that it's best to be prepared for all eventualities, just in case. Cyrus will probably agree with me that we'll try not to kill them if we can avoid it."

"Those were the orders we got, yes," Caesar said and stopped abruptly when he turned his head towards a low noise from up the hill. All of them followed his gaze. Still in shadow, but clearly visible towards the light night sky, they could see two persons carrying a third. They all scrambled up to their feet, meeting the pair halfway.

"She's heavier than I thought," Cyrus huffed as he let over the burden to Omega. She took the body on her shoulders and with ease went over to the tent, letting the woman down on the ground without any hassle. Miriam saw Roxy's lifeless face and shuddered.

"Is she dead?"

"No," Oona answered, "we just tranquilized her. She came looking for the girl." Her face was closed as she gave the unconscious young woman on the ground an emotionless glance. "It was a good thing that you shot that man, Claire. It seems likely that the girl was going to be sacrificed."

"What?" Both Olwen and Miriam spat out the word.

"That's what she said when she cried out for Jesus. 'We don't have time for more games. It's after one. They're waiting for her at the sacrificial table'."

"*Mother, accept our offering...*" Miriam whispered, feeling cold to the bone. "But... children..."

"I guess that's what happens to disobedient children, Claire," Cyrus broke in, looking weary. "You remember Paulina's statement, eh, that children who don't give in just disappeared? There are probably lots of them buried all over the place. Sick bastards." He exhaled and tugged at his hair. For a moment, silence lay heavily over the camp. Then Cyrus shrugged and grimaced. "Anyway, let's have a short briefing before we go in."

After cozily bedding Roxy in a sleeping bag, not so cozily handcuffing her, Omega put the unconscious woman in a hollow behind the tent. Olwen examined her briefly before joining the others. "She'll probably sleep through the night. Those tranquies are quite powerful. I'm happy that you managed to get her alive."

Both Cyrus and Oona nodded. Cyrus took a sip from a juice pack and looked at all of them.

"The plan is very simple. We'll divide into the two teams we've been working: Oona, Claire and I are Team A. Olwen, Caesar, and Omega are Team B. As far as we know, there are only three more adults on the farm at this point. Team A goes into the barn where the older woman and the children are. There are two more men we don't know the location of. It's Team B's task to make sure they don't call for reinforcements. You need to locate and incapacitate them. When you have secured the farm, you come to the barn and

253

help Team A out. Olwen is P.I. Whatever she says is an order and has to be followed. Any questions?"

"Shoot to kill?" Oona asked.

"If necessary, yes. We'd like to take as many as possible alive. When it comes to the children, shoot only to injure if you have to shoot at all. They're the real victims here, after all. Anything else?"

"We've got three tranquilizers left," Oona said. "Who takes them?"

"You. As far as we know, the woman in the barn is Margery Phillips. We need her alive if there's any chance at all. The men are superfluous."

A grim silence spread out in the small group before Cyrus got up. "Let's get our gear together and move out."

They divided into the two different teams before they left the base camp. Miriam saw Caesar, Olwen, and Omega disappear into the dark shadows of the hills before she followed Cyrus and Oona down toward the short side of the barn.

Everything was eerily silent. Not a sound slipped through from either the barn or the house. A dim light was lit in one of the lower windows of the house, but that was all. She looked at the other windows, only slightly reflected by the ragged clouds overhead. Anyone could be standing there watching them. Goosebumps appeared on her arms, and a cold shiver ran down her spine. Cyrus' and her footsteps sounded alarmingly loud to her ears suddenly, but Oona could have been a ghost floating soundlessly down the hill.

They climbed over the low fence and walked cautiously towards the barn wall, three dark shadows that blended into the night around them. It took them just a couple of seconds before they reached the rough planks. Cyrus held up his hand to signal a short break, and all of them checked their guns and the rifle. Through the wooden wall, a faint sound reached them, heightening and leveling down, again and again. Cyrus made another signal, and they all began to move towards the right corner, which he quickly glanced around and then waved affirmatively to them as he slipped around it.

The enormous barn door was closed, and a weak flickering light shone through the narrow slots. Oona and Miriam stopped at the right side of the door while Cyrus carefully moved to the left side. They stood in silence for half a minute, concentrating, focusing, before Cyrus drew a deep breath and slowly opened the door with the rifle in steady hands.

The flickering light and the chanting became stronger. Miriam could see the backs of black clad children some thirty yards further down in the barn. No one seemed to notice them. She made the okay sign towards Cyrus, who nodded and slid in. Oona followed like a shadow behind him, and Miriam swallowed hard, her adrenaline pumping and her skin heating, as she raised her gun and snuck in through the narrow opening, carefully closing it behind her. It was hot and humid inside. Her pores opened immediately, and sweat broke through. Oona and Cyrus stood still as statues with their backs at the wall, staring towards the children. As she turned to watch, the chanting became higher, more intense, almost painful in its tone.

The older woman from the procession stood on a podium, her hands in the air, shaking as she ferociously chanted something deep down in her throat. Beside her was a rough stone altar covered in big, dark spots. A huge knife lay in the middle of it, gleaming with a dull reflection. Miriam recognized it. It was the same kind of knife they had found in Henry's closet. She shuddered and thought with relief of the girl up in their camp.

With a last gurgling sound, the woman opened her eyes and searched through the now silent crowd and then gazed at the closed barn door with a frown. Miriam froze and forgot to breathe for some seconds. When the woman turned towards the children with a growl, a physical wave of fear made them shudder. She turned to the front row and pointed carelessly at one of them. A high whining shriek came from

255

the child as the closest ones pushed him forward. He stumbled and fell over the podium. With strength worthy a young weightlifter, the woman grabbed the child by the neck and with one smooth move lifted him up on the altar, took up the huge knife, and cut his throat. Black blood spurted from the opened wound as the woman shouted out some kind of incantation.

The next second everything seemed to happen all at once. Miriam felt a gush of air as a bullet flew just past her cheek and the woman slumped down like a sack of moldy potatoes on top of the tiny lifeless body. The chanting wavered down and stopped, insecurely. Cyrus, with the reeking rifle in hand, started to move forward towards the children. Then the barn door opened, almost gently, in the corner of her eye. A foul smell gushed in, making her choke. The children immediately turned their heads towards the door and started to scream in terror. All over each other, they tried to run towards the opposite wall, trampling some of them down under their feet. Cyrus turned to watch as well. His eyes widened, and his mouth slacked as the rifle fell from his hand. In the corner of her other eye, Miriam could see Oona slowly moving towards a dark nook, gun in unsteady hands, pointing towards the door. It felt like moving in jelly as she turned to look, taking a couple of steps away from a racy dark-brown tentacle that was waving in the air an inch from her face. Her mouth opened, trying to scream, but nothing was heard. Her legs just collapsed under her in an itching, watery clot. Helplessly she tried to crawl away from the towering mass of tentacles filling up the door. Somewhere behind them was a body covered with mouths that were opening and closing ceaselessly as if they were hungry. Green goo dripped slowly to the ground from them, leaving a syrupy trail behind the creature as it smoothly moved forward on hoofed feet.

Tears of terror flowed from her eyes as the tentacles reached closer to her. In the corner of her eye, she thought she saw Cyrus fumble for the rifle, but she knew he would be too late. The moment the tentacles gently touched her foot, she wet herself. She didn't even register the sound of a bullet smacking into the wall at first, but the tentacle immediately stopped caressing her and lashed out, hitting Oona over the head. Miriam wasn't sure if the cracking sound when it hit the other field researcher was just in her head or if the tentacle had actually crushed her skull, but Oona collapsed lifelessly to the ground.

Cyrus finally managed to grab the rifle, but before he could use it, another tentacle grabbed him harshly, lifted him up in the air, and brought him close to its body. The shrieks that welled out of him again and again as one of the mouths bit down on his neck and started to suck violently were sickening. Miriam's hand reached down to her own gun as if with a will of its own, but before she even managed to touch it, the sucking stopped, and the enormous tentacle caressed the sobbing, screaming man as it mildly put him down beside Oona.

She could see how the creature ducked to get through the door and decidedly headed towards the altar without acknowledging any of them anymore. It lifted up the older lady and cradled her as it turned around and headed out of the barn again.

Left behind was chaos.

Epilogue 1

Henry rose out of the sofa as she closed the door behind her.

"How is he?" he asked with a clearly concerned voice.

She sighed and ran a hand through her hair, the gesture painfully reminding her of Carl.

"He's getting better. Still not talking, though. The psychiatrist that Dr. Bernard has recommended is considering letting his daughter visit him. He loves Sarah more than anything, as I understand. Maybe that could make him turn the scale. Hell, I have no clue! I'm not a shrink!"

"Easy, Mimi, easy." He was at her in two steps, hugging her comfortably. "You know Cyrus. He won't give up. In the end, he'll be too stubborn to let them win."

She took a deep breath, thinking of Carl's pale face and dull red hair as he was sitting at the window, staring out at nothing, then thinking of Cindy in her straightjacket, violently trying to hurt herself, and how she never got out of the ward. Carl wasn't like Cindy. He was stronger.

As if he could read her mind, Henry said: "Do you remember Cindy?" She nodded. "I really loved that girl and how she worked that brain of hers, but in the end, she proved too soft. Cyrus has his weaknesses, but softness isn't one of them."

"Cindy wasn't soft!" Miriam protested. "She was half-eaten by spiders and made a cocoon for their eggs! Carl wouldn't have remained sane after that either! None of us would!"

Caesar flinched, but she didn't know if it was because of her tone or because of the use of Carl's name. Whatever it was, she felt as if she couldn't care less. She just wanted to be alone.

"I just meant that her brain was too sharp to be able to handle... Hrm, that didn't come out as I meant. Goodness, I know Cyrus is smart! I just..."

Miriam held up her hand to stop his rambling. "That's okay, Henry," she said coldly.

Henry sighed and rubbed his face harshly. "I'm sorry," he mumbled, but she just shrugged, too exhausted to be happy or even care that he apologized for once. In the deep silence that followed, she went over to the window, pressing her forehead towards the chilly glass, desperately trying to shut out the memories of that night that haunted her every moment.

"Mimi…" Henry hesitated.

"Yes?" she said without turning around, once again wishing that she were alone.

"Um… well…" He swallowed audibly. "I know this isn't the right time or place, but…" He hesitated and Miriam turned around, looking at him tiredly. He avoided her gaze and tapped his index finger nervously on his leg. "I was going to… I've been thinking… It's been some time now…" Again he paused and had a slightly desperate expression on his face.

"Yes?"

He inhaled deeply and looked her straight in the eyes. "Will you marry me?"

She could feel her jaw drop. "What?"

"Yes, you know; marriage. Like… well… marry me?" She just stared at him without really understanding what he was saying, and he looked nervously at her, swallowing visibly. "I mean, I'm not part of team C2 anymore. I can marry you now." There was another silence where she really tried to say something, but her brain was just blank. Small sweat drops appeared on Henry's forehead, and he cleared his voice. "I realize that I've been terrible to you during this project, jealous and all that, but that's good, you know, because then you know I'm human…" She blinked and stared at him. He moaned. "Oh God, of course, I'm human! I'm NOT an alien! You know I'm not an alien! Mimi, stop looking at me like that! Please!"

He buried his face in his hands. As if in a dream, Miriam took the few steps towards him, reached out and

259

clasped his hands gently in hers, caressing them. Then she put her hand under his chin, making him meet her eyes. Tears welled over when she saw all the tenderness and love that he felt for her in his face. She took a deep, shuddering breath and dried away her own tears with an irritated gesture.

"I don't know, Henry," she mumbled. "I... just don't know. I think I... I... need some time alone, to learn to stand on my own two feet for once. Not leaning on one man or another."

He just stared at her, unbelievingly. "You... you don't want to marry me?"

She bit her lip and watched his sudden pained expression. Then she closed her eyes and rubbed her face. "I'm sorry. I'm so very sorry."

The silence grew thick and the seconds ticked by, turning into minutes. She had no idea what to say to make it easier for both of them, and she avoided looking at his shocked face. Eventually, he sighed heavily and seemed to try to compose himself. When he took her hands gently in his and caressed them, she looked up at him, surprised.

"Don't be sorry, Mimi. In a way I'm... really happy for you. You... you have changed during this project, in a positive direction, and developed traits I always suspected were there, but never knew how to help you unlock."

She couldn't answer. She just threw her arms around him and realized that she still loved him, probably always would. It was just not the right path to walk now.

"I love you, Mimi. Don't forget me."

She shook her head and heard a laugh trying to find its way out. "You're funny," she mumbled into his neck.

He smiled into her hair and, when he released himself from the embrace, he had tears running down his cheeks. She had never seen him cry before, and it shocked her more than anything else. A guilty feeling hit her hard, as Henry cupped his hands around her face, looking her lovingly in her eyes, before turning around and walking out the door.

As it closed behind him a huge relief filled her, and she felt free, as if she had been chained without knowing it.

Epilogue 2

Instead of rain, which would have been more appropriate, Olwen thought, the sun shone in abundance from a cloud-free sky. She and Omega stood a bit behind the family. It wasn't a big gathering, just Oona's mom and dad and younger sister. There was also an old friend from the Rangers present, as well. Mike had been Oona's best friend and lover. He looked awkward as he stood beside her, trying to hold his tears back. Olwen pressed his arm gently.

"It's okay, Mikey. She would've loved the thought of you spending tears on her."

The sound that came from his throat was nothing more than a gurgled laugh. "I know, Sal. I just wish that I once, just once, had told her that I love her."

His voice broke, and he started to cry in deep, sobbing breaths. Olwen threw her arms around him and leaned her head towards his chest, wishing that she could cry too.

The reception afterward was short, but Olwen, Omega, and Mike did not stay. They stepped out together, leaving Oona's family to their grief. As they walked down the stairs, Olwen caught a glimpse of a man standing in the shadow at the corner of the walkway. She suddenly smiled with fluttering heart and patted Omega on the arm and nodded towards him. The younger woman followed her gaze, and her whole face brightened up.

"Mike," Olwen said, "can you wait by the car, please? There's someone here we need to see."

"Sure."

As the two Field Researchers walked over to him, he straightened up and greeted them with a smile.

"Olwen, Omega. I'm glad to see you again, even if I wish it were under happier circumstances. I'm sorry for your loss." His voice was as deep and soothing as she remembered it to be.

"We too are very, very sorry," Omega said, her voice trembling.

"So, what brings you here, Caesar? Not just to pay your respects, I guess," Olwen inquired.

"No, not only for that, even if it would be enough. And it's Armand now, not Caesar."

Olwen raised her eyebrows in surprise. "Well now, congrats then."

"Thanks. Let's go to my car and talk."

During the short walk to his non-descriptive-looking car, the thoughts raced through her head. So, Caesar had been promoted. She had never heard of something like that happening before, even though she figured those things did occur every once in a while. That meant that if he was here as a representative of the Faculty, something serious had happened. Her stomach clenched, and she shared a worried glance with Omega. She did not, really did not, want another project this close to the other one. They just lost Oona! Please, let them grieve for a while first so they could manage to pull themselves together!

In the car, Caesar... no, sorry, Armand, placed himself so he could view both of the Field Researchers. He cleared his throat. "First of all, our project went relatively successfully. We managed to capture Roxy Phillips, even though she refuses to talk, and one of the male guards, Robert Sunder. He talks, all right, so now we have a pretty clear picture of what was going on, and it's not pretty." He rumbled around in his briefcase and handed them a report each. "Everything's in here. You can read it later. In short, the children who survived are all traumatized, naturally, and under the supervision of a psychiatrist who is also a GFS Researcher, which of course makes it easier for us. They will need to be adjusted to a normal life before they can be adopted. We'll see how that will turn out. Some of them are pretty brainwashed. It's... frightening... Truthfully, I don't know if they ever will be adjusted." He fell silent a moment

263

and looked old and sad with wrinkles more accentuated than Olwen remembered.

"What about the girl?" Omega asked urgently. "Did she survive?"

"Ah, yes, the girl..." Armand cleared his throat. "In fact, she did." Olwen joined Omega in her cheering and a broad smile lit up her face. "Her name is Lydia Ericks, nine years old. They call her 'the miracle girl' because she shouldn't have survived. Her injuries were too severe, and she lost too much blood, and the time before she came to a hospital was too long, but she beat them all, seemingly too stubborn to die."

"Good girl," Omega said gently, and Olwen nodded.

"She'll never be able to have children, but according to her doctor, she has the most amazing attitude, and she let him know that there are so many orphaned children out there and 'someone needs to take care of them.'"

Omega and Olwen watched him stunned, and then Olwen shook her head admiringly. "I'm happy that she'll live. Really happy. Claire did the right thing, shooting that man."

Omega nodded in approval.

"Hm, yes..." Armand frowned for some reason that escaped Olwen. Then he continued: "There are records of previous children, now all grown up, who will be taken in for questioning. It would be terrible if these formerly collected children continue what we just put a stop to at the Phillips' farm. According to Margery Phillips' personal records, many of them work in influential positions. One of these is the psychologist at the Alaska Department of Health and Social Services. She will be questioned about two apparent suicides and one disappearance among her patients. Concerning Margery Phillips' husband William and son Warren, they were not at the farm, as we initially thought. The prisoner, Robert Sunder, told us that they were part of the team that operated here before we got the lead to Alaska. William Phillips was killed by Cyrus on July sixteenth, and Warren Phillips committed suicide on July seventeenth." Armand paused, seemingly lost in his own thoughts, before shrugging and turning towards them again. "Anyway, our biggest concern now is Margery Phillips and what happened to her after she disappeared with that creature. According to our male prisoner, it's called *Her Child* and is supposed to be a minion to something even worse. I won't go into any details right now, but they can apparently be summoned by blood sacrifice. We need you to go out and locate her. She's too dangerous to be permitted to roam free if she's still alive." Olwen couldn't help sighing. Armand looked sympathetically at her. "It's too soon, I realize that. This is not a case of capturing her, though, just trying to locate her. You won't be alone either. You will have two new researchers in team O6. Dr. Bernard has let me know that Cyrus will be fully recovered in time. Right now, he's functioning again, and the psychiatrist tells me that he needs something to concentrate on. This project will be perfect for that. He'll be part of your team as FR Octavius. Claire will become FR Ophelia."

Olwen couldn't help a huge smile showing as her heart jigged happily in her chest. Omega smiled too where she sat in the back seat and leaned closer towards him.

"That's great news, Caesar!" she said. "We really like both of them. Thank you."

He smiled back at Omega, but Olwen thought he looked sad. "Yes, we thought that it would be nice for you to get people you are already familiar with, and more importantly, know that you can work together with. You, Olwen, will be P.I. of the team. Cyrus… sorry, Octavius, is not mentally stable enough yet to take on any leadership role. You, on the other hand, have plenty of experience being principal investigator, and you have the Faculty's full confidence in your ability."

Olwen couldn't help blushing at the praise, especially since it was so unexpected.

"So when do we start?" Omega asked.

"Well…" Armand looked at his watch. "There's a plane leaving at eleven p.m. tonight. I'm quite sure that you'll be able to catch it if you leave for home now. Everything is cleared with your superiors." Olwen and Omega shared a look, and Armand smiled at them, handing them a plane ticket each. "Best of luck to you. Remember, you're not to engage in anything, just locate her and keep her under observation until help arrives. If anything unexpected happens, like *Her Child* showing up, your orders are to disengage and get the hell out of there. Don't even hesitate one second. Understood?"

Olwen couldn't help feeling a pang of relief. "Yes, sir!"

"Good." He dug into his pocket and brought out a plain, white business card each for them. *Armand* was the only thing written on it, and a phone number. "I'll be your contact. Don't hesitate to call me, even in the middle of the night." He scrutinized them, and they nodded. Suddenly that rare smile of his, both mild and warm, that always made Olwen feel so happy and well cared for, lit up his face.

"All right then," he said. "I believe you have a plane to catch."

About the Author

A.E. Hellstorm was born in Sweden, but spent several years of her youth in Portugal and Greece, before returning to Stockholm, her city of birth.

As a young adult, she took a diploma in Creative Writing, as well as a Master of Arts in Scientific Archaeology.

In 2005, she and her husband moved to Canada together with their cats, and have lived there ever since.

In Canada, she took a diploma in Arts and Cultural Management, and in Photography. She opened her photography business *Flying Elk Photography* in 2012.

In the Hands of the Unknown is her first published novel, but she has had a play, *Marsvindar*, staged at Rosenlundsteatern in Stockholm, Sweden, in 1992, and she has also participated in two anthologies: *Karbunkel* in 1994, and the *2014 Wyrdcon Companion Book*.

Other than that she is a vivid roleplaying enthusiast, and she was deeply engaged in the Swedish larping community during the 1990's and early 2000's. In the year of 2000, she organized the Greek mythology-based larp *'The Song of Mycenae'*.

When she doesn't write she enjoys curling up in a recliner with a book and a large cup of tea.

65282817R00162

Made in the USA
Charleston, SC
20 December 2016